coming up
for air

coming up for air

NICOLE B. TYNDALL

Delacorte Press

Text copyright © 2020 by Nicole B. Tyndall
Jacket art copyright © 2020 by PedroTapa

All rights reserved. Published in the United States by Delacorte Press, an imprint of Random House Children's Books, a division of Penguin Random House LLC, New York.

Delacorte Press is a registered trademark and the colophon is a trademark of Penguin Random House LLC.

GetUnderlined.com

Educators and librarians, for a variety of teaching tools, visit us at RHTeachersLibrarians.com

Library of Congress Cataloging-in-Publication Data
Names: Tyndall, Nicole B., author.
Title: Coming up for air / Nicole B. Tyndall.
Description: First edition. | New York : Delacorte Press, [2020] |
Audience: Ages 12 up. | Audience: Grades 7–9. | Summary: "A coming-of-age story about a girl with creative aspirations and the star swimmer who charms his way into her life, centering on themes of addiction, loss, and the tumultuousness of first love— and how to find strength when everything falls apart"— Provided by publisher.
Identifiers: LCCN 2019040832 | ISBN 978-0-593-12708-7 (hardcover) |
ISBN 978-0-593-12709-4 (library binding) | ISBN 978-0-593-12710-0 (ebook)
Subjects: CYAC: Dating (Social customs)—Fiction. | Photography—Fiction. |
Drug abuse—Fiction. | High schools—Fiction. | Schools—Fiction.
Classification: LCC PZ7.1.T965 Co 2020 | DDC [Fic]—dc23

The text of this book is set in 11-point Berling.
Interior design by Trish Parcell

Printed in the United States of America
10 9 8 7 6 5 4 3 2 1
First Edition

To my mom, for fighting for us

after

Senior Year

autumn

CHAPTER 1

"Please, I need to see him." My throat is tight and the desperation in my voice hurts my ears, but I force the words out. "I know what you're going to say, but, just . . . *please?*"

The thirtysomething nurse standing in front of me in light blue scrubs answers patiently. "I'm sorry. His paperwork is clear. I can't let you back."

I feel like I'm watching, listening, from far away. This woman is my total opposite. She's calm and composed, and it makes the frustration inside me reach new heights. I want to yell, *I'm not hysterical!* Which I realize will probably only make things worse. I force myself to stay quiet. To think before I speak.

I can't argue with her. She's right. It's well after three in the morning. But I couldn't sleep. I couldn't stand *not* being here. And I guess I thought maybe the hospital operated by different rules in the middle of the night. Nighttime can have that kind of magic. Braden is the one who taught me that, but those are his tricks, not mine.

I take a deep breath. "Can you just . . . Does it say my name, specifically? Does it say 'Hadley Butler'?" I look around as I ask, hoping I won't find any familiar faces.

Her expression, full of pity, cuts like a knife. "It says 'no visitors.'"

"*None?* None at all?"

"Just his parents."

Panic surges through me. I search the room. "Are they here?" *Of course* they're here. Their teenage son is in the hospital, where else would they be?

"They're resting in the med inn." Relief courses through me. I might get away with visiting without anybody knowing.

I look back up at the nurse. The hospital lights are harsh on her face, casting unforgiving shadows under her eyes and on her cheekbones. My fingers, hanging empty at my sides, long for the familiar weight of my camera. If I were to photograph her in this light, it would be easy to frame her as a villain: the Gatekeeper. But it's not her fault, I remind myself. She's not the bad guy.

"Can you just tell me if he's stable?"

"I can't share medical information with anyone but family."

"Is there *anything* you can do?" I plead, my questions piling atop one another like bricks of an abandoned haunted house. I can't help it. Because if the tables were turned, I'm positive that he would find a way to visit me. Rules have never meant much to Braden Roberts. But I did. Despite everything, I know that.

Hope drains from me when I meet her apologetic eyes.

I try one last thing. "If I gave you a note, would you give it to him? I mean, I know he can't read it now. But it'd be there

4

for him, you know, when . . ." I trail off. I'm not sure how to finish the sentence.

I feel at my pockets. Before I drove over here, I sat in my bedroom and frantically scribbled three different versions of a letter. One pathetically details how much I love him; another is an apology, long and rambling; and the shortest one is furious, cursing him for his weakness—cruel and unfair, maybe, but I meant every word. I was going to choose one in the moment, but, really, the only way to be honest would be to give him all three. I fish for them with my fingers.

The nurse sighs. "I . . . I think you should probably just head home. It's late, and doesn't school start tomorrow?"

How am I supposed to start senior year without him?

She doesn't wait for an answer, continuing, "If you're looking for more information on Mr. Roberts—"

"His name is Braden." *And if he were awake, he'd charm you into having all the visitors in the world.*

She takes a long look at me before she says, "If you want more information on Braden, I suggest you reach out to his parents. I'll make sure they know you were here."

I take a step backward. "No. Um—" *Shit. Shitshitshit.* "It's okay." Braden's mom made it perfectly clear that she did *not* want me here. She might even think I'm the reason her son is in the hospital at all. *And maybe I am,* a small, scared voice whispers from the depths of my mind. I shake my head, gaze unfocused on my feet. "No, it's okay. I guess . . . I'll just go."

I can hardly believe that for all the ways I can claim Braden as my own, none of them will get me past those doors.

I walk away slowly, noting each step that takes me farther away from him, wondering how I will survive the wondering.

Did he see it coming? Did he feel it, the moment he lost control? Was he afraid? But most of all: *Is he going to be okay?*

"Hey, miss? Um, Hadley? Right?" The nurse's voice finds me down the hall, just before the exit.

As I turn, a small optimism sparks inside me. "Yeah?"

"He's eighteen, your boyfriend?"

"Ex-boyfriend." My voice cracks on the word. "But yeah."

She nods. She knew his age; it's on his chart. Her eyes are kind. "Right now, it's up to his parents. But as an adult, Braden can make the choice for himself, who he wants to see—once he's able. If your behavior is any indicator . . ." She pauses. "I bet he'll contact you, when he can."

I open my mouth to argue that, after today, he might never want to see me again. And I definitely shouldn't want to see him.

But then her words hit me.

She's saying that he'll call me once he's conscious. *When, not if.* She thinks he's going to be okay. Relief burns my eyes.

It's ambiguous. It might not really mean much. And I wish that I could see that he's breathing, that he's here, but I understand that this information is a gift. She isn't supposed to tell me anything at all about his status. I mean it when I say thank you.

Even with that small piece of information, I still feel defeated as I get into my car. The feeling only deepens when I notice my Great Lakes University portfolio, my most important college application, sitting on the passenger seat. Over the past few weeks, I've spent hours and hours getting it ready, debating each photograph in every way I can imagine. I pull the book onto my lap and open the front cover, knowing he'll be there. He'll be healthy, alive. *So alive.* My eyes fill, and all I can make out is a smear of peach. Remembering him like that, electric and urgent, makes my insides riot.

For just a moment, I let it take over—the kind of angry crying that feels like it's escaping too fast and too hard, like bats swarming from a cave. I picture hundreds of them, hairy and the color of ash, flying out of my twisted mouth. I watch their imaginary wings flap in circles around my car, until suddenly I can't stand it.

I throw my door open and grab the bound photos, march to the closest garbage can, and slam the book into it with a satisfying clang.

I'll make a new portfolio. Without him. Or maybe *just* of him. Or maybe I won't make one at all. Great Lakes has been my longest-standing goal, a worry and desire constantly lingering just past my fingertips, but compared to life and death, it's nothing at all.

I take a deep breath, slamming the car door closed behind me. *Get ahold of yourself.* I sit up straight and wipe my eyes in the rearview mirror. I tilt my head up and down, staring at my reflection, letting the shadows on my face echo the ones I saw on the nurse's earlier. I look like a Francesca Woodman photograph: haunting and haunted.

I check my phone. It's three-fifty-two in the morning.

Fifty-two minutes since I arrived.

Time is supposed to heal. But I'm not sure exactly what *should* heal in this case. Maybe some parts of it need to stay broken.

He and I need to stay broken.

I turn the key in the ignition, knowing I should head home

but hesitant to leave him there, alone. I move in a fog until somehow, I reach my driveway.

When I open the side door of the house, I don't even bother to muffle the jingle of my keys or the thud of my purse on the floor. Nobody stirs to ask me where I've been. You'd think I'd be used to the quiet by now, but the reality is lonely and hollow. Feeling like a ghost of myself, I move to my room, shut the door, and crawl into bed.

One night has passed, and so far, time isn't holding up its end of the bargain.

before

Junior Year

autumn

CHAPTER 2

Becca syncs her phone to the speaker, and an upbeat song fills her kitchen, lit with October sunlight. "There. Happy, Ty?" she asks.

Tyler, sitting with us at the table, nods. "So much better."

"I'd never heard it so quiet in here," I add, looking around the room. Tyler and I have been coming to Becca's house since middle school, and without its signature chaos, it's almost unrecognizable.

"Yeah, the boys are terrorizing someone else. And I think my parents are at the restaurant." Becca scowls. "But they could have cleaned up a little before they left." There's a huge stack of dishes soaking in the sink. I don't know where Becca got her hyperorganized gene, but it isn't from Mr. and Mrs. Gomez.

Becca and I both work at her parents' diner, Belavinis, which used to serve solely Greek-American food. When Becca's grandpa passed away over the summer, her mom inherited the restaurant, and she wanted to put a new spin on things. She and Becca's dad are trying to make it their own.

I glance toward the sink. "Did they come up with anything, um, Greek Mexican?" They're trying to incorporate Becca's dad's family cuisine into the mix.

"What?" She follows my line of sight. "Oh. No, the menu battle rages on."

"Speaking of food . . ." Ty sits up in his chair. "Anybody else hungry? I could order some pizza."

"Can't. I'm supposed to get takeout later with my mom and sister," I answer, sighing. "Remy's upset because her latest conquest broke up with her. Or, I don't know, cheated, maybe?"

Becca looks surprised. "I didn't know she was dating somebody."

I shake my head. "I probably just hoped he would go away fast enough that I wouldn't have to tell you. And *she* probably didn't tell you because it's Wyatt Coleman."

Becca's perfectly groomed brows meet. "*Wyatt?* When did that happen?"

Ty pulls at the drawstrings of his hoodie. "Isn't he the guy who . . ."

I confirm his suspicions. "Yeah, in the hot tub. With those girls from Richmond."

Becca straightens her pile of papers, organizing our human biology worksheets, which, weirdly, are all about fetal pigs. We took regular bio last year, but this class is an elective, and it's been surprisingly hard. "Well, Remy isn't afraid of . . . a challenge, I guess."

I snort. "You mean she thinks she can rehab every jerk who looks twice at her?"

"What does Judd say?" Ty asks, referencing my brother, Remy's twin.

"We barely talk about it anymore. Remy doesn't listen, so there's no point."

Becca doesn't seem concerned. "I'm sure Remy will be fine. She's smart." Her eyes are scanning the diagram in front of her. "She can handle herself."

"Debatable," I mutter, a little annoyed. Becca always defends Remy, even when she doesn't deserve it.

Becca doesn't notice, though, and instead pulls up her long, dark hair, and I know she's done gossiping about my sister. She secures her pony with a velvet scrunchie, looking like she's ready to get to work. "Okay, well, if you're hungry, Ty, I'll order something to eat, but only *after* we finish this."

Tyler groans. When we decided to hang out here after school today, I don't think either of us pictured doing homework. Not on a Friday afternoon, anyway.

"Come on, it's not that bad," Becca insists. "Look, we can start with the stomach." She leans over the diagram, her neat lines labeling the organs of the digestive system.

"Well, on the bright side, nothing suppresses an appetite quite like dissection," I tell Becca. I shudder a little in disgust at the memory of her in class. She was merciless with the knife.

She's unfazed. "Just avoid thinking about the smell, and you'll be fine."

"And *that's* it, I'm never eating again."

I look to Tyler to back me up, but he must have checked out when Becca honed in on our homework. He's muttering to the song playing, and scribbling lyrics onto the sole of his shoe, a pair of beat-up Vans. I kick his other foot.

He jerks to attention, lifting his head of cropped, dark hair.

"Oh. Um. Yeah, Becs. It's the weekend. Do we really have to do this right now?"

Becca looks between us, her lab partners and closest friends. "I have less than an hour before I have to go work at the swim meet, and then you guys are free to do whatever you want. But, Hads, you're the one who was worried about the test on Monday. And if we do it now, it's fresh in your mind."

Becca and I are both in NHS, the National Honor's Society, and while Becca's grades get her there with ease, I'm hanging on by the skin of my teeth.

She continues, "Studies show that if you review the material shortly after you learned it—"

"Yeah, all right," I interrupt her, trying to avoid a lecture. "That's the gallbladder." I point out on the diagram.

"Yes! Okay, just a few more. And then we can move on to reproductive."

"Fun."

A loud, campy song starts playing on the speaker.

"What is this?" Tyler asks.

I turn to him. "There's a song you *don't* know?"

Becca sighs, incredulous. "It's from *Waitress*." When we don't react, she adds, "The musical? Sara Bareilles?" She looks at us and decides we're hopeless. "My choir group performed it last year? It's a huge hit on Broadway!" Her phone buzzes. "Hold on, it's Greg."

Becca takes her boyfriend's call and leaves the room.

Ty hits his pen rhythmically onto his notebook. "I really have to stop agreeing to come over here after school. Homework on a Friday is criminal."

"She's such a good influence," I agree with dismay.

"Ugh," he groans, "it's the worst. Except that my science grades are basically the highest they've ever been." Science has never been Tyler's strong suit, and this class is in addition to our chemistry class. But I loved regular bio so much last year that I convinced Ty and Becca to sign up for this one too. I'm still sort of surprised that Ty agreed. Maybe he just didn't want to be left out.

"Yeah," I answer, "and between the two of you, I might not *totally* fail the math on the ACT." We've been studying together a lot this fall, and I'm praying Ty's and Becca's precalc expertise will save me.

"You still have months to work on those practice tests, Hads. And I don't think your photography program will mind if you're not the best at the Pythagorean theorem."

He's talking about Great Lakes University, and I appreciate the vote of confidence, but I'm almost certain he's wrong. It's a supercompetitive liberal arts school, and a total long shot. But they have this killer photography program, and I'm dying to go there. I've been working hard since freshman year, when my photography teacher told me about it. Students get to spend a semester in *Paris*. Anytime I want to give up on remembering some elaborate formula, I picture myself in a beret, snapping shots of the hilly, Montmartre streets. It makes the decision simple: keep studying. I want to see what those places look like in real life.

"I hope so," I reply. "And you're totally going to get into Columbia College." Tyler wants to enroll in their music-business program.

"And Chicago isn't too far from Great Lakes U."

I feel my grin spread. "Well, I *obviously* can't go to school too far away from Lakebook's first-chair trumpet player."

"You know, Hads, of all the ways you describe me, that's definitely the coolest." His voice drips with sarcasm.

"Would you prefer eighth-grade second-place mathlete?"

He gives me a level look. "No. No, I would not."

"How about—"

He cuts me off. "Badass guitar player? That would work. Or even accomplished pianist, if you're feeling fancy."

"Nah." I smirk. "I like mine better."

Ty makes a good-natured, disapproving face, then nods toward Becca's room. "Hey, um, Becs is working tonight, and I think Greg was out sick today, but I'm up to hang if you are. We can forget about school stuff. Want to come over later? After your dinner, I mean. We could camp out on the couch and have a *Kill Bill* marathon?" Then he furrows his brow. "Or, wait, should we pick something else? 'Cause of all the crappy shit the producers did to Uma Thurman?"

I love that Ty considers that kind of stuff, but in this instance, I think it's okay. "*Nobody* should miss seeing Uma kick ass. It's not her fault they're shitty."

He smiles. "So you're in?"

"Yeah." I glance out the window, taking in the bluster moving through the trees. "Staying in sounds good."

Becca comes back into the kitchen, her fuzzy pink sweater catching my attention. She tends to dress somewhere between a sorority sister and a Disney princess. Her phone is still pressed against her ear, and her expression is pained.

"Is Greg all right?" Ty asks.

16

"One second," Becca says into the phone. Then she looks at me. "Hadley, um, don't kill me."

"Why would I kill you?"

"Greg is supersick. Like, you don't even want the details."

I can see the question forming on her face. "You're kidding, right?"

She pouts, an expression dramatic enough for the stage.

"Does the concept of Friday night really not mean *anything* to you?" I ask.

"I know. *I know.* But he doesn't want to be alone. And working the meet will count for your NHS hours just as easily for you as it does for mine."

Her big, puppy-dog eyes are impossible to say no to. "Ugh, all right. Just let me ask if I can keep the car longer," I say. "Remy might kill me for no-showing, but whatever. It's already her second breakup since school started."

I'm normally more sympathetic to my sister, but my own boy problems are still a little fresh. My ex, Noah, ended things in August, right before he went off to school. It wasn't exactly a shock, but I have to admit, it hurt more than I expected. And ever since, every time Remy is upset over some guy, I kind of feel like I'm reliving my own issues.

"You're the best, thank you!" Becca gives me a quick one-armed hug, leaving me in a cloud that smells like her hair spray, and then returns her attention to her phone, moving out of the room again.

Ty looks at me. "You're a good friend."

"We both know she would do it for me."

"Yeah." He nods. "She would. And no worries, we can rain-check Uma."

"No, let's just do it after. The swim meet can't last all night, and *some* part of our Friday should be fun."

His mouth curves. "All right, cool."

I text my siblings in our group chat, asking about the Jeep. My phone buzzes, seconds later.

Judd: I'm at that Magic the Gathering competition all night, so it's cool with me.

Remy: Fine, whatever, I'll just drown my sorrows alone.

Judd: You have Mom, Rem.

I feel a wave of gratitude for my brother, always the peacemaker.

Remy: No, she bailed. She got her wine delivery thing, and her and Dad are with the neighbors.

Judd: Dad's drinking wine?

Remy: No, he brought one of those jugs of beer he likes. Craft something? I don't know. Who cares? The point is that everybody is abandoning me.

I grimace at the thought of Remy alone and click to video chat with her. Easier to read how bad her mood is. A few seconds later, there's a cheerful *bing*, and my sister's face fills the screen.

When Remy's not mid-breakup, she's usually so put-together that looking at her makes my T-shirts and air-dried hair feel frumpy. But not right now. My sister's dark curls are in a frizzy knot on the top of her head, and her normally perfect eyeliner is smudging all over her cheeks. Paired with the sharp look in her eyes, she's downright scary.

"Ugh, Rem, you look . . . upset."

"You mean I look like shit," she snaps.

"I didn't say that!" *But like . . . kinda.* "Are you okay?"

"Well, no, Hadley, I *told* you. Wyatt—" Her voice cracks as her eyes go glassy.

Uneasiness sloshes in my stomach. "I'm sorry. . . ."

"Look, it's fine. I'm not exactly shocked that you don't get this, with your dating strike or whatever."

"I'm not on a *dating strike*, Rem. That's not a thing. I'm just taking a little break. Junior year is important for college apps."

"I've heard your little speech, Hads."

I swallow my frustration. "And I *do* get it, Remy. I just went through the same thing." *Expect Noah and I dated for five months, not five minutes.* "Give me a little credit, please?"

"Yeah, sorry, whatever. It's just not a good night for everybody to be so freaking busy."

"I'm not trying to blow you off. We didn't even have any plans other than dinner! But Becca just—"

She interrupts me. "Whatever. I'm fine. It's fine. I'm watching Bravo, and Abigail said she could come over later, when she gets off work." Abigail is not only Remy's best friend, but one of Judd's closest friends too. I feel a wave of relief that she won't be alone.

"Okay, well, I really am sorry. And it's not like I'm going to a party or something. I'm working a swim meet for NHS."

Remy's eyes narrow, attention suddenly focused. "Wait. The *boys* swim meet?"

I shrug. "I don't know. Why?"

"Because if it's the boys' team, that means *Braden Roberts* will be there."

I can't keep all these random guys straight. "Who? I thought you were upset about Wyatt?"

"I am! Ugh, Hadley, you're so clueless sometimes. You

must know who I'm talking about; he's like one of the hottest guys in your grade." It's an effort not to look at Ty, wanting to roll my eyes at her dramatics. "He's new, totally crushed the captain's record at tryouts. . . . Don't you watch the morning announcements?"

"Not really."

"I don't know what you're going to do without me next year." She shakes her head, and I must not look convinced, because she adds, "I'm just trying to warn you, okay? That guy, Braden—he's friends with Wyatt, and from what I've heard, he's even worse than him. And Braden was a dick to Chrissy, who's literally the nicest. Apparently, our school is overflowing with assholes."

I scoff. My sister and I don't exactly have the same taste in guys, and this information isn't exactly relevant. It sounds like she wants me to gossip more than anything else. "Maybe *you* should go on a dating strike, Rem."

Remy rolls her eyes. "I don't think so. It's my senior year, and I plan on living that shit up. And my show's back on, so I'll talk to you later."

The screen goes black.

I look at Ty. "Well, that was . . . predictable. But it looks like I'm off the hook."

Ty opens his mouth to answer, but then Becca comes barreling back into the room. Before I can even tell her I've gotten the all clear, she starts on me. "Okay, so, Hads. You're going to be selling tickets. It's supereasy. They're five dollars apiece, and you just keep track of how many you've sold—tickets are numbered—and how much cash you've taken in. At the end of the meet, everything has to balance."

"Like our shift report at the restaurant?" I ask.

"Exactly." She nods.

"Yeah, all right. When do I have to leave?"

She grimaces.

"Are you kidding? *Right now?*"

"No. I mean, Coach does prefer that you're early. But you have a solid five minutes before you have to go," Becca says.

"You are *so* lucky I love you."

"I really am." She beams, giving me a swift hug and then throwing her ponytail back behind her.

I let out a deep sigh.

"Later, Butler," Ty calls to me. "See you tonight."

❄   ❄   ❄

When I get inside the school, there's a table set up for me in the hallway at the pool's entrance. I've never been to a swim meet before, so I'm not exactly sure what to do. And because I followed Becca's instructions and arrived early, there aren't tons of people here yet; mostly just a group of guys in team sweats, their families, and some significant others.

A muscular bald man with a whistle around his neck approaches me. "You don't look like Becca Gomez," he says. I don't think there's a staff member at this whole school who doesn't know Becca.

"Oh, yeah. I'm filling in for her. I'm Hadley, um, Butler."

He nods. "Coach Jones."

"Is this my station?" I ask.

"Yes, ma'am." His voice echoes down the hallway. "Did Gomez talk to you about what to do?"

"Yeah, I think I'm all set." I take my jacket off, set my camera on the table, and settle into my seat.

"All right, well, let me know if you have any questions." He taps his fingertips against the table.

"Thanks. Um, good luck? Tonight?" I'm not sure what the right terminology is for a swim meet. The only school events I usually go to are in the auditorium—Becca's shows or Ty's concerts. Somehow, *Break a leg* feels like the wrong thing to say.

Coach, unfazed, continues down the hall.

"*There* he is!" one of the swimmers shouts as the school doors open.

A tall, broad-shouldered guy walks inside. "Hey, man. You ready?" Instead of a varsity jacket, he's wearing a leather one. The collar is up in the back, pressing into the nape of his neck where it meets his blond hair. The way he moves—with long, sure strides—makes it easy to picture him in the water.

"I'm ready to see if you live up to the hype, Roberts," the swimmer replies.

At his name, I sharpen my attention.

The guy my sister warned me about, Braden Roberts, answers with unmistakable confidence. "I always live up to the hype."

When he walks by my table, he meets my eye. Then he smirks. Like because I'm looking at him, he caught me at something. It's suddenly clear to me what Remy meant about bad news.

Before I can think how to react, Coach Jones's voice booms, "All right, team, in the locker room! Now! Let's go!"

For the next hour, ticket sales ebb and flow, and from my seat outside the pool, the meet mostly consists of a lot of echoing and cheering. I spend my time reviewing pictures on my camera from a yearbook shoot I did last week. When the event finally comes to a close and the last lingering attendees head out, I stand and open the cash drawer to count the money.

"Miss Butler," Coach Jones says by way of greeting, "I'm going down to the office for the key to lock up. Almost done with that? Anything I can help with?"

I barely look up, nodding and continuing to count as I answer. "I'm good; almost done."

"Okay, just drop it in the office when you finish."

"Will do."

The sound of Coach's squeaky shoes fades, and I continue with my task. After a few moments of quiet, I hear a door creak open, followed shortly by a loud whisper. "Now!"

The entire swim team, clad in matching sweats, explodes out of the locker room and out the side exit of the school. The last guy out is carrying a bundle in his arms.

"What the hell?" I mutter out loud.

Through the glass door, I can see the boys run to the last group of cars in the parking lot. They pile in and let the tires screech as they peel out.

Sighing, I restart the counting of my stacks of bills. I'm almost done, and my heart rate is almost back to normal, when a voice behind me mumbles, "Hey."

I jump, scared out of my thoughts. When I turn, Braden Roberts is standing in the middle of the hallway.

In just his Speedo.

Reflexively, I take a step backward.

This—okay, *not-bad-looking*—guy is wearing nothing but a green swimsuit, sneakers, and a towel.

And that towel—which could have been used to cover some skin but decidedly *is not*—ropes around the back of his neck, not hiding anything. I don't even realize my eyes are moving down his body, until I have to jerk my gaze away at his hip bones, stopping before I see anything else—anything . . . bulgy.

"Um, hi," I answer, trying to suppress the burn on my cheeks. *Oh my god. Cheeks. Don't think about cheeks!* But I can't stop the voice whispering in my head: *What does the back look like?*

I almost laugh out loud.

Stop it!

I make a promise to myself to behave like someone who can see all this boy-skin without totally losing her shit. Not that I've ever had the opportunity before. Me and Noah kept things pretty PG. But I definitely don't want to give this guy the satisfaction of a reaction. Not after Remy's warning. Or after the way he smirked at me.

I stand up straight and, forcing my eyes from his body to his face, realize I have to add an item to my list: a smile. He's also wearing a shit-eating, you're-totally-busted smile.

Freaking hell, get it together, Hadley!

He holds that gesture for a heartbeat longer than necessary, and my blood cells climb over one another to get to my face. I shove them back down, readjusting my attitude, putting it in place like a shield.

He starts to explain himself. "So I guess the team has a tradition of stealing the new guy's clothes and taking off while he's in the shower? First-meet hazing, or something like that." He lifts his phone in the air; they must have texted him this information. "But if you ask me, the captain's still a little pissed I knocked his name off the record board." He's clearly proud of himself. "I was hoping somebody was still here."

"Um, all right, well, Coach is in the office." I expect him to head over there, but he doesn't move. "I'm pretty sure the rest of the team left together. I'm not sure how you missed it. They weren't exactly quiet."

Braden shifts his weight to his other foot and thoughtlessly rubs at his left shoulder. I try not to notice the way his fingers dig into the muscle. The whole thing is irritating, the way he looks completely at ease, basically naked, in a hallway that was full of students only hours earlier. A hallway I walk every day. I mean, he's essentially living the most common nightmare of all time. *I* should be the one who gets to act casual.

I try to call him on it. "You know, you do a have a towel. You could cover up."

He raises his eyebrows. "You're right. I could." But he doesn't.

"But you'd rather show off?" I counter.

He studies me for a moment. "Was that a compliment?"

"Um, no?"

"But it wouldn't be showing off if you didn't think I looked good."

25

God, he really is obnoxious. "You know, this is a really crappy way to get somebody to help you."

He laughs. "You're right." He pauses. "So, the thing is . . . I sing in the shower."

"What?"

"It's why I didn't hear them leave. I was playing music on my phone." He gestures to just above his head and draws a flat line with his hand. "I had it sitting on the wall between the showers, and . . . I was singing." I know what he means; the girls' lockers have the same showers, with the thick walls between them. Suddenly I have an all-too-clear image.

"Well, that's *a lot* of information about you."

"Yeah. I guess it is." He flashes a boyish grin. "Can you believe that they thought this whole thing would be *embarrassing*?" At first, I think he's being arrogant. But then I'm not sure. Maybe there's a hint of self-deprecation too?

He takes a step closer and leans into the table, resting one hand on its surface. He's close enough that I can see his eyes are hazel. "Look, I'll survive the embarrassment." Humor traces his lips. "I think so, anyway. But I have a problem."

"Okay . . ."

"I don't want Coach to know what happened, or they'll call me a narc, but I don't have a ride."

"Which is why you're asking me," I finish for him.

"Yeah." He looks down at my car keys sitting on the table.

"What about your parents? They just left without you?"

"Couldn't make it. Work stuff."

I frown. "They didn't come to your first varsity meet?"

He laughs. "This wasn't— I mean, I was on varsity at my

old school. Since freshman year, actually. And my mom wrote me a card."

Can I just leave him here? Somehow, the mention of his mom makes it harder to say no. I sigh. "All right, fine, I'll give you a ride. Just let me give this to Coach and we can go."

His shoulders visibly relax. "Thank you." He reaches out a hand. "I'm Braden, by the way."

Feeling strangely formal, or maybe just grown-up, I take his hand. His cool skin envelops mine for just a moment before he lets go.

"Hadley," I answer, and his lips curl upward in satisfaction, like he somehow earned my name. I want to tell him that he hasn't earned a damn thing. That I see through his whole . . . deal, I guess. Except that, okay, I did just agree to give him a ride. But that's all he's getting from me.

❊   ❊   ❊

I move down the hall, drop off my NHS responsibilities, and say goodbye to Coach. Then I grab my stuff. "Ready?"

He leads the way, and we walk toward the side exit of the school, with me trying desperately not to look at *the back.*

"So are you psychic or something?" he asks.

I jerk my eyes up. "What?"

"The camera." He gestures to my DSLR, slung over my shoulder. "Just had a feeling you were going to see me like this?" He arches an eyebrow.

I snort-laugh. "I didn't even know you until five minutes ago."

"Yeah. Hence, psychic." He half-heartedly puts a hand up

between us, standing still now, instead of moving toward the door. "Either way, I would appreciate it if you didn't use that on me during this *very* embarrassing prank."

"That won't be a problem."

"Then why'd you bring it? If you aren't going to take pictures."

"I don't know. I just did. Come on, let's go."

"So you just carry that giant thing with you everywhere you go?"

"It's not giant—"

"Compared to you it is," he interrupts.

I continue, "But yes, basically. I do. *Come on.*" I step in front of him.

"Why?"

Frustrated, I turn. "My god, do you always ask so many questions? I brought my camera because I had to work all last summer to afford it, and I like keeping it close." He still looks unsatisfied, so I add, "And it's pretty much my favorite thing ever. Okay?"

"Whoa. Favorite thing *ever?*" Braden looks it over again, glancing at the pins decorating the strap. He stops on one in particular. "Does that say . . . ?"

Some of my irritation fades as I realize which pin he's looking at. I have to hold back my laughter, but I keep my face as neutral as possible. "'Brains are the new tits'? Yeah. A friendly reminder from Mom to, you know, prioritize."

Braden doesn't move. "From Mom?"

"Well, technically it's from my sister. It's a joke. She has kind of a dark sense of humor."

"My mom makes me put a dollar in the swear jar if I say *tits*. Or, well, she used to."

The swear jar? I almost tease him for it before I realize what that means.

"Wait. Why in the hell would you ever say *tits* to your mom?"

"What, you can, but I can't?"

"Yeah." I nod. "Exactly."

He gives me a questioning look.

"When you have them, you can talk about them."

His eyes shift a bit lower.

"Oh my god!" I move around him toward the exit. *Remy is right.*

He objects, "You're the one who brought it—well, *them*, really—"

"Have fun walking! Try not to let any important append-ages fall off!" I shove the door open, my leather boots crunching on the fallen leaves.

Braden chases after me, but when he steps outside, he lets out a hearty "Holy mother of shit!"

Wonder how many dollars that would cost him.

"Hadley, wait, hold on!" he shouts as he regains control of himself. I turn and give him a pissed-off look.

He puts his hands up in surrender, looking sheepish. "I'm sorry. I was just messing around. Honestly." His eyes are sparkling, and I realize he's enjoying this. "Let's go, okay? Together? *Please?* I'll race you. It will make you *my* favorite thing ever."

"I'm not *racing* you. I'm not five. And I'm definitely not a thing."

He drops his head, shaking it. "Sorry. *Man*, I'm really messing this up. I am honestly not this much of an ass. Not usually, anyway."

I take in the sight of him, standing in the leaves in his Speedo, bouncing his weight from one Nike-clad foot to the other. Just looking at him hurts, what with the October air biting all over. I curse Mom for her overactive empathy gene, one of her more annoying traits that I inherited.

"I'll let you take my picture." He offers, as if it's a prize, and I can't tell if he's joking or not.

I look at him doubtfully for a moment. Honestly, I'm not sure what makes me do it. Maybe I just want to feel the familiar calm of standing behind the lens. Or maybe it's because he does look damn good in that Speedo, and *the picture* won't be able to annoy me. Whatever the reason, I lift my camera, adjust the settings, and snap a quick shot. And when I glance at the image on the view screen, it stops me in my tracks. Under the school lights, Braden is glowing; pale skin surrounded by every shade of orange, red, and yellow foliage.

Whoa.

In this picture, Braden Roberts looks just like a subject of my all-time favorite photographer, Ryan McGinley. In his *Fall* and *Winter* series, he shot these young people running and climbing around, naked, outside. But it's not really about them being naked—not to me at least. It's more that they're bursting with all this energy, like they're freer, more *alive*, than anybody I've ever seen in real life.

Until Braden, right now.

I can't help but look back at him, the real version of the guy in the picture.

I take in the sight for a second too long, before I force myself to stop.

"What?" he asks.

"You just . . ." I trail off, staring at the screen. "Nothing. Come on, let's go."

Braden gives me a curious look. "Must be a pretty good picture, huh?"

I start toward the car. "Well, I'm a pretty good photographer."

Braden catches up, but I turn away, because suddenly, watching him feels like tapping into a live wire. Unnerved, I unlock the Jeep, and we get in.

My car has never felt this small, ever.

"You, um, all right?" The leather is cold even through my layers.

"Well, I don't think I lost any appendages. Yet."

I bite my lips to hide my amusement as I turn the key in the ignition. Ignoring his glow-in-the-dark thighs, I blast the heat, adjust the vents, and mess with the radio. "So, um, where am I taking you?"

"Team sleepover at Pebbleridge. Do you know it?"

Pebbleridge is known not just for the expensive houses that make up the subdivision, but also for the giant lake situated right in the middle. Kids from my school are always sneaking in to swim or fish off the dock, which you aren't supposed to do unless you actually live there.

"Oh, yeah, my friend Tyler, he lives in that neighborhood. I'm actually going tonight too."

The car shrinks farther, and Braden's voice gets closer. "Friend, huh?"

"What?"

"Tyler, he's just a friend? Not your boyfriend?"

"Oh, um. Yeah." I shake my head. "Or no, I guess. Not boyfriend." I back the car up, pulling out of my parking spot. "I was dating this guy, Noah, but we broke up a few months ago." I don't know why I'm telling him all this. But there's an energy radiating from him. And something inside me keeps stirring in response. It's making me nervous and weird. "Why?"

"Just curious." It's quiet for a beat before he asks, "You're not going to ask about me?"

"You mean if you have a girlfriend?"

"You're not curious?"

"No. And you don't."

"And how would you know?" His voice is playful and defensive.

"Just do. You don't seem like the girlfriend type." Remy didn't say much, but I know how to read between the lines.

"Why not? I'm a good catch. Fastest fish in the sea." He smiles at his terrible joke.

"Yeah, fastest to swim away," I counter.

"It's not like that!"

"Oh, I think it's exactly like that." I give him a look, but catching his eye makes my stomach flutter. I sit up straighter and focus on the road. "Can we talk about something else? Or not at all?"

"Not at all works fine for me."

Relieved, I settle into my seat. And after a couple seconds, the quiet takes on a life of its own. Eyes fixed on the road, I'm still painfully aware of him. The way he's using his breath to warm his fingers and then running his hands up and down his legs.

Quickly, I steal a glance. He's covered in goose bumps. I'm surprised to feel a small pang of guilt as I think of my boots, jeans, sweater, and jacket. I groan as I start to work my coat free, planning to offer it to him.

"Do you want help?" he asks, reaching to pull my arm free of the sleeve.

"No."

He withdraws. "All right, sorry."

I give him a sharp look as my coat finally untangles from around me. I toss it on his lap. "Here. I don't want to crash because I'm worried about you freezing to the seat or something."

He adjusts my coat on his legs, looking pleased. "Thanks, but we both know that's definitely *not* what's distracting you."

"You know, you really need to get over yourself."

"You don't know me well enough to say something like that."

"I know *plenty* of guys like you." *My sister has dated almost all of them.*

"I've got news for you, Hadley: you don't know anybody like me." When he says my name, I swear I feel a spark jump from him to me.

I try to ignore it. "Just buckle in."

"Whatever you say." He stretches the seat belt across his bare chest until it clicks into place.

And for the rest of the short drive, I keep my eyes fixed in front of me and reassure myself that I am nothing at all like Remy.

CHAPTER 3

I watch my sister in our bathroom mirror. "Seriously, Rem, *sloths* move faster than you."

Remy is smearing concealer under her eyes. She's still pouty. "Well, that's funny, because I look more like a raccoon."

"How much longer do you need?"

"Just a few seconds, okay?"

I'm too annoyed to answer. "Judd!" I call down the hall. "Are *you* almost ready?"

All I get from his room is a grumble.

This is useless.

Remy and Judd both applied early to Michigan State University, and ever since they got their acceptance letters, their interest in high school has plummeted. Remy committed, and Judd is still deciding, but neither of them is any help at getting me to class on time.

The smell of bacon wafts through the house, and I descend the stairs and make my way to the kitchen. If I'm going to wait for them, I might as well get something to eat.

"Morning, Hads," Mom says cheerfully. Her dark hair is pulled back into a low bun that hovers just above the collar of her white shirt, which she paired with a gray skirt and matching suit jacket. She looks every bit the lawyer, aside from her bare feet.

I pull a piece of bacon off the plate on the counter. "Morning," I answer, taking a big bite. But then I have that horrible memory of the fetal pig and choke.

"You okay?" Mom asks, moving a step closer.

I take the coffee mug from her hands and, with a bitter gulp, wash the bacon away. I hand the cup back. "Thanks. Sorry, just biology ruining my breakfast."

Her nose wrinkles as we eye the sizzling pan. Mom knows all about the dissection; I've complained about it every day since we started. This particular assignment is seriously ruining my favorite subject. Inability to eat bacon might be the last straw.

"You ladies okay over there?" Dad's sitting at the table, a bottle of cold brew next to his open laptop. His clothes are much more casual than Mom's: dark jeans and a Polo T-shirt. If all else failed, I'd know it's a weekday by his straw-colored curls that are gelled into submission. And despite the fact that I can't see it from here, I'd be willing to bet that the screen is mostly black, filled with green lines of text.

"Yeah," I answer, "swallowed down the wrong pipe." No need to ruin bacon for him too.

Mom hands me a plate and gestures for me to pass it to Dad. I set it in front of him. "How's the Matrix?"

That's Dad's favorite joke when he's coding: I'm in the Matrix. It's not exactly funny, but he repeats it so often that we've adopted it.

"Not bad. Just finishing up before my meeting," he says, taking a particularly fatty piece of meat. "It's a yearbook day, isn't it?"

"Yep." I nod, turning away. Mom gets an eyeful of my disgusted face and snorts with laughter.

Chewing, Dad asks, "What's so funny?"

"Nothing," Mom and I answer in unison.

Then Mom turns to me, gesturing up the stairs. "How late are they? Do you need me to take you? I can go into work early."

I look at my phone. "No, it's okay. I'm already screwed, anyways."

"I'm sorry," she says. "I'm sure Becca's not going to be thrilled."

"Yeah, she's going to be pissed. But she'll get over it."

A couple minutes later, Judd and Remy make their way downstairs. Remy is fully dressed, outfit curated from head to toe, and Judd looks scruffy and ruffled. Remy works at this boutique in town, and I swear she might as well be getting paid in clothes. Judd and I just didn't get that gene.

In some ways the twins couldn't be more different, but when they look at me, it's hard to ignore their resemblance. They have matching blue-green eyes, the same build—long and slender—and the same dark, curly hair.

Remy looks me up and down. "You know, Hadley, if you wanted, I could help you pick out an outfit for school."

I look at her flatly, comfortable in my Keds, boyfriend jeans, and sweater. "Let's just *go*, please."

Fifteen minutes after we should have left, we say goodbye to our parents, and finally make it out the door.

Automatically, I get into the back seat of the Jeep. Judd doesn't really care whether he gets the front seat, but it's become a habit, because Remy always objects—claiming seniority—when I try to take shotgun.

My sister adjusts the driver's seat. "Hads, you know when you don't put it back I can hardly even get in."

She's not that much taller than me, but I let it go. "Sorry. Thanks for letting me use it so much this weekend, guys."

Remy turns. "You were gone a lot."

I exhale, tired of her attitude. "I had the swim meet and a group project. Remy, if you're mad at me for bailing on Friday, can you just say so? Because you said it was fine."

To my surprise, Remy's attitude falls away. "Wait, I forgot to ask, did you see that guy?"

"What guy?" Judd asks, suddenly interested.

"Braden Roberts." Remy side-eyes Judd. "Even Wyatt—who is the actual scum of the Earth—said he's bad news, so that's when you know. And they're friends! I told Hadley to stay away from him." Remy digs in, trying to prove her point. "I saw him break up with Chrissy McMillian at Wyatt's homecoming party in front of everybody. She was crying, and he totally didn't care. He was talking to some other poor girl by the end of the night. The whole thing was intense."

Somehow, this information makes me feel disappointed and relieved at the same time.

I change the subject so I don't have to dwell on the confusing mix of emotions. "Did Abigail end up coming over on Friday?"

Remy and Judd exchange a look.

"What?" I ask.

Judd answers, "Remy may have convinced us to do something . . . sort of stupid, after I got home."

Remy scoffs. "Oh, please. Judd, don't act like it was all me! We were harmless. Just egged Wyatt's car . . . a little. No permanent damage or anything. Well, except to Mom's organic eggs. But it made me feel better."

I object. "Um, and why exactly didn't you invite me?" It'd have felt good to get a little retribution on one of these jerks.

Remy sounds exasperated. "Yeah, right. Like you would have come."

"Of course I would have!"

"Okay, you're right, maybe you would've. And you'd have taken pictures of *us* throwing eggs and not lifted a single one yourself."

"What?" I look to Judd to defend me, but he puts his hands up.

"Sorry, but Remy has a point. And then you would have had evidence. Of just us."

"I would have totally thrown an egg," I argue.

"All right, whatever you say," Remy says, like she couldn't believe me less.

A little pit settles in my stomach. *Do they really think I'm that boring?*

Judd adds, "But the pictures definitely would have been dope."

Somehow this makes me feel worse. "Well, we'll never know since you guys went without me."

"God, you know, Hads, you are so grouchy this morning. You should try meditating or something," Remy says.

When I finally walk into my yearbook meeting, nobody's there. I text our group—Becca, Ty, and Greg—and head to the caf to see if they're getting breakfast. Ty is sitting alone at the corner of a long table, lost in thought.

"Hey, Ty."

He looks up from his notebook.

I flop my stuff next to him. "How mad is she?"

He smirks, still looking a little absent. "She's not thrilled."

"I can't believe I missed it entirely. I'm going to kill Remy."

"Becca will get over it. And you should probably go tell Mr. Patel that you're still in. Becca's all freaked that he'll take our club status away without four people."

This summer, Becca went to a two-week leadership camp and came back determined to make our college applications stand out. Which is why when the yearbook club didn't generate enough student interest this year, Becca suggested the four of us keep it from extinction.

"Thanks for the heads-up. Where is she?"

"She took Greg to the library to help him with his Spanish homework. I got your student profile assignment for yearbook, though. Hold on." Ty turns a page in his notebook. "Here."

Tyler's all-caps handwriting says: *BRADEN ROBERTS.*

"You've *got* to be shitting me."

"Um, no. Why?" He looks at the name again. "Oh, shit, is that the guy Remy mentioned on Friday?"

"Yeah. And I met him too. I drove him to some house in your neighborhood, actually. Right before I came over."

He looks surprised. "You did?"

"It's a long story. Doesn't matter." I grab my phone to check the time, but instead notice the date. My heart sinks. *No wonder Ty is sitting over here alone.* I look at him more closely. He's picking at the seam of his disposable coffee cup.

"Ty. It's your mom's birthday." The last one she was alive to celebrate was four years ago, before she unexpectedly passed away from a brain aneurysm. "I'm sorry. I'm such an idiot; I just realized. How are you doing?"

He takes a deep breath. "I'm all right. Thanks for saying something, though."

Which is basically Tyler-speak for *Nobody else did*. Which, unfortunately, doesn't shock me. Becca and Greg don't always pick up on stuff like that. And in their defense, it's easy to not think about losing a parent. Until it isn't.

I try for a happier note. "Remember the day we met?"

Ty exhales, amused. "When you barged in on me in the nurse's office?"

"I was so surprised," I say, laughing. "I basically jumped out of my skin. It was *always* empty."

"And I thought you were going to apologize, but you were just *pissed*."

I cover my face with my palm. "I know, I was such a mess. I thought the world revolved around me." I had recently found out that Mom had breast cancer, and the nurse told me that whenever I was upset, I could take a minute in her office. And Ty's mom had just passed away, and the nurse told him the same thing. He definitely had more of a right to be in there than I did, but he never made me feel bad about it.

"You know, I kind of liked that you yelled at me," he says.

"What? Why?"

"Yeah, I mean, everybody was treating me like I was made of glass or something." His lips curve. "Not you."

"Not me." I shake my head, still embarrassed, even though it had been in seventh grade. "I don't know what I would have done without you that year, Ty."

Mom ended up needing a surgery to remove the tumor from her breast, but no chemo or radiation, thank god. She's been okay since then, but I can't remember ever being so scared. And those first few weeks of school—when the hallways were filled with shrieks, laughter, and endless gossip about who kissed who over the summer—Ty and I kept finding ourselves alone together in the nurse's office, quietly bonding over our fear and grief.

"Cancer, death, yelling," he teases. "*Totally* normal way to make friends."

I smile. "I'm still not sure why you put up with me."

He rubs his forehead with the heel of his hand. "Me either, Butler."

"And how's your dad?" I ask, knowing Ty worries about him during this time of year.

He shrugs. "It's kind of hard to tell. He seems the same. You know, tall, serious. Doctor-y."

"That's good, right?" I ask. "That he seems like himself."

"Yeah." Then he sits up straight and his fluid movements go stiff, almost robotic, transforming himself into a goofy version of his dad. "But, Miss Butler, mental health, while often invisible to the outside world, is just as important as physical health."

"That was too good," I say again with a laugh. "Spot-on."

He continues in the perfectly articulated Dr. West voice, "I am a man of many, diversified talents."

The first bell rings. I have seven minutes to get to first hour, and with my late-rising chauffeur, I'm tardy way too often.

"Ugh, I've got to go. But that second impression got totally creepy, FYI," I say as I swing my backpack over my shoulder. I still have to get to my locker to ditch it. No bags in class.

Ty's voice is mock-serious. "And now she's insulting me on my dead mom's birthday. Still as ruthless as you were in seventh grade."

I object. "You said you liked it!"

"Oh, I'm *deeply* messed up. Mommy issues."

"Oh my god, that's not funny." I shove him affectionately with my shoulder. "Hey, for real, I hope today doesn't totally suck, okay?"

"It'll be all right."

I hold up my phone. "Say the word, and I'll meet you in the nurse's office."

❀　❀　❀

As Ty and I part ways, a voice bellows over the rest. "Hey, Hadley!"

My stomach drops; with what emotion, I don't know. I turn and find a way-too-cute guy gesturing with his chin for me to come talk to him.

"I can't be late!" I shout in his direction.

He motions again: *come here.*

I know I can't avoid my assignment forever. *I might as well get this over with.* In the crowded hallway, walking toward Braden feels like swimming upstream.

We meet halfway, and he quips, "Funny seeing you like this. Daylight. Me fully clothed." Even with his jacket on, I can clearly see his shirt clinging tightly to his chest.

"Yeah," I answer flatly, "hilarious." The automatic doors slide open and close as students hurry inside, bringing in the chilly autumn air.

"Not a morning person, huh?" he asks.

"That's what they tell me."

"Okay, well, I'll keep it short, then, I guess. Coach said you wanted to interview me?"

Another student rushes by, nearly knocking me over. But Braden steadies me, a firm grip on my elbow. "Oh, um, thanks." I look down at his hand. It takes up nearly half my arm; probably good for swimming. I push down the thought, and he lets go of me. "Just for the record, I got *assigned* to interview you."

He doesn't seem to care about the difference.

I continue, "Look, I don't want to be late for first hour, so can you just meet me in the library today during study hall? We can do a portrait in the gym? After?" If I get this done right away, maybe Becca will be less mad at me for missing the yearbook meeting.

"Can't," he answers, "I have to make up a test."

"Okay, what about tomorrow?"

"I usually do my homework in study hall."

"You don't do your homework at home?"

He laughs. "Are we getting this interview thing started early?"

I look at him, trying not to notice the bold, straight lines of his face. Everywhere except his lips.

He continues, "I have practice after school. With school and work and swim and everything, my life can be pretty scheduled. It sucks."

I force myself back into the present moment. "Okay, well, when, then?"

"I can meet you at the Starbucks in town tonight? I have, like, an hour after dinner."

The warning bell rings—one minute until class starts. "Okay, fine. What time?"

"Seven-thirty?"

"See you then." And before he can say another word, I turn on my heel, determined to stop looking at his freaking face. As I'm frantically shoving my bag into my locker, I have an idea on how to make this interview worth my while.

※　　※　　※

It's a quarter to eight, and when I walk into the coffee shop, Braden is already inside. He's leaning against the cream-and-sugar station, and when he sees me, he stands up straight. "Hey, I already ordered, but I was just thinking I should have waited. Can I get you something?"

He's wearing that leather jacket, and I swear to god, it's like the guy has *always* just gotten out of the shower; the scent of soap clings heavily to his skin.

"No, um, thanks." I shake my head. "I'm good. I'll get it."

I order a mint tea, and when I rejoin him, Braden is holding a frozen drink piled high with whipped cream.

"What?" he asks.

"I didn't say anything."

The green straw sits between his teeth. "Tell that to your face."

"I just . . . I think I expected you to get a black coffee."

"Gross. Why would I do that?"

"I don't know. To be macho or something."

He shifts his weight. "You really think you have me figured out, huh?"

I'm spared from answering because my tea's ready. When I grab it, Braden starts up the stairs, and we situate ourselves in a back corner near the fireplace.

"So," he asks, scooping out whipped cream with the end of his straw, "you have some questions for me?"

"I do."

Because while Braden was allegedly making up a test, I went into the library and looked up different ways to interview people. After some research, I settled on the Proust Questionnaire, because it claims that it reveals the true nature of whoever you interview. And, hopefully, once I see that he's exactly the kind of guy Remy warned me about, I'll stop picturing him in that freaking Speedo. Or worse, as a Ryan McGinley photograph. Free and alive and—*stop it!*

"You ready?" I ask.

"Hit me."

"Okay, first question: What's your idea of perfect happiness?"

He frowns. "What?"

"Did you not hear me?"

"No, I heard you, just . . . um, okay. Perfect happiness?"

"Yep." I can't help the satisfaction at catching him off-guard.

He rubs at his face. "I guess . . . a full-ride scholarship to the University of Michigan, for swimming, obviously." He pauses. "Or, well, actually, if we're talking perfect happiness, to Stanford—it has the top swim program in the country. And they have even higher academic standards than U of M, which is already hard."

I open my mouth to reply, but he shakes his head.

I watch it occur to him. "Or, no, wait. No, forget school. Perfect happiness would be standing on the top podium at the Olympics. Definitely. Final answer."

"Oh." That's not exactly revealing. "Um, really?"

"No," he says seriously before breaking into a laugh. "What do you mean? Of course, really."

"Is that actually a possibility?"

His gaze holds steady. "Maybe. My times are good. I work hard."

Despite myself, I'm kind of impressed. I didn't know he was *that* good. "Well, okay, then—a medal at the Olympics," I repeat as I write it down.

A flicker of a brow. "Why do you make it sound like that?"

"Like what?"

"Like it's, I don't know, *not* the coolest thing ever? Because the Olympics are literally—"

I laugh, interrupting. "You don't have to explain the Olympics to me."

"Are you sure?" he teases. "'Cause you seem confused. It's this epic, worldwide—"

"Okay, okay, I know what the freaking Olympics are. I just . . . I don't know. As happiness goes, isn't it a little . . . impersonal?"

He looks baffled. "There's nothing more personal."

I scoff. "How?"

He sits up straight, leaning closer. "Training your body, mentally pushing yourself as hard as you can—harder, even—to accomplish something great. It's your whole . . . self. What could be more personal?" His jacket pulls tight across his shoulders.

Stop looking at his freaking shoulders. You're on a mission. Focus.

I try to think of an answer closer to what I would say. "I don't know, like . . . eating dinner with your family? A good conversation with people you love?"

"Eating dinner with my family? A conversation? Instead of an Olympic medal? Are you serious?" The look he's giving me is so intensely focused, so perplexed and amused, that I don't know what to say. When I don't answer, he continues, "Hadley, okay, if eating dinner with your family is your idea of perfect happiness, let me tell you something: you should think bigger."

I defend myself, bristling at his words. "It doesn't ask what your greatest goal is. It asks about happiness."

"Isn't that the same thing?"

"No. Not to me." How are we fighting, already? It's been less than ten minutes since I walked in. "I don't know. Whatever."

"I stand by it," he asserts. "Winning a gold medal at the Olympics is definitely my idea of perfect happiness."

I fold. "All right, I wrote it down."

"Great."

"Okay, um, next. What's your greatest fear?"

"Losing at the Olympics," he shoots back without even thinking.

I drop my pen. "Braden. Your biggest fear, *ever*, is being talented and dedicated enough to qualify for the *ultimate athletic competition*." I notice him smile at my definition of the Olympics. I continue, "But not being one of the top three *in the entire world*? That's *the* scariest thing to you?"

"Kind of, yeah."

"That's . . . That can't be true. What about being murdered? Or death in general?" He doesn't look convinced. "Or what about, god forbid, *not* qualifying for the Olympics *at all*?"

"These questions are sort of intense."

What it sounds like he means is *You're intense.* "I went with the Proust Questionnaire," I reply.

"Proust?"

"I don't know—a French writer."

"What does a French writer have to do with anything? Aren't you going to ask me about my records or the team?"

"No."

"Isn't that the point of an athlete profile?" he argues.

"I'm a cofounder of the new yearbook club. I get to decide what the point is."

His grin is self-satisfied. "Oh, well, I didn't realize I was being interviewed by the *cofounder.*" His whole body loosens up as he teases me.

"Well, you are." Trying to move with dignity, I fidget in my seat.

He bites his straw. "So you *did* want to interview me for this."

"No. I was late for the meeting, and—"

"Sure, Hadley. But this would be a lot more fun if you could relax a little."

And when I see the next question, I find that I do feel more relaxed. *All right, Braden, let's have some fun.*

I read from my notebook: "'What's the trait you most deplore in yourself?'"

He sets his drink down. "*Deplore?* You want me to tell you what I hate most about myself so you can put it in the yearbook?"

I can't help the small amusement on my face. "I could get you started with some suggestions."

"Man, you are ruthless." But it doesn't sound like an insult.

"You're actually not the first person to call me that today," I counter, feeling a growing buzz in my stomach.

"I'm not surprised."

"*So . . . ?*" I ask, having fun for the first time since I got here.

"So . . . ?" he repeats.

I do my best impression of Becca. "The student body has a right to know that their star athlete has insecurities too. It's . . . humanizing."

He meets my eyes for a fraction of a second too long, and

a spark jumps between us again. "I guess I could always work on my breath control. Mine's good, but Coach thinks it could be even better."

"That's not real."

"Tell my coach that."

"Okay, well, it's technical. How about something personal?"

He narrows his eyes. "Why do I feel like you're getting at something specific?"

I shrug.

"No, come on, spill. I can handle it," he insists.

I decide to just lay it out. It's part of the reason I'm here; I can't deny I want to know the truth. "All right. Well, if I'm being honest, I was thinking you might admit that you . . . I don't know, could be an asshole to girls. Like how you broke up with Chrissy at Wyatt's homecoming party."

He shakes his head, somehow amused. "Chrissy? Seriously? Have you been sitting on that one?"

"Just wondering, is all," I say innocently.

Braden looks at me like he's putting together a puzzle. Eventually, he asks, "Don't you think you're being a little hard on me, Hadley?"

The contents of my stomach spin. I don't know why, but I didn't expect him to call me on it. I feel like I've been caught, and I hardly even know what I'm doing. Maybe I just thought he was too arrogant to care. I try for some bravado. "I thought you could handle it."

"I can."

"Well, good."

Thinking, Braden leans back in his chair, balancing it on

two legs. "So that's the type of answer you'd like for these questions?"

I can't exactly say that I want to put the details of his breakup in our yearbook. But I do want to establish that he might be the actual worst; give myself enough of a reason to get a grip and ignore him.

"I mean, I'd like some actual honesty, yeah."

Suddenly his chair falls into its rightful position. "Look, I'll make you a deal, okay? I'll answer a couple of that French guy's questions. But only because you have a really messed-up idea of who I am." He pauses. "And only if you answer them too." He's radiating that same energy from Friday night, and something about it makes me want to lean into this. Into him.

I swallow. "I'm not the one being interviewed."

"And I agreed to talk about swimming, not to be grilled about my greatest fears."

I mean, that's sort of fair. "That doesn't mean I have to tell you anything."

"You're right. You don't." His brows furrow. "But will you explain one thing?"

I give him a weary look, but then, knowing I haven't exactly been especially nice, I nod.

"How can just eating dinner with your family *possibly* be your idea of perfect happiness?"

"I didn't say it was." My voice sounds sharp.

He's calm in return. "No, you didn't, but you suggested it."

And maybe it's an attempt to prove him wrong, or maybe it's because his voice dropped into this low version of itself when he said *suggested*, but for whatever reason, I find myself answering honestly. "My mom had cancer. She's okay now, but eating dinner with my family—my *whole* family—it's not something I take for granted."

"Oh."

I find myself filling the awkward space with words. "My parents like to cook together. And it makes the whole house smell like onions and garlic, or whatever they're making. And Remy and Judd, my siblings, fight over who gets to choose the music, and we set the table for everybody with these colorful dishes, and I just . . . I like it. It's no Olympic medal. And I don't know if it would be my exact answer for *perfect* happiness. But it's not far off either."

I'm surprised to find his attention so focused. "What would make it perfect?"

"I don't know. Nothing's perfect."

"Come on. Try."

"More family, I guess?" I meet his eye, uncomfortable with the sudden scrutiny. "Like, extended. And friends. And their families. More food." He laughs a little, and it loosens up something inside me. "Maybe in the summer, on the patio? With some lights strung up. And Remy's playlist. Not Judd's."

"Those are your siblings?" He rests his elbows on the table, drink forgotten.

"Yeah. They're twins, actually. Seniors this year."

"Your family sounds fun." He nods. "You're kind of making me want to come to this dinner."

I don't know what to say.

"But that would ruin the perfect part, right?"

I bite my lip. "You're right."

He laughs. "Whoa, I was joking, but—"

"No, I mean, about before. Being hard on you. I was doing that. Sorry."

He lifts a shoulder. "I said I can handle it."

"I know, but . . ." I think about explaining, but decide against it. "Just . . . sorry. It wasn't cool."

"Thanks." His lips curve up.

"All right," I tell him, "now it's your turn to answer something way too personal."

"Hey, I just asked you what you asked me."

"Hold on. Let me find a good one."

"Wait. You're just going to choose your favorite? That doesn't seem fair." He moves closer to my side of the table, attempting to read the list. I pull my notebook in toward my chest, trying to ignore the smell of his leather jacket and his soap. "Can't I just talk about happiness too?" he asks.

"No, you already did that one, and I think you were actually telling the truth."

"I was. . . . Okay." He sits up taller. "All right, then, bring it on. Give me your worst."

"Okay." I decide on a question, and read it out loud: "'On what occasion do you lie?'"

He scoffs. "That's it?"

I warn, "I don't want some bullshit answer about how you lie when your mom asks if you've done your homework."

"I don't think I really lie."

"Oh, please. Everybody lies."

Braden readjusts in his seat and thinks for a minute. "Okay, I guess I lie . . . when the truth isn't good enough."

" 'When the truth isn't good enough'?" I repeat, trying to understand. "What does that mean? Isn't good enough for who?"

"For me."

"I'm not sure—"

"Like, okay . . . If we have a brutal practice—which we do, all the time—and Coach asks me how I feel, after, I always say I feel great. No matter what, even if my tendinitis is killing me"—he rubs at his shoulder—"or my muscles are so tight they're burning. I just . . . I stand up tall and tell him I feel awesome. The other guys on the team, they'll show that they're done. But I never do." He pauses. "And it's not a pride thing, even though that's part of it. It's because I shouldn't be as tired as everybody else. Not if I want to be the best. Which I do. So I lie, and Coach gets to go home feeling confident about me, and I work harder, until the truth is good enough. Until I can tell him I feel great, and mean it."

I study him, watching his finger trace the lines in the table. "I think I get that."

He looks surprised. "That's it? You're not going to hassle me about it?"

"Nope."

He laughs. "Man, you're really hoping I'm going to tell you about Chrissy, huh?" He pauses again. "Wait, is that why you were so irritated with me on Friday? Do you know her or something?"

I snort. "No, that was just my natural reaction to your charms."

"That good?" He shakes his head. "Well, I'm sure I was coming off like an asshole. I get all revved up after a meet."

After talking about lying, I decide to tell the truth. "If I'm being totally honest, my sister was Wyatt Coleman's homecoming date. And she may have witnessed some things."

"Wait, *that's* your sister?" I decide to ignore whatever he meant by that.

I nod. "But they broke up."

"Oh, well, good." He relaxes into his seat. "Wyatt's . . . not the best guy."

All right, *that's* surprising. "My sister said you were friends."

"Not really. But I mean, I'm new. It's taken me a minute to figure out who's actually cool. I hung out with him for a couple weeks. And he wasn't."

Maybe that's why Wyatt told Remy bad things about Braden, because he dropped him. "Um, yeah. Can't say I disagree."

"Live and learn." He looks at me. "About Chrissy, though. I'm curious. What makes you think I'll tell you the truth? I just told you I lie."

"I don't know, try me."

"All right." But then his eyes flicker over to my camera, sitting at the corner of our table. "Wait—" He finds the strap and points at the pin he noticed at the swim meet: Brains Are the New Tits. "You said your sister had a dark sense of humor. This is for your mom."

Nobody has ever put that together before. I look up at him. "Oh, um, yeah. It is. We thought she might need a double mastectomy, so Remy got the pins for the three of us. She thought it was funny, I guess. But my mom only needed a lumpectomy; a smaller surgery. So now it's just a weird pin from Remy."

"Your sister sounds cool. Way too cool for Wyatt."

"She is. Most of the time. When she isn't a hot mess. Or moody."

"I can't picture someone related to you being a mess. I mean, you're the *cofounder* of the *yearbook* club."

I laugh, despite myself. "Yeah, Remy's not really a joiner. She does her own thing. Kind of fearless. It gets messy sometimes."

"Messy can be fun," he counters in a way that sounds like a challenge.

"You *would* think that."

For reasons I still don't understand, the air charges between us.

"So, um, you were going to tell me about Chrissy?"

"Oh right. Well. Okay. I might have accidentally led her on, like, a small amount."

Of course he did. "I thought this story was going to be redeeming."

"I never said that. But the thing is, when I'm into somebody, I'm direct. Like, there's no speculating with me. I had two girlfriends at my old school—not at the same time, obviously—but they would back me up on this." I find myself wanting to ask a bunch of questions, but I hold back. He continues, "And okay, I guess Chrissy didn't know that. She had been texting me, and I was sort of responding, sort of not— just bare minimum to not be an asshole. And I guess that sort of made me an asshole, because she thought it was way more than it was."

I study him, skeptical.

"Look, I'm not going to win any awards here for being the best guy in the world. At the party, she had a couple drinks, and I realized she had a totally different idea about what was going on than I did. I mean, she wasn't my date or anything. We had never even hung out one-on-one. So I explained to her that I wasn't really into it—very nicely; honestly. And, well, she was drunk and upset, and it turned into a . . . thing."

"Like her crying in the middle of the party?"

"I mean, yes. And she was also yelling at me, *a lot*. And she hit me with her purse."

I choke on a laugh. "Sorry."

"Yeah. I don't know how I get the bad rep out of that night, but, you know, people assume." He pauses in a way that's heavy with meaning. Then he asks, "If I answer some more of those questions, do you think I could change your mind?"

We look at each other, and it's making me edgy, because I can't figure him out.

"Are you going to tell me the truth?"

"Yeah." He nods. "Yeah, I'll tell you the truth."

And for whatever reason, I believe him.

"Okay, then, maybe," I admit.

"Good." He smiles. "Hey . . . this is kind of weird, but now that you maybe think I'm slightly less of a dick . . ." He looks at me like it's a question.

I assess him, and after a beat, I nod.

He relaxes a little, continuing, "I've been wanting to ask: Can I see that picture you took of me?"

I could show him; it'd be easy enough to scroll through on the view screen. "Um." I hesitate, feeling like it's personal. But the picture is of him. "Yeah, okay. I'll show you."

I find it, and remember again how naked he was. I haven't actually let myself look at it since that night. I hand my camera over. He takes it gingerly, holding it with both hands.

"Oh." It's a short, small sound.

My heart rate picks up. "It's not exactly my best work. I mean, I took it so quickly, and just the one shot—"

"No, it's . . . it's awesome. That night, your reaction was . . . I don't know. I wasn't sure what to expect."

"You seemed pretty confident at the time."

He looks at me doubtfully, before returning his attention to the screen. "You're good at this. Can I look through a couple more?"

Mentally, I run through my last few days of pictures; mostly just shots of my family. "Sure, and thanks. I like it."

"I can tell."

"You can tell?" I echo, surprised and unsure what he means.

"Yeah, I don't know." He's quiet for a minute, and then explains, "Like, when I'm swimming, I'm giving it everything I have because I love it. I want to be the best so that I can keep doing it. And I mean, sure, I'd love a scholarship—"

"Or an Olympic medal?"

His eyes spark. "Yeah, that too. But mostly, I just want to stay in the water. And that looks different from somebody who's in the pool to check a box for a college app, you know?" His eyes find mine. "Not everybody gets what it feels like to throw yourself into something, but I think . . . it seems like you've thrown yourself into this. Like, these don't look like snapshots. They look like art."

I'm suddenly at a loss for words.

"Sorry, is that weird?" he asks.

*Only because it might be the nicest and most unexpected com-
pliment I've ever gotten.*

I shake my head. "No. It's not weird at all."

I let him look through the rest of my images, explaining
my thoughts behind a couple of them, and we end up staying
there for an hour longer than we were supposed to, abandoning the Proust's Questionnaire entirely. And the longer we
talk, the more I realize I might not have a good reason to hate
this guy at all.

CHAPTER 4

Ms. Klein is talking about salivary glands, in humans this time instead of fetal pigs. Or, I guess, actual saliva. Whatever. I'm not really listening. I can't stop thinking about something else.

Someone else.

All day I've been on edge, wondering if I might run into Braden in the hallways. I can't seem to stop thinking up all the different ways it might happen, if I do see him. What he'd say, what I'd say. I keep getting deep into this whole fictional conversation before I realize what I'm doing and curse myself. I don't know what's going on with me. It's like I'm being pulled in two directions at once. Sometimes I'm desperate to see him, and other times I want to avoid him until graduation. It's unnerving. I was never like this about Noah.

I sneak a glance at my phone, wondering how much longer I have until lunch, and I have a text from a random number. I slide my finger across the screen: I think I have late-onset frostbite.

As I'm reading, another message appears. Don't bother looking it up. It's definitely a thing.

What?

Then it occurs to me.

Except, it can't be; I didn't give him my phone number. I type frantically, heart racing: Who is this?

Did you run around outside with more than one guy in a wet Speedo?

Um, no. No, I did not. I answer: As a matter of fact . . .

He replies: You owe me if I have frostbite.

Late-onset frostbite is for sure not a thing. I struggle to keep my expression neutral as my thumbs form the words: Plus, that was a week ago! And it wasn't even that cold. You're fine. And btw, I totally saved you. You owe me!

He answers in a series of messages: Oh, right. That's what I meant. Buzz: I owe you. Buzz: I could make it up to you. Buzz: Do you like pizza?

Is he asking me out on a date?

Are there humans who don't like pizza?

I grin self-consciously into my lap as I watch him type: Fair point. How about tomorrow? 8pm? *Holy shit.* He *is* asking me out. Buzz: We can bicker in a new place.

I stifle my laughter. *Shit.* I promised myself I wasn't going to do this for a while. I think I've mostly recovered from when Noah broke up with me, but my stomach still drops whenever I think of him walking away.

My heart hammers. The truth is that some part of me has already made up its mind. It's not like it's a full-blown relationship; it's just one night. I can sort the rest out later.

I type: Okay.

61

Barely a second later: That's a yes?

Don't make me regret it.

I watch the ellipses form on my phone: I'll pick you up this time.

You could also maybe wear clothes this time, I tell him.

He doesn't even pause before retorting: You'll just have to take your chances. Text me your address before then so I know where to go.

Oh my god.

I'm floating but also might be sick.

Is dating still a thing? I guess he didn't actually use the word *date*. But that's what this is, right? I can't think of anybody going on a date. Last year, when I started hanging out with Noah, it was at school stuff, NHS, and then we hung out in groups. I think we were official before we ever went out to eat together.

Ms. Klein interrupts my thoughts. "Hadley, I'm giving you my best spit material. Would it kill you to pay attention?"

"Sorry, Ms. Klein." I slip my phone into my pocket, trying to calm myself down.

There is no actual chance in hell that I will be paying attention to anything at all until I can go over every single detail of this with Becca.

❄   ❄   ❄

"No, I'm sorry, but that's a joke, right?" Remy's eyebrows draw together.

"What?" I look down at my flannel and jeans. "It's October in Michigan! I can't exactly wear a sundress."

62

"No, you're right. But you could look more like . . . a girl?" Becca pipes in as she leans against my dresser, watching me in the mirror.

Remy swallows a laugh, and I give her a nasty look in return.

Nerves fire in my gut. "What if I don't *feel* like looking like a girl?"

Remy and Becca always gang up on me about clothes. They have since we were little, back before her family moved and Becca still lived down the street. It's just that I'm most comfortable in boyfriend jeans and flats. My only kind of girly tendency is my nail polish—but usually black—and I guess I have an affinity for rings. I like the way they click against my camera.

I check back in with the mirror. All right, so the outfit isn't exactly trendy. But it can't be *that bad*. I look at Remy's face, which is all but saying *It can and it is.*

I'm not going to win this argument. All day, I've just been getting more and more nervous, and standing here, being critiqued, puts me over the edge. I collapse backward onto my bed. "Maybe I should just cancel."

"What?" my sister and best friend ask in unison.

Remy shakes her head. "Hads, I know how excited you are. At breakfast, you were smiling at your eggs."

Shit. If Remy knows I'm into him, she'll be like a dog with a bone. And I don't want to have to answer to her; I'm confused enough answering to myself.

But she's right. All morning, I kept picturing Braden walking through our front door, and it made me feel like I might explode into a cloud of butterflies. Which, if

63

you ask me, might be a good enough reason on its own to cancel.

"You're the one who said he was an asshole, Rem. And I'm not even sure if I like him. It's possible I hate his guts." I think I'm really trying to convince myself more, not her.

Becca rolls her eyes. "You clearly don't hate his guts."

Remy jumps in. "And it sounds like I got some details wrong. Plus, I should have known that if Wyatt didn't like him, that was *good* news." But then her expression turns serious. She sits down next to me. "Look, I think I know what you're doing."

"What am I doing, Rem?" I ask in a voice snottier than I mean to use. She glares at me. "Sorry," I grumble.

She considers me carefully. "I think you might actually like him, and that freaks you out. And we've seen my track record." She laughs. "I get why you'd want to be smarter than me."

"I don't think I'm smarter than you."

Except maybe I do, at least about guys.

Or at least, I used to.

Remy looks at me doubtfully. "I'm not mad about it, all right? I sort of get it, even if I don't agree. We can be different." She puts up a hand, as if she knows I'm going to object. "And I know I give you a hard time. And it's not necessarily bad that you're careful. I just don't want you to be careful for the wrong reasons, you know?"

"Not really," I say, irritated. Remy steals a glance at Becca, and I snip at them. "If you guys are going to talk about me, you should at least do it out loud."

Becca takes over, her voice gentle. "Sorry, Hads. We're not

trying to talk about you. . . . Okay, I won't speak for Remy, but I'm glad you went out with Noah. Glad you put yourself out there. And just because you guys broke up, it doesn't mean you shouldn't ever try again."

"Exactly." Remy sits up. "And I get it too. After Mom, that scare . . . the idea of losing somebody—it's really hard. More real, I guess."

"What? Who said anything about Mom?" I look around, afraid she might've heard. I don't want Mom to think she messed me up or something. Because she didn't. And she's fine. All of that's behind us.

"Hadley, I just . . . It's okay to not be perfectly cautious sometimes. I know you don't exactly subscribe to this, but if Mom's stuff taught me anything, it's that life is short. You're seventeen. You like a guy—"

"I might not like him!" I protest.

Amused, she repeats, "*You like him.* Go out with him, at least this one time. The world will not end. I promise. And then, if you decide you don't want it to go any further, that's cool too. It doesn't have to change your whole focusing-on-school thing."

"Remy, can you, just for once, not act like my therapist and be my sister?"

"Tough love, Hads. It's important. Plus, a therapist would be too nice. You totally need me."

And even though it's the last thing I want to do, a laugh fights its way out of me. "A therapist would definitely be nicer," I confirm.

And with that, the energy in the room relaxes. The way it normally is between her and me.

I look between my sister and best friend. "Okay, well, if the world does end, I'm holding you two responsible."

"Deal." Remy looks satisfied. "All right, now that we've gotten that out of the way, let's see a new outfit."

I shake my head. "I give up. This is, like, the fifth option I've shown you guys. Just pick something. As long as it doesn't involve glitter, I'll wear it."

Becca makes a happy, high-pitched noise and goes to my closet. Remy opens my underwear drawer.

"Um, Rem, aren't you supposed to be, you know, anti-underwear exposure? Like, in general, but *especially* the first time Braden and I are hanging out?"

She smirks. "Well, Hads, he did show you his. Isn't it your turn?"

"Remy! I am literally never telling you anything again."

Becca's laughter fills my bedroom. "In Hadley's defense, it wasn't *technically* his underwear. . . ."

"Thank you."

"It was even smaller," she finishes wickedly.

They cackle.

"It's official. I hate you both."

Mom approaches, hovering at my doorway. "How's it going in here? We're getting close to pick-up time, aren't we?"

Excitement and terror tangle in my chest. "If everybody keeps making a big deal out of this, I swear, I'm going to—"

Mom laughs, shaking her head. "He must be really cute."

I look up, pained. "He is."

Becca and Remy jerk their attention back to me.

"What?" I ask.

"Nothing," they insist.

"Remy, for real, can you stop digging through there?"

"No, look, I was going to explain. I'm just trying to find something that matches. And it isn't for him—it's for you. Confidence starts with your first layer."

I'm as red as a tomato. I try to make my face communicate a whole sentence: *Can we not talk about this?*

But then Mom says, "I always make sure I match when I have a big case."

I look at her, betrayed. "You too? Really?"

"Sorry, honey."

Becca plugs in Remy's curling iron and calls me over to sit in front of the full-length mirror. Then she moves behind me and selects a strand to curl while I fidget with my rings. Becca eyes me and then looks to Mom. "So, Mia, any interesting cases lately?"

Mom sighs. "Well, I'm helping this twentysomething woman fight for full custody of her kids. The dad is an abusive mess. Honestly, it's heartbreaking." She turns, and her face is resolved. "But I'm going to win."

"Good," Becca and I say in unison. Then we look at each other and laugh. It's a relief to expel some of my nerves. I know Becca changed the subject so I could have a minute out of the spotlight, and it makes me swell with gratitude.

Becca pulls a hand through my hair. "I don't understand why women would get involved with guys like that."

Mom breathes out. "It can be complicated."

"Sounds simple to me: leave," I comment, twisting my thumb ring.

"I'm glad you feel that way." Mom looks to Becca and Remy. "Both of you too?"

"Absolutely," Becca replies.

"*Of course*, Mom." Remy sounds exasperated as she digs through my clothes.

After a brief silence, Mom says, "Hey, Hadley, you know if you really don't want to go, you don't have to."

"What?"

"Tonight"—she looks at Becca and Remy again—"if it's not just nerves, if it's something else, you don't have to go."

"Oh." I shake my head. "No, Mom. It's nothing. I want to go." I'm biting my stupid smile into my mouth, and my cheeks are pink in the mirror, and I'm considering hiding under my bed, but I can't stand the idea of Mom worrying about me like that. "I . . . He's— I don't know. I want to go."

She looks at me, knowingly. "Okay."

Remy and Becca are also looking at me closely now. The butterflies spread, taking over my insides entirely. "Will you guys stop it already? Any outfit updates over there?" I ask Remy.

"Not really. Although you do have *three* different Buffy T-shirts." Mom is the only one who finds this amusing; Becca loves Buffy almost as much as I do. Remy stops rifling through my clothes. "I'm not sure what I'm even doing in here. Hold on, I'll be right back."

A beat later, she reenters my room with a cropped olive-colored sweater in her hands.

She holds it up. "Option one: it would show a little bit of skin, since it's off the shoulder, but it's still completely weather appropriate and not too much."

"Love it." Becca nods.

I'm shocked. "I actually do too."

Remy beams. "Perfect. But also, if you stain it, you will literally have hell to pay."

"What a new and totally unexpected threat."

Remy rolls her eyes. "You're lucky I'm letting you borrow it at all. Mom, can you grab her those jeans too?"

Mom tosses them over.

After Becca finishes my hair, I take the clothes and get changed.

When I step in front of the mirror, Becca lets out a happy sigh. "So much better."

And as much as I hate to admit it, she's right. Long, beachy waves fall to the lowest part of my rib cage. The sweater is fitted and hangs off my shoulders slightly. And the cropped jeans make me feel like myself; they're loose and high-rise, and go surprisingly well with Remy's top. I look like a more put-together version of myself.

Remy leans against the wall. "Not bad."

Suddenly the doorbell rings. The bottom of my stomach drops out. I look at three of my favorite people, panicked. "He came to the freaking door? Do guys usually come to the door? Why didn't he text?" I can hear how frantic I sound. It's like I've never done this before.

I check my phone; it's three minutes after eight. No new messages.

Remy's voice is calm, steadying. "Hadley, it's fine." She hands me my high-heeled black booties. "Wear these. I don't want to hear it. You are not wearing those Keds."

Mom looks me over one more time and gives my shoulder

a squeeze. "I'm going down there before your dad does any permanent damage."

I slip on the sneakers. "If I'm going to do this, I'm going to do it as myself."

It's just pizza, just one date.

And if it doesn't go well, I never have to see Braden Roberts again.

CHAPTER 5

Braden is standing in the foyer talking to my parents, strikingly at ease. Like making-Mom-laugh-level at ease. If Mom is charmed by him, I will never, ever hear the end of it. I hope she's just being polite.

I take a closer look. Braden's in that same leather jacket, with the collar up, and underneath it, he's wearing a black V-neck sweater, with dark jeans, and his Nikes. His hair is pushed back, and his hands are in his jean pockets.

He looks even better than I expected.

His eyes follow me down the last two stairs. "Hey, Hadley," he says, like he didn't just learn my name days ago. "I was just telling your parents how you saved me at the meet last week."

All at once, I feel both my parents direct their attention toward me. "I'm a regular Supergirl, I guess." I give Braden a look. "You ready to go?" I ask as I open the door. I want to get out of here. I'm nervous enough without an audience.

Braden takes the hint and quickly says goodbye. Even from

outside, I hear Mom's peppy "Nice to meet you! Bye, Hadley!" It's her I-want-details-later voice. No chance.

When the door finally clicks shut, I look at him. "You came inside? To meet my parents?"

He shrugs, looking down at me with amusement on his face.

"Did you not want me to come in? Are your parents strict or something?"

"No, definitely not. It's fine, I just . . ." I trail off and then look up at his face. "Hi," my mouth says without my permission, and I feel my insides melt. *What the hell?* I curse myself.

"Hi." He barely furrows a brow. "Everything okay?"

"Yeah. Totally." *I can do this. Without making a fool of myself.*

We're quiet for a minute, still standing on the doorstep, when he nods in the direction of his car, a black sedan parked behind Becca's. "Let's go?"

"Yeah. Okay."

We walk in silence. I take deep pulls of the cool night air, avoiding piles of damp, fallen leaves as we walk. He unlocks his car, and we get in.

The quiet remains.

He doesn't even have the radio on.

I wait for him to say something.

He doesn't.

I try to think of something to say.

I can't.

Braden looks relaxed. *How can he possibly feel at ease right now?* I can feel my nervous energy practically bouncing around the car.

I let the big, bulking quiet stretch on as he adjusts the heat, then I notice his auxiliary cord. "Hey, is it cool if I plug my phone in with that? Ty sent me a new playlist today—it's a thing he does when he finds stuff I might like. We could check it out?"

He pulls the gearshift into drive. "Sure, go for it."

I haven't heard of the first song, but I trust Tyler's taste. A slow beat fills the car, and I'm too nervous to pay much attention.

Braden's voice breaks up the nervous chatter in my head. "Are you sure there's nothing going on with you and him?"

"What?"

His eyes spark. "This song is about a guy who thinks he's called dibs on a girl." He looks over at me. "But she's with somebody else."

"What? No. It's not like that. And Ty would never call dibs on a girl anyway."

"No?"

"Girls aren't like a front seat. You can't *call* us."

He laughs. "Don't look at me; it's not my playlist."

"This is just one of his favorite bands."

But Braden doesn't answer and instead gestures for me to listen. And now the lyrics are making my skin feel itchy and uncomfortable. I skip the rest of the song and move on to the next.

Braden chuckles, and I quickly reply, "Shut up. I'm not saying you're right. It's just too slow."

"Whatever, it's cool. I like a little friendly competition."

I have literally no idea how to answer that, so I don't. We're quiet for a moment before he changes the subject. "Hey, about before, coming into the house. I was just trying to be polite. I'm sorry if it was weird."

I take a deep breath, trying to figure out how to clarify my feelings. "No, it's fine. I just have this thing. I don't know how to explain it. I kind of . . . don't like official stuff? It makes me . . . uncomfortable."

Was that even coherent? What I should probably say is that I don't like how out of my comfort zone I am. That I'm sort of freaking; that my best friend and sister seem to think they know why, but I'm still trying to sort it out. And that I want to get rid of the feeling that a million different expectations are floating between us. Mostly, I just want to downplay the whole thing so I can relax.

Braden gives me a confused look. "You mean because I'm taking you out?"

And you make me feel too many confusing things. "Just getting my parents involved . . . It's a whole scene. Which makes it *way* harder to pretend that this is all just a normal thing. You know, not a big deal?"

My mouth has fully run off on its own, making nonsense excuses.

He stops at a red light and turns to look at me. "You want it to be no big deal?"

"I guess so, yeah." I meet his eye and hardly register that the light shining on his face changes from red to green. For just a second, he doesn't move. When he finally turns back to the road, I exhale slowly.

My thoughts race, but he interrupts them. "Do you just

mean how a first date is a little . . ." He's looking for a word. "I don't know . . . forced? Kind of weird?"

I sink in my seat with relief that he understood at least part of my concerns. "Exactly."

"Well, if you want, we can pretend we've done this before."

"What?"

"If the whole Official First Date thing freaks you out, we could skip it."

"We can just do that?"

"We can do whatever we want. It's our date. What number feels less . . . pressure-y? Three? Five? Eight?"

"People go on eighth dates?"

"They probably just call it dinner at that point."

I watch his hands slide across the steering wheel as he makes a left turn. He has long fingers and short, clean nails. And despite the fact that I planned on going on *no* dates, now or in the near future, I'm surprised to find that this idea actually does ease my nerves. "Eight sounds like too many—how about five?"

"All right, fifth date it is." He pauses for a quick, cocky smile. "Man, you must be into me to go out with me five times."

I shoot back, "We could make it zero, instead." My voice sounds scolding, teasing, and it's the most I've felt like myself since he picked me up.

It's almost as if he's watching my personality slide back into place. "I'm kidding. Just kidding," he assures me.

A few minutes later, we pull into Pieces and Pies. It's all windows on three sides, and it's lit up in green, red, and white. Braden puts the car in park. "Best pizza in Michigan."

At the restaurant, he opens the double doors in a way that forces me to walk under his arm, allowing him to look down at me as I pass.

Waiting at the hostess stand is a curvy blonde, whose eyes light up at the sight of us. Her reaction is definitely not for me. *Great.* I hear Braden curse under his breath.

"Brade!" she squees. The name tag on her vest says "Alice." She moves to give him a hug, eyes sweeping over me, but Braden turns to the side and puts only one arm around her. The difference is subtle, and more satisfying than it ought to be.

Braden steps away from her and sets a hand gently at the small of my back. "Hey, Alice, this is Hadley."

Her mouth goes slack. "I've never seen you guys here before."

Technically, there's nothing rude about what she said, but it's definitely a challenge of some sort. Braden rises to it. "Yeah, we haven't been here yet. But we've been out a few times. Right, Hadley?"

I nod. "Totally." I shouldn't be encouraging him, but I can't help myself.

"How many was it again?"

I just shake my head, forcing back my laugh.

Alice's eyes give me a once-over again. "Oh. Well, you didn't mention it, Brade." Then she grabs two menus from the back of the hostess stand. "Here, this way."

She leads us to a small two-top in the middle of the restaurant. I trail her, watching the effortless way she moves. Her vest stops right at the smallest part of her waist, and her hips sway as she walks. Even in her ugly uniform, this girl is seriously pretty. She slaps the plastic menus down at our seats.

Braden looks at the table. "Hey, Alice?"

She presses her lips together. "Yes?"

"I was kind of hoping we could have table twelve." Braden gestures with his head to the booth at the back corner of the restaurant.

"Ugh, Brade. You are *so needy*." But she doesn't actually look annoyed. She picks the menus up, her fake nails clicking on the plastic, and walks over to Braden's desired booth.

"Thanks, Al."

"Have fun." Her hips swing again as she saunters away. And, to his credit, as Braden slides onto the sticky faux leather of the seat, he doesn't pay much attention to her.

Situated in the booth, we pick up our menus. I'm distractedly scanning the pasta section when Braden's menu hits mine and pushes it down, away from my face. He's leaning in close to me, his elbows on the table. "Sorry about her. I checked the schedule, and she wasn't supposed to be in tonight."

I didn't know he worked here, and I'm ready to ask him about it when somebody says, "Hey, Varsity." It's equal parts mocking and friendly.

I look up, even though nobody in their right mind would ever call me Varsity. The voice is coming from a cute, dark-haired guy about our age.

Braden answers with a hand slap. "Hey, man."

The guy is wearing a Pieces and Pies T-shirt, with a towel draped over his shoulder. He and Braden complete a complicated handshake, and he turns to me with a friendly expression on his face. "And *you* must be Hadley. The reason I'm working tonight." He looks pointedly at Braden, who laughs.

Braden introduces us. "Hadley, this is James. James is a sophomore and captain of the junior varsity swim team. He's covering my shift tonight."

"And Braden is the worst, and captain of nothing," James says cheerfully.

Braden ignores the insult and lowers his voice. "By the way, dude, thanks for warning me about Alice."

"Yeah, sorry, man. She traded with Lauren, I think. Probably because she didn't know you already traded with me." He directs his attention back at me, speaking conspiratorially. "The poor girl has it bad for Varsity here." He claps Braden on the shoulder. "But she's all right. Even if she has terrible taste in guys. No offense," he says to me. "Don't let her crash your . . . thing."

"None taken," I answer cheerfully. "I can barely stomach him."

Braden raises his brows. "Even on our very official date?"

"Can you not?" I say.

Braden looks at James. "Apparently, I found the only girl in the world who doesn't want to acknowledge that she's on a date with me."

"Right, the only one," James deadpans.

I laugh too loudly, and seeming to have made up his mind, James gives Braden an approving look. "Shit, Brade! I like her." He looks at me. "I like you."

"Um, thanks."

"You should try to keep her around. I could use somebody else to knock you down a few pegs."

I expected Braden to stop James before he even finishes the thought. But he doesn't. I'm so surprised at first that I don't realize he's waiting for me to answer.

I object, "I barely agreed to tonight!"

Braden leans back in his seat. Looking at James, he shrugs. "She's not sold yet. So be cool, man."

James replies, amused, "Smart girl. Because you do know what this guy is like, right?" He points to Braden with his thumb. "*Conceited ass* doesn't even begin to cover it. Like I said, the worst," James concludes.

Braden smirks. "Every time you call me the worst, I'm taking a dollar from your tip."

"So, what—I'm down from five to two? I think I'll be all right."

"Oh, we're up to three times now?" Braden says. "I only counted two."

James turns toward me. "I'm sorry. Just because you chose to eat with this guy doesn't mean you should get bad service. Have I mentioned, Braden is the worst?" James holds up three fingers in Braden's direction. "He distracted me. Can I get you something to drink? Maybe to take the edge off being out with him? I could probably dig up something with a bite in the back."

"Easy," Braden mutters, rubbing at his shoulder, but James only looks encouraged.

"A Coke, please?" I ask.

"Coming right up." And he heads off without taking Braden's order.

I gesture toward James's back. "So you guys are friends, right?"

"Yeah, we met at club swimming over the summer. He's pretty much my best friend. But don't tell him I said that. Wouldn't want it going to his head." He crinkles his eyes and slides the menu back and forth on the table. "So, Hadley. Very important. What kind of pizza do you like?"

I look down at the giant menu and close it, overwhelmed with options. I had enough trouble with my outfit. "Pepperoni?" I shrug. "I'm not that picky. I pretty much just like pizza as a rule."

"Like all humans?"

I can't help but grin at the recollection of our texts. "Yeah." The air between us pulls tight. "But no pineapple. Fruit does not belong on pizza."

"Agreed." He nods approvingly. "Okay, so how do you feel about pepperoni, green pepper, onion?" he asks as he points at the list of toppings on the first page of the menu. Then he looks up at me to see my reaction. In this light, his eyes look more green than hazel.

"That's actually my favorite."

We smile at each other until James leans between us, dropping a Coke in front of me, and another soda in front of Braden.

"Hashi," Braden says to James, "can you get us the usual? Don't forget the sides."

"Oh, please, Roberts. I never forget the sides." They bump fists.

As James walks away, I ask Braden, "Hashi?"

"Short for Hashimoto."

"Ah." I pause. "And I forgot to ask you the other day, how'd it go with your teammates after I dropped you off? Everything cool with them?"

"Yeah. Honestly, their little prank worked out for me." He looks meaningfully at me. I study my hands. He continues, "Plus, it gave me an out for dying my hair."

"Dying your hair?"

"It's a stupid tradition. The team bleaches their hair a couple weeks before conference, then everyone shaves it off, right before. Some people say it makes you swim faster, but it's crap. I fight it every year; I don't need to change my hair to swim fast." He runs a hand through his, *all right*, kind of nice hair. "And I told them that their prank and my lack of narc-ing should give me a free pass."

"That's a really weird tradition."

"It is. But most of the guys' hair is so fried from all the chlorine they don't really care."

There's a beat of quiet, the two of us leaning into the booth. Before I can think myself out of it, I blurt out, "Can I ask you something?"

He runs his fingers through his blond strands. "No products, air-dried. Just one of the lucky ones, I guess."

"Not about your freaking hair."

He laughs, and I realize belatedly that he was kidding. He nods. "What is it?"

"Why did you ask me out?" My eyes shift over to the hostess stand, and I catch the movement of Alice's head as she quickly looks away. She picks up a rag and pretends to clean some menus. "You evidently have other people interested. People who are . . . nicer to you?"

Braden follows my gaze, and Alice drops her stack of menus. They clatter loudly to the floor. When I turn my attention back to the table, Braden is focused on me.

"I'm not really into nice." He pauses and then shakes his head. "It's boring. And there's seriously nothing worse than boring. Plus, I happen to love both attention and a challenge, and when you saw me in a Speedo, you told me to cover up."

I bite my lips to keep them from turning up. "That bothered you?"

"Well, yeah. I get it, but it wasn't exactly the ideal reaction. And we go to the same school; I wasn't some creepy stranger."

"Jury's still out on that one," I respond, but he looks at me like I proved his point. I ignore it. "So if I start giving you attention, telling you how great you are, you'll be satisfied and move on to your next victim?"

"And by *victim* you obviously mean *date*."

"Obviously." I smirk.

His eyes narrow. "Are you fishing for compliments?"

I lean my head back in exasperation. "Not even. I'm just trying to figure you out."

He studies me for a second before he answers, "Well. Since you're fishing, I guess I like your honesty. I hate getting my ass kissed. And mostly, I think I like all the opportunities to show you how wrong you are about me. A new challenge every couple minutes. The dream." He turns on his megawatt smile.

"So would you like me to vocalize all my bad thoughts about you, then?" I tease. Except the truth is that I like what I just heard. Because he basically said that he'd rather have a sparring partner than a cheerleader.

Amusement sits on his lips, but his words are more serious.

"And I liked the way you talked about your family. How they make you happy."

"You said that answer was boring."

"I lied," he says, sliding to the edge of his seat, closer to me. "I think it's part of the reason I went to your door today. Talked to them and everything. I wanted to be able to picture what you described."

Maybe I am kind of wrong about him, because I would have never guessed any of that.

The way he's looking at me is so intense. "And I don't know . . . Don't you think there's something between us?"

It feels like a strong magnet is pulling me toward him. I swallow. "Maybe."

"If we were really on our fifth date, what else would I know about you?"

"I don't know. What do you mean?"

"Start me out with the basics. We sort of skipped regular stuff, because of your French writer guy."

I can't help but laugh. "I guess you're right. Um, okay, well . . . I've lived here, in Lakebrook, forever, since kindergarten. And I told you about my family."

"What else?"

"Um, I've had the same friends as long as I can remember. You know about Tyler, but there's also Becca Gomez and Greg Miller—they're dating each other. Do you know either of them?"

He shakes his head.

"Well, you *would* have met Becca. She was supposed to work the meet last week, but Greg got sick and I had to cover for her. And I work at her family's diner, Belavinis, so we have that in common, I guess. Both work at restaurants." The restaurant is hectic around us, full of loud voices and young employees hustling from table to table. "What about you? Do you like working here?"

"Yeah, I do. I sort of need to be busy. I've always worked, because I tend to get into trouble if I have too much free time."

"Of course you do."

"Nothing too crazy, though. Well, except . . ." He pauses dramatically.

I sigh. "Except what?"

He shrugs. "It was years ago. Like, I was just a kid—twelve or thirteen, maybe. And I was hanging out with these guys on the baseball team and these idiots said I wouldn't be able to do it, so obviously I had to prove them wrong."

I give him a half-annoyed *continue* look.

"So. I may have thrown a rock—a pebble, really . . . at a fire truck."

"As in the vehicle that helps firefighters save actual lives?"

"That's the one. The pitcher said I couldn't hit the center of the logo, which I did—bull's-eye." He meets my gaze. "Oh, don't look at me like that. Nobody was *in* it." He laughs and then grimaces. "But our dumb asses got caught. The actual firefighters weren't that far away, which we didn't know, and they heard my—really, very little—rock slam into the side of their truck."

"You were such a little shit!" I clear my throat. "What happened?"

"Well, it was technically government property—so I had to talk the police out of charging us with a minor felony."

I burst out laughing. "So you were brought into the police station, for a felony, at *twelve*?"

"I may have been thirteen."

"And . . . ?"

"And I pleaded my case. And I gave them some sad eyes and we were on our way—I mean, after a lecture and calling our parents. I was grounded for a month, but my criminal record remains clean. Plus, I proved that idiot pitcher wrong."

"Which is clearly the most important part."

"You already know me so well."

"So you're telling me I'm on a date with a felon."

"A *fifth* date."

"My mom will be so proud. Actually, are you sure you haven't met her before tonight? She *is* a lawyer. Maybe she defended you for dognapping? Or blowing up a mailbox or something?"

"Nah. Not my style. But I did take a victory lap of fifth grade." He grins. "Couldn't pay attention. Swimming helped with that a lot, though. And that's it. The extent of my troublemaking past." His eyes glint before he continues, "Otherwise, the big stuff: my family has lived here for six months. We moved after sophomore year ended. And my mom had to restart her catering business when my dad got the job here, so they've been busy lately. Which is why they weren't at the meet."

"Moved from where?"

"Outside Chicago." He takes a sip of soda. "How'd you get into photography?"

"It wasn't until a couple years ago. Science was al- ways my favorite subject, and freshman year my counselor suggested I try photography, since it's basically just the law of reciprocity—like, focusing and controlling the light." I shrug. "And I got really hooked. I think it's something about making the world look the way it feels."

His brow wrinkles.

"What?"

"Just . . . before. When you were fishing for compliments." I roll my eyes, but he adds, "The photography thing. It's . . . it's cool to hang out with somebody who might get how I feel about swimming, but with her own thing. You know?"

And I do know. It's one of the reasons I like hanging out with Tyler and Becca so much. Because they both have things they love, and we talk about them all the time. And I have to admit, the way he described competing in the pool . . . It made me feel the same way.

Braden says, "Like, you just made it sound interesting in one sentence." I'm surprised to find that his expression is so sincere.

I can't help feeling like I've done this with him before— the talking, the laughing, the teasing. It's easy. It's fun.

And then James drops our pizza between us, breaking our gaze, and sets down a shaker of crushed red pepper and a side of ranch.

Braden and I talk and laugh while we eat. I learn that he is an only child; that he's focused on the University of Michigan for a swimming scholarship; and that his favorite class is his advanced English course, Modern Thought and Literature, because he likes debating philosophy with his teacher. Each new fact feels like a clue—some fitting easily with who he seems to be and others taking me by surprise, like the English class. Before I know it, it's hours later, and the restaurant looks like it's shutting down. At the first small lull in our conversation, I tell Braden, "We should probably get going."

He looks around at the busboys wiping down the empty tables. "Shit. You're right."

"I think they might technically be closed."

Braden checks the time on his phone. "Ha, they are." Then he meets my eyes. "I can't believe we've been sitting here for three hours. It went by so fast."

And I don't know whether to be comforted or scared to know that he's as lost in this as I am.

❉   ❉   ❉

Several minutes later, Braden pulls into my driveway and turns to face me. The song on the radio floats between us as he watches me.

"I had fun tonight," he says.

"Me too," I say quietly.

He's still looking at me through the dark, and I squirm in my seat, all too aware of what could happen next. I'm doing everything I can not to look at his mouth.

I simultaneously want him to kiss the life out of me *and* want to run far, far away and never look back. "I'm just going to get out of the car, before it's a whole thing, okay?"

"Okay." He nods.

But I regret saying it, and for just a second, I'm desperate to stay. I force myself to find the door handle. "Okay. Um. Bye."

But as I'm standing outside, before I can shut the car door, I hear his voice. "Hey, Hadley. Wait." He's leaning toward me, golden hair falling over his forehead. "I just thought you should know. For me, tonight, total big deal. Best fifth date I've ever had."

"Yeah?" I bite the inside of my lips until they hurt.

"I'm going to make it six."

"You can try."

We look at each other, quiet. "All right, then, I'll try."

And as I move to head inside my house, I feel like I'm floating on air. The minute I close the door, my phone buzzes. What are you doing tomorrow?

CHAPTER 6

I'm putting my bag in my locker on Monday morning when Braden approaches and leans against the metal door.

"Hey." His expression is boyish, sweet. It's the simplest thing he could have said, but my whole body reacts.

I haven't seen him since Friday. I couldn't hang out on Saturday, because my family already had plans, and I was starting to worry. *Did he take it personally that I said no? What if he realized I'm not as interesting as he thought? What if he could tell how into him I am and decided the challenge was over?* My mind found so many ways that this might blow up in my face.

"Hey," I echo, trying not to sound as relieved or happy as I feel.

"So." He takes a half step closer. "I want to tell you something, but I'm afraid you're going to make fun of me."

A thousand contradicting feelings clash together when I look at him. Teasing feels safest. "I think you might be on to something."

"Hm." His eyes crinkle as he assesses me. "Never mind, then." He starts to walk away.

My reaction is immediate. I close my locker and hurry to catch up. "Fine! Okay! I won't make fun of you."

He stops. "You promise?"

I nod.

His voice is low. "I was just going to tell you that I've never looked forward to Monday so much." He glances around the hallway, but nobody is paying any attention; just a few scattered students getting ready for first hour.

"What?" I study him, afraid to feel flattered.

He tilts his head and shrugs. "Yeah."

The warning bell rings, cutting through the tension between us.

Still facing me, he takes a couple steps backward. "I'll see you later, Hadley." And as quickly as he appeared, he's gone.

And the whole week is like that—Braden appearing for brief moments in my otherwise normal days, and those instances feel more vivid than everything else put together. I find myself looking for him around every corner, jumping at every text, every male voice, anything at all that could be him. Nothing has really happened, aside from some serious flirting, and by lunch on Friday, I feel a little crazed.

I do my best to put him out of my mind and take a bite of my sandwich. "No, I get the assignment, Bec. I just don't know why she always has us do dioramas. Like, when in the hell are we ever going to need to know how to do a freaking diorama?" I laugh over the noise of the cafeteria.

"Fair, turning a shoebox into a scene from *Animal Farm* doesn't really seem like a marketable skill," Becca says.

"Right?"

But the rest of my thought leaves, because I swear to god, I smell his soap before I see him.

"Hey, Hadley. Can I sit with you guys?" Braden asks, chomping into an apple.

A thrill runs through me. "Hey, I thought you were in the later lunch today."

"I am," he admits before sitting down. "You're Becca, right?"

"That's me."

"Braden. Maybe Hadley mentioned me?"

I shoot Becca a look, and she's quick on the uptake. "Sorry, no."

Braden turns to me. "Really? Nothing at all worth mentioning?"

My smile is so big and wide it might actually crack my head open. "Nope."

"Well, I guess I have to step it up, then, huh?" I watch his lips, and I catch myself wondering how his mouth would feel. When I look into his eyes, he smirks.

He knows.

I turn to Becca, trying to get out from under his freaking spell, but she's looking at us intently. Plotting.

Shit.

"Braden, why don't you come to my house tonight?" she asks him, all faux innocence, "I'm having people over, and Hadley will be there, if you want to join." I look at her, unsure if I want to kill her or kiss her. *Do I just want to kiss* everybody *right now?* She doesn't falter. "Plus, we could use some help after school, setting up. My boyfriend, Greg, has to work, and I don't want to make Ty move all the firewood alone."

"I can definitely help." He looks at me, hopeful. "If that's cool with you, Hadley?"

My eyes can't seem to stay off his lips. "Um, yeah. Yeah. I mean, if you want to."

"I do." He turns back to Becca. "Hadley can text me your address?"

Becca says, "She's got it."

He looks at me. "Well, then, it's a date." He raises his eyebrows. "Number six."

❊   ❊   ❊

We're standing outside the linen closet at Becca's house. The door is thrown open, and blankets, pillows, sleeping bags, and every kind of sheet and towel are all bursting past the doorframe.

"So what's this for, again?" Braden asks.

"Braden. You're killing me." Becca has her hand on her hip, assessing the contents of the closet. They're already acting like best friends, and she will definitely be getting a speech about loyalty later. She continues, "To start, the blankets go on the trampoline."

I help explain. "Becca always tries to get us to stay out there all night, but we've never made it. The trampoline is too far from the bonfire, and it's completely freezing. So we need every blanket we can get." I turn to Becca. "We know it would be more logical to convince Becca that we don't actually need to be out there that long, but . . ."

"It's tradition," Ty concludes. A corner of his mouth lifts, and he glances in my direction.

Suddenly afraid Braden might think I sleep next to Tyler, I clarify. "The guys have to leave at some point—rules of the house. And the latest Becca and I have ever made it is four in the morning, even in the summer. Our success rate is directly linked to the number of blankets."

Braden makes a skeptical face at Ty. "If they've never done it, is it really a tradition?"

"It's a tradition that we *try*," I tell him, now feeling defensive. "Becca always picks a night that is, like, almost unbelievably too cold for the first bonfire of the year. I guess we should be grateful she chose October, instead of mid-January." I look at Becca, but she just smiles innocently. "And we get food that we can cook on the firepit, so s'mores, and hot dogs, and we bring tons of sleeping bags onto the trampoline, and . . . just hang out, I guess."

Becca jumps in. "And Tyler always makes a special playlist for the occasion."

Braden looks at me pointedly, but I don't return his gaze.

Tyler nods in agreement and adds, "And Hadley almost always gets grossed out by the burnt hot dogs and orders pizza."

"Pepperoni, green peppers, and onions?" Braden asks.

I nod, but Tyler contradicts me. "Usually just pepperoni."

"And Greg pulls up that astronomy app." Becca's voice goes dreamy.

Tyler brushes her off. "Yeah, yeah. We know, you're dating."

Becca points to the bundles in Braden's and Tyler's arms. "Okay, I think that's enough blankets and stuff for now. We can bring those down and see if we need more."

Braden gestures with his head to the staircase. "Sounds good. After you, ladies. And Tyler."

An hour later, the patio, chairs, and trampoline have all been cleared of fallen leaves, and the wood for the bonfire is stacked and ready to be lit. I'm grateful that Becca's choir friends and Ty's friends from band won't get here until later, because I'm shivery by the time we come back inside. It will be nice to warm up for a bit.

Becca and Tyler go to get some snacks from the storage room, leaving Braden and me alone in the living room. My stomach flutters as he sits next to me on the couch, placing his arm across the back. I pull a blanket from the armrest, and Braden adjusts it to cover us both. I feel his attention on me, but I'm too nervous to return it. I distract myself by trying to get some feeling back into my fingers.

"You're never going to warm them up like that." He reaches for my hands and eases my cotton gloves off. Then he takes my fingers and presses them between his.

"You need skin to skin. And friction."

He moves his hands slowly back and forth over mine and brings them to his parted lips, blowing hot air onto our curled fists. Then he pulls our gathered hands to his cheek and leans his face against them. My rings press gently into his skin. "Better?"

My heart hammers as I nod.

"Hadley." He falls into silence. "I've been thinking. . . ."

"What?" I say, breathless, afraid to move much at all, and it's like I'm standing on ice.

His voice lowers to a whisper. "There's something here. Between us."

I'm suddenly afraid of where this is going. *If he says it out loud, there's no taking it back.* "Braden—"

"I like you."

I inhale sharply. I should be thrilled. He's doing and saying all the right things, but instead of happiness or relief, all of my fears are piling up. I pull my hands away. "Braden . . . I should have told you sooner, but I sort of promised myself I wouldn't get involved with anybody for a while. And—"

"What?" He interrupts, but he doesn't look upset. In fact, when he speaks, his words are playful. "Don't you think . . . Isn't it a little late for that?"

I bury my face in my palms and then peek out above them, studying his hazel eyes. *His stupid hazel eyes. Yes. Yes, it's too late.* "Maybe," I manage.

"'Maybe'?" He's incredulous.

"Yeah." I nod.

"So exactly how long did you plan to avoid getting *involved*?"

"Like . . . all of junior year?"

His eyebrows shoot up. "Oh."

And then I start to ramble. "It's, well, I told you about my ex, Noah. He and I just broke up not that long ago. In August. And it sucked. And I didn't even really like him, not like—"

Trying not to smile, Braden's lips press together, and I realize what I almost admitted.

"I mean," I continue, feeling the blush spread against my cheeks, "I had everything all planned out." The air goes out of me. "And then I met you."

"And then you met me," he repeats, turning the words into something lighter. It almost sounds like a question.

There's a sharp pain in my gut. "Braden, I have no idea what I'm doing," I admit.

"Neither do I," he says. He leans closer. "Look, Hadley, I'm not trying to push you into anything. If you want me to back off, just say the word."

But, the thing is, I can't.

I look at him and force myself to address what's scaring me most. "You like me?" The words feel like delicate glass.

He nods. "Yeah." This time, he's the one watching my mouth. We're so close, he's whispering. "But I could try to stop, if you want. I could try to be your friend."

I swear I can feel his breath on my lips.

Suddenly I'm desperate to take it all back. I shake my head. "I don't think . . ." But then I trail off because he's tilting his head ever so slightly. Without thinking, I lean a fraction of an inch closer to his face.

"Hads!" Becca barks my name from the other room, and I jump completely out of my un-kissed skin.

I knew they weren't going to be gone forever, but I have a sudden, strong urge to take out my best friend.

Braden pulls away as Tyler comes around the corner with a bag of popcorn and a jumbo bag of M&M's, Becca trailing him. Tyler seems to sense that he interrupted something, but Becca is clueless. "Tiebreaker. Mixed together, for the ultimate salty-and-sweet medley? Or separate and boring AF?" She looks pointedly at Ty.

Braden's elbows are resting on his knees, and he's gently pressing his knuckles against his lips.

"Separate," I answer, just to spite her. It's petty, I know, but her *timing*.

Her eyebrows furrow, and she looks around, wondering what the problem is. She and I usually stick together against the boys. She looks at the lack of space between me and Braden and understanding clicks behind her eyes. She gives me a *sorry-sorry-sorry* face, and I widen my eyes in a look that I hope tells her I love her but also that she is freaking roadkill.

"All right," Braden says, standing. "I think my initiation hazing is done?"

"Yeah, Roberts." Tyler nods. "You've done your part."

"Okay, so I promised my mom I'd be home for dinner, since she's actually home tonight, so see you guys again around eight?"

"Later," Tyler answers.

And suddenly Braden is walking away. He's standing with the length of the coffee table between us. "See you, Hadley."

"I'll be here." It's a small voice that I've never heard myself use before.

Then he turns and ascends the steps two at a time.

When he's gone, Becca smirks at me and flicks a single piece of popcorn into her mouth. "It is *so over* for you," she says, obliterating the popcorn between her teeth.

❧   ❧   ❧

I'm sitting as close as I can to the bonfire without having to worry that my blanket is actually going to ignite. It's been hours since Braden left, and despite my best efforts, I'm still thinking of him every time I join my hands together in front of me. I keep catching myself looking at my fingers. Waiting for him, I feel a little unhinged. I check the time again. He should be back soon.

"Hadley? Where are you right now?"

I look up at Ty. The warm light of the fire bounces off his face, bringing out the gold undertones in his light brown skin. He's wearing hunter green joggers with a black crew neck, and his Vans are bouncing to the beat of the music. I pull my camera from the chair next to me and snap a shot. In this moment, he somehow looks totally himself. "Sorry, I'm just . . . distracted," I tell him as I click the shutter again. Ty doesn't even react; he's so used to me taking his picture.

I review the last image and notice a funny expression on his face. I put the camera down and give him my full attention. "What did you say?"

"I asked if you listened to it yet."

I make a sheepish face. "Listened to what?"

"Man, you really are in your own world. The new playlist."

My stomach drops. I have been avoiding this since Braden's weird comments about it. "Oh. Um. Listened-ish. I didn't know where I was going, so I had my GPS on, and it kept interrupting." It's not a lie—that did happen; it's just also not the whole truth.

"Oh. Well, you should try it again. The songs are . . . They're good." He tries to meet my eye, but I can't quite manage it.

"Okay. I will," I answer too quickly, and then try to change the subject. "Anyway, what's up with that girl I saw you with in the hallway today? After band? Anything happening there?"

"What? Oh, Amber. Nah."

"Why not? She's so pretty." This whole conversation feels

phony, so forced, but Braden has gotten into my head and messed up what would normally be an easy exchange with Ty.

"Yeah, I don't know. Hey, did you happen to at least hear the last song?"

"Um, maybe?" I open up Spotify.

"You should make sure you have the right one; it's called 'Flexuary.' Greg named it, obviously." He laughs under his breath. *Greg named it; it wasn't just for me.* I feel my posture relax.

Greg, who must have been off with Becca, lands with a thud on the chair next to Ty and interrupts him. "'Cause we're flexin'.'" Greg flexes a modest bicep covered in layers of sweatshirt. The firelight bounces off his teeth.

"What did you do—hear your name and come running?" I tease.

They ignore me. "Yeah, we are," Ty says. Greg slams a friendly fist against Tyler's shoulder.

Then, as if he just noticed me sitting here, Greg looks between Ty and me. "Shit. Wait. Did I walk in on you *still* trying to educate Hopeless Hads on music?" The weird tension with Tyler is new, but this conversation is not.

I defend myself, laughing. "Greg. Hopeless? So harsh. Just because I'm not writing an essay on the world's best lyrical double entendres doesn't mean I'm a total lost cause." Ty and Greg spend hours on Genius, fanboying over the most creative verses.

Greg shakes his head. "She's just never going to develop the sophisticated tastes that we have."

"'Cause you're notoriously sophisticated, Greg," I shoot

back. But then it occurs to me that my supposed ignorance could work in my favor, just in case Braden was onto something with Ty. I try to play it off. "But I guess I kind of see what you're saying. I wouldn't say I'm *hopeless*. But words have never been my thing." I gesture to my camera. "I'm better with visual art."

Ty gives me a weird look, but Greg doesn't even glance over. "Yeah, see, Ty? The rest of us have accepted it. You've got to let it go." Becca must hear him from the trampoline, because she starts singing the chorus from *Frozen*. A few of her choir friends join in as she gestures wildly with her arms, hardly visible from underneath her pile of blankets. I think she may have been sipping from Greg's water bottle. Filled with . . . not water.

I swallow my laughter and turn to Greg. "You should have seen that one coming."

Greg sits up tall. "I'm just glad *my* girl appreciates a strong lyric."

His emphasis on the word *my* makes my stomach turn.

I can feel Tyler looking at me, and I sneak a glance over to him. The fire dances in his amber eyes. Then the song playing around us ends, switching to something with a catchy beat.

"Shit, Ty!" Greg interjects. "This track is insane. I haven't heard it in so long. I'm going to go turn it up." And then he heads inside where Tyler's phone is connected to the speaker system.

The uneasiness between Ty and me remains.

He turns to me. "Don't listen to Greg. We don't all have to be into the same stuff. But I think that what he means is that every song tells a story, and sometimes they can say . . .

I don't know. Like, say something that's almost impossible, otherwise." He's looking at my face, and I suddenly think of the soles of his shoes, words trapped between him and the concrete. "I just mean, you might think of them differently— the songs—if you pay more attention."

I feel my heartbeat pick up, and I'm not sure how to answer. I can't stand feeling this way around Ty anymore, so I try to shake it off, lighten the mood. I move my body back and forth to the music and make up nonsensical lyrics.

He looks me over. "All right, I won't give up on you yet, Butler."

I feel my face fall before I can stop it, and I can tell Tyler notices.

Shit. What the hell is happening?

We're quiet for a minute before he drops all pretense. "You like that guy, don't you?"

"What?"

"Hads."

I can't lie to Tyler. "Yeah," I admit, "I do."

"But you're not happy about it?"

I laugh, shaking my head. "No."

"Why not?"

"I don't know. I didn't want to deal with any of this—at all—this year. And even if I did want to, you've met him! He's *so* not the kind of guy that I pictured myself with."

The silence stretches a little too long to be comfortable. "What kind of guy did you picture?"

"What?" But I heard him. "I don't know. Someone less . . . Somebody who doesn't leave a trail of crying girls behind him. Or who isn't a total cocky asshole."

Ty laughs. "Is all that true?"

"Honestly? Not really. Which is sort of shocking? He said he had two different girlfriends at his old school, each only for a couple months, but it sounds like things didn't end badly or anything. Oh, except the cocky part. That part is definitely true." Then I tell Tyler what I've been too scared to consider, even in my own head. "Remy thinks I'm protecting myself. Being defensive. After my mom's thing. That I'm afraid."

Ty studies my face. "What do you think?"

"I mean, maybe it does have something to do with that." Somehow, saying it out loud feels like a betrayal. *It's not Mom's fault.* I pick at my nail polish.

Ty nods. "I get that. And okay, honestly, he might not be the guy I pictured for you either. But, Hads, being scared . . . That isn't a good reason to push somebody away."

That fear rushes over me. "How do I tell the difference, though? Like, if I'm just freaked out generally or if I actually have a bad feeling about him?"

"I don't know. I guess you just have to try. Shit happens, and you deal as it comes. But it's stupid to have feelings and not do anything about them." His gaze is heavy. "I think you'd regret it."

I try not to feel everything he isn't saying out loud, and focus on what he is.

He has a resolved look on his face. "You deserve to be happy. You shouldn't miss out on that, just because of something bad that happened in the past." His voice is weirdly formal, like it's a declaration. "I want you to be happy."

My insides squirm, guilt and revelation mixing a confusing cocktail. "Thank you, Ty."

He looks more relaxed now, as if he said what he set out to say. "Yeah, no problem."

"But nothing's really happened yet. We'll see."

"It seems like it's going to. And, Hads, it's good."

We're smiling nervously at each other, and when Greg comes back through the door to the patio, he isn't alone. Braden stands next to him, moving the night sky out of the way to shine in the dark, and suddenly I just can't deny how I feel.

"I'm going to . . . ," I start.

Ty nods. "Go."

❋   ❋   ❋

Braden watches as I move toward him.

"Hey." I bite my bottom lip. "So you obviously know Greg now."

"Obviously," he answers.

Greg looks back and forth from Braden to me, then glances at Ty. "Everything cool?"

I nod. "Yeah. Everything's cool."

"Okay, good. Then I'm going to let you . . . do whatever this is."

I laugh as Greg walks away. *Whatever this is, is right.*

Braden gives me a conspiratorial look. "I wanted you to myself, anyways." He tilts his head toward the sliding glass door. "I got you something."

"Yeah?" I take a step closer to him, and he wraps my fingers in his. I try not to worry about anybody who might be watching. For the second time today, there's a flutter in my stomach; butterflies waking.

As he leads me inside, the warmth of the room brings a tingling sensation back into my limbs.

"Sorry I'm late. My mom made a big deal about family dinner tonight," he says. "And I wanted to make a pit stop after."

Braden continues through the basement and toward the laundry room. I can hear the dryer running before we cross the threshold, and I know it's because Greg put blankets in there earlier, hoping to bring them out later, toasty warm. He loves to be the hero.

When we walk in, there is a stack of pizza boxes sitting on top of the washing machine next to half-eaten bowls of M&M's and popcorn. The room is warm from the dryer, and smells like tomato sauce and garlic.

"You didn't get to go home for dinner. And Becca mentioned that her parents wouldn't be back from the restaurant until later. And since you usually end up ordering pizza anyway, and I, you know, have connections, I thought I'd hook you up."

I let his hand go and open the box on top. Pepperoni, green peppers, and onions. I whip around, smiling from ear to ear, and pieces of my hair graze his shoulders. "Tha—"

He puts his hands on either side of my face and catches the rest of my gratitude with his lips.

Everything inside my body forgets what it's supposed to be doing in order to focus on the touch of his mouth against mine.

I sigh into him, and then I feel the breath go out of him too. He moves even closer, until the washing machine presses against my hips. I shift my weight onto my toes, and wrap my arms around his neck, letting my fingers brush against the ends of his hair. His hands graze my sides, fingertips moving up to my face, cupping my cheeks.

Fighting this would be like fighting the tide. I don't have to worry about defining it right now. Better to dive in, waves washing over me, letting the cool water render me weightless and free. Better to enjoy this moment, right now.

I don't know how long we stay like that, caught up in each other. Moving our careful hands to new places. Memorizing every small sensation.

Eventually, when I pull away to look at him, his eyes are question marks. "I'm sorry. I should have asked first. Was that okay?" He puts a hand on the back of his neck. "I . . . And you're so . . . And earlier, it seemed like . . ."

"Yeah," I say breathlessly, nodding. "Yes, it's—"

And then he kisses me again, before I can finish my sentence.

CHAPTER 7

The bell on the door dings, indicating the exit of our sole remaining customers.

"They're gone!" I call into the kitchen, sticking the bill into my apron, which sits at my hips like a wide belt.

"Yes!" Becca cheers, and a beat bounces from the kitchen into the dining room a few seconds later.

A smooth voice fills the restaurant, sliding against the tables and up the walls. The song is in Spanish, but I immediately recognize it. Becca and Alberto—Becca's cousin and a cook at the restaurant—love this song.

As I collect the dishes, I rock back and forth. My good mood makes everything better. I push the swinging kitchen door open and drop my full tray at the bussing station. As I round the corner, I find Becca and Alberto in a playful sing-off.

Becca cheers when Alberto finishes a flawless verse. "*Madre mia!* Alberto! Not bad!"

He brushes his shoulders off.

Becca sashays up to me. "Oh my gosh, Hads, are you dancing at work? With minimal prompting? Yes, I am feeling this." She looks me over carefully. "I thought you were *so tired* today."

"I am," I say, grinning.

My phone rang around eleven last night, and Braden's voice was in my ear. He made my cheeks burn as he told me all his thoughts about my lips, my hair, and the way we fit together. By the time we finally hung up, it was rounding on three in the morning.

The chorus starts, and I sing along the best I can manage.

Becca looks at me with approval. "Okay! That was sort of Spanish!"

"Sort of!" I cheer, spinning. I grab the bucket of rags in bleach water to go finish bussing that table.

But first I get a washcloth and squeeze out the excess liquid. Becca's back is to me, and I can't resist. Twisting up the rag, I snap it right between the back pockets of her jeans. She squeals and looks for something to use in retribution, but I shimmy away, pushing the kitchen door open with a dramatic hip bump.

And then stop, mid–dance move.

Because Braden is standing at the front entrance.

"Hey, Hadley." The force of his smile hits me right in the chest.

"Oh! Um, hi."

How long has he been standing out here?

Before either of us can say anything else, Becca calls from

the kitchen, "I hope you don't think you got away with that, Hads! Because brace your cheeks, I'm coming for you!"

Braden lifts his eyebrows.

She continues, totally oblivious, "And, watch out, 'cause I just found that big-ass spatula."

The door dramatically swings open, and she crashes right into me, kitchen utensil in hand. We steady ourselves, and Becca notices Braden. "Oh. Shit! Sorry! Hi. *Totally* didn't know anybody was here."

Braden eyes the spatula. "Kind of figured."

Becca tucks her arms behind her back. "Alberto, can you turn it down? We have a customer!" The music fades.

Braden looks like he is doing everything he can to keep from laughing. "I didn't mean to interrupt you . . . uh, working."

"No prob," Becca answers, because I'm too busy staring at him.

"Are you guys . . . open? I was hoping to get some food, maybe say hi to Hadley." He looks at me, and his voice drops. "I didn't see you at school today."

"We're open," Becca says, elbowing me. "Hadley, how about you help our customer?"

I shake my head. "Sorry. Yeah."

Oh, hello, brain. Welcome back.

Becca disappears back into the kitchen.

Braden looks around the empty restaurant. "So . . . is there room in your section?" He tries to hold his laughter back, but it's a lost cause. "I'm so glad I didn't text first."

I swat him with the towel. "You're the worst. Come on. That booth in the back corner."

He leads the way, and I tighten my pony as we walk,

pulling it high on the crown of my head. I smooth my Belavinis T-shirt and retie my apron, then grab a menu from the hostess stand. I drop it in front of him as he slides into the booth.

Not trusting myself, I put on my best waitress voice. "I'm so sorry for our lack of professionalism before. But welcome to Belavinis, sir. Is this your first time dining with us?"

"Thank you." Mischief crosses his face. "As a matter of fact, it is."

"Great! Welcome. Do you need a few minutes to look over everything?"

"I might." He picks up the menu. "Do you have any recommendations?"

I tilt my head and feel the end of my ponytail graze my back. "It depends. Are you looking for something specific?"

"Actually, now that you mention it. . . ." He drops the menu. "I am."

My pulse speeds up.

His eyes land on my lips. "What about you, miss? Anything sound particularly good lately?"

I feel a little dizzy. *This isn't fair! I don't stand a chance with him looking at me like that!* Slowly, I nod.

His expression is wolfish. "I hoped so."

"Yeah?" I say breathlessly.

"Yeah. I hate eating alone."

"What?"

"So, two burgers, then? With fries? And a Coke, for me."

I snort.

"I'm sorry," he says, "is there something wrong with that order? I thought we were on the same page?"

All right, I can play along.

I put my hand on the table, pressing my weight into it, and lean closer to him. "No problem at all, sir. I was simply under the impression that you might want something a little more special. Something you could only get"—I look down at my name tag—"here." I stand upright. "But it's my mistake. I can certainly accommodate that very basic choice."

I turn on my heel, but before I walk away, his fingers wrap gently around my wrist. It feels like lightning. "Wait," he says.

I turn to him.

"Hadley, I really do only want it . . . here?" His expression is so frustratingly cute. I want to scrub it right off his face.

I pull my lips into my mouth. "Good to know."

"Okay, last thing."

"What?" I laugh.

"Just to be clear. I totally do want that burger, though. Along with your company, and your—"

"I'm on it," I interrupt. I can't hear him talk about me like that right now or I'm going to combust. I start to take a step toward the kitchen, but his fingers tighten around my wrist.

When I turn back, he's smiling big. "It's just that I had two practices today, and I'm starving."

I can't stop myself from mirroring his happy expression. "That's very interesting and all." I lean into his side of the booth. "But if you want me to get you some food, you're going to have to let go." There is zero percent of me that wants that.

"I'm having conflicting interests."

For a moment, I'm lost in him, until . . . "Wait. You had practice before school today too?"

He nods and slides his hand down to my fingers, tracing them with his.

I try to pay attention to my words. "But you didn't get any sleep last night."

His thumb moves across my wrist, and he raises a shoulder.

"I didn't mean to keep you up—"

"It's good. I promise."

With the way he looks at me, I'm suddenly in danger of exploding into a fit of hysterics.

I need to get out of here.

"I'll be right back with your food."

Safely in the kitchen, I give Braden's order to Alberto, then hang on to the prep counter like I just finished a marathon.

"What's wrong with you?" Becca is eating a plate of fries.

"*Shhh!* He'll hear you."

"Oh my god." She rolls her eyes.

"Becca, how can I possibly—like, how is it humanly possible to feel so idiotic and so happy at the same time?" I ask in an urgent whisper.

"You have a crush." She says it like it's the simplest thing in the world.

"No. No, that's not what this is. I had a crush on Noah, and I *never* felt like this."

"Okay, Hads, let's get something straight. You thought Noah was *nice*. That guy out there"—she points to the door with a fry—"he's a lot of things, but he's definitely not *nice*. He's a completely different species."

I can't help but remember Braden saying something

similar at Pieces and Pies, that he thought nice was boring. "God, this is embarrassing." *And wonderful.*

"Yep," she affirms.

"I hate it."

"Big, fat crush." She offers me her plate, but I shake my head. "Also, did you just leave him out there by himself?"

I lean my chin into my hands. "Yeah. Trying to act normal is exhausting. I needed a break."

She looks at me frankly. "But you're also dying to go back out there."

"Completely."

"Here." Becca grabs two cups and fills them with ice and fountain Coke. "Take a breath. Bring these out there. Sit with him. I promise, you will survive."

I grab the drinks. "It doesn't feel like it."

She doesn't bother replying as she practically pushes me out the door.

I walk toward Braden with a slushing fountain Coke in each hand, and he puts his phone down as I reach the table, looking at me like I'm a slice of our famous coconut-cream pie.

Okay, I think. They might have a point.

Nice might be overrated.

❊   ❊   ❊

"Are you sure you don't mind?" I ask Braden as I gather my stuff.

He opens the door. "I'm sure."

When Braden finished eating, Becca told me I could head

home, even though there was still cleanup to be done. Normally, I wouldn't take her up on it, but she insisted when I told her Braden offered to drive me.

Outside, the sun hangs low, splashing the sky in golds, pinks, and blues. I take in a breath, relishing the cool air. I beat Braden to his car and lean onto the passenger door, admiring the evening sky. Instead of unlocking it, Braden leans next to me.

"Hey."

"Hi."

He turns to face me. "Hadley?"

I want to catch his voice and keep it in a jar by my bed.

Wow, okay. This guy is turning me into a legit psychopath.

I can't think when he's so close.

"Shit." He turns away. Is he laughing?

I'm frozen. "What?"

"The way you're looking at me . . ." He shakes his head. "I feel like I'm losing my mind."

Fear pulses through me. "How am I looking at you?"

He searches my face. "No. It's good. I . . . I like it."

With a strange mix of urgency and courage, I slide my hand to the back of his neck, pulling him into me. I can't fight it any longer.

He slips his hands into my open coat, wrapping an arm around me and pressing his fingers against the small of my back. The other hand sits at my hip, gripping a handful of my T-shirt. His fingers graze bare skin at my side. For a desperate moment, I'm completely lost.

"Wait, Hadley," he whispers against my lips. Still tangled together, Braden presses his weight against me, against his car. Our chests rise and fall against each other. For a moment, the only sound is our rapid breathing as he studies me with wild eyes.

Finally, he laughs.

I cover my face with my hand.

"What even . . . ?"

My heart is still hammering. *Thank god he feels it too.* "I don't know," I tell him, "I've never—"

His brows scrunch together. "No, me either."

It's like we remember at the same time that he's still got me pinned against the car, and he takes a few steps back. The air rushes in, sending a chill up my spine.

"Should we . . . ," he starts to ask. "Should we talk about what you said the other night? I don't want you to think I wasn't listening."

I shake my head. "No, that's the last thing I want to talk about right now." *Not yet. Just let me enjoy this for a minute. We can sort it out later.*

"Are you sure?"

"Definitely."

"So this, right now, this is okay?"

I nod. "Very okay."

"Good." He looks me over. "Because I really don't want to take you home yet."

I take in the sight of him against the backdrop of colorful sky. "I actually have an idea," I tell him. We're cutting it kind of close, but I think I can make it work.

"Perfect."

"I didn't even tell you what it is yet!"

"Doesn't matter, as long as we get to hang out longer."

* * *

A few minutes later, Braden pulls into the empty parking lot of the local state park. When he turns the car off, he asks, "So what are we doing exactly?"

"I haven't taken your portrait yet, for the yearbook profile. And the light is perfect."

"Now?"

"Yeah. Come on. I'll show you." I open the door and grab my camera. I start on the path into the woods, gesturing for him to follow me.

Slowly, the forest unfolds at our feet. The dirt is blanketed in dry, fallen leaves, and the dark lines of the trees climb and web, reaching for the low sun. It should be ugly, dying, but without most of the foliage, there's just enough space for a golden glow to come through, haloing the branches. In the less dense parts of the woods, the light shines unobstructed, streaking the air in long, delicate lines. The sun makes it all come alive.

"Wow." He exhales.

"Cool, right?"

"Yeah. How'd you know?"

"It's the golden hour, when the sun looks like this. And I've taken photographs here before." I start to change my camera settings, lowering the shutter speed.

"It's the golden hour right now?"

"Yeah, after sunrise or before sunset. It's never actually a whole hour, though."

"Do you do this kind of thing for all your yearbook subjects?"

"No." I snap a shot of the landscape and quickly review the exposure. "I don't." I'm going to need to steady my hands, but if I can manage it, these pictures are going to turn out beautifully.

"So who did you photograph here before?"

"Just the trees."

He smiles in response, and I snap a shot.

"Hey! Wasn't ready."

"Too bad. Come on, we've got to move fast."

"How long does it actually last?" He looks around. "Like this."

"It's hard to say. It's all about the angle of the sun at the horizon, and the types of particles that the light passes through in the atmosphere."

"So you never really know?"

"Right. You just know that it's temporary. And awesome. And to make the most of it while you have it." I walk him over to a tree, closer to the small pond. "Here. Lean against that."

"That's it? Lean?"

"That's it." I frame my shot, opting to keep the sun in the background of the frame, letting the light spill behind him.

My god.

He shifts his weight. "This is kind of weird. Should I look at you? Smile?"

I keep my camera pressed to my face. "Am I making *Braden Roberts* uncomfortable?"

"Come on, cut me a break."

Getting under his skin will never get old. I answer his question, "Neither, actually. Just sort of stare out in the distance. . . . Okay, except don't act fully pissed."

He laughs.

Click.

I love it before I even check.

"Okay, now actually turn around and lean on the other side. I'm going to have you face the light for a couple."

"Wait. Before we take more of me, can't I take a couple of you?"

I shake my head. "Nope. Not the way this works, Roberts."

"What do you mean?"

"It's too hard for me to be objective when I'm in the picture. I promise, I've tried. But it throws me off."

He looks at me doubtfully.

"Can you just follow a very simple direction, please?" I ask.

"One day, I'm taking your picture," he says.

"All right, one day."

And then, with a pointed gaze, he does as I ask, putting a hand up to shield his eyes from the sun.

"Oh, sorry. Yeah. You can keep them closed. I'll tell you when to open."

My footsteps crunch as I approach him, and he blindly reaches out to me. I let his hand settle on my waist and touch my fingertips to his jaw. I marvel at it, hands on one another so casually. "This way, just— Yeah. Like that. Perfect." I take a step back, and his hand falls away. "Can you cross your arms?" I zoom in. "Okay, all set. Open your eyes."

I snap as quickly as I can. Because *wow.*

While I'm reviewing the images, Braden moves beside me. "Are they any good?"

I tilt the screen. Braden looks exactly how he's been making me feel all day long, like he's shining from the inside out.

Looking down at the camera, his face is filled with such surprise that I find myself wondering if I missed something. "What is it?"

"Nothing . . . um—"

"You don't like it? It's not a big deal; I can delete it. Perks of digital."

"No." He takes the camera from me. "I like it a lot, actually."

"Then what's with the weird look?"

"I'm not—"

I reach for my camera, but he wraps an arm around me, keeping it out of reach.

"Are you *blushing*?"

"I did *not* blush," his says.

"I swear I saw a little pink."

"It's just that light you love so much."

I play along. "Oh, the light. Okay."

"Yeah."

"Sure."

He leans his head into my shoulder, words muffled. "I like the way you see me."

"You're not exactly hard to photograph."

He lifts his head, a questioning look on his face.

I laugh. "That's all you're getting from me."

"I'll take it."

But there's still something there, something I can't quite place. "What is it?"

"Nothing." He looks a little nervous. "I've just never seen myself like that. And I don't know how you did it, but it looks like . . ." He exhales deeply. "It looks like you like me. The same way that I like you. And with everything you said the other day . . . I just—I guess I didn't expect that."

And my stupid heart, the one that's meant to be locked away, softens. I take a step closer to him. "You thought it was less?"

He shrugs.

And then, for today, for right now, I decide to give in. I take his face in my hands and say, "Maybe I should do something about that."

CHAPTER 8

I push the metal lever to the lowest setting on the Kitchen-Aid and start to mix the dry ingredients in without really looking, because I can't pull my eyes away from the truly hideous color of the fondant Becca is making. I wrinkle my nose. "Becca, I hate to tell you this, but that looks like pee."

Tyler barks a laugh, looking up from his bowl of Mom's spaghetti. By the time the two of them got here, our family had already eaten dinner, but Mom can't help feeding everyone who visits. Ty's so used to it, he didn't even wait for her this time; he just fixed himself a bowl.

Becca shoots Ty a vicious side-eye, and he grimaces. "Sorry," he mutters. When she looks away, he risks a glance back at me, nodding.

"Come on, back off my cake, guys!" Becca flashes her phone in front of us. "It *totally* matches the picture." Then she sets it down, clearly defeated. "Ugh. Maybe I should have just made Jell-O."

I immediately feel guilty. "No, I'm sorry. This is a great

idea. It's just not done yet. He'll think it's hilarious." Hilarious is pretty much Greg's highest praise.

"Chocolate cake over Jell-O every single time," Ty says.

I nod.

Becca shrugs, still unconvinced, when Mom walks into the kitchen. Her hair is in a neat ponytail, and she's wearing a lavender sweater. Her feet are bare, and she has a perfect, dark pedicure. Sometimes, when I look at her, I wonder how we can be related. Like Remy, she's always so put together, and I'm pretty sure I have pee-colored frosting on my face.

"Hey, guys!" she greets us.

"Hey, Mia, thanks again for letting me borrow your mixer." Becca looks around. The counter is covered with scattered utensils, spilled flour, and egg cartons. "And pretty much your entire kitchen. I promise we'll clean up."

"Oh, honey, it's no problem." Mom opens the fridge and pulls out a Tupperware of cut strawberries, then sits on a barstool at the island. "Hadley said you're making a cake for Greg's birthday. I can't believe you kids are turning seventeen."

"Well, I'm not," Becca sighs. "I hate being young for my grade."

"One day you'll be grateful for being young." Mom looks at each of us. "So what's going on tonight, other than baking? Just hanging out?"

My parents have always had an open-door policy with our close friends, so Ty, Becca, and Greg never really need a reason to be here. We spend a lot of time at each other's houses, doing homework, watching movies, whatever.

Ty looks at Mom. "Yeah, we've hardly seen Hadley at all this week."

"I've seen her at work," Becca says as she stirs her frosting. She sounds like she's trying too hard to contradict Ty, and I feel a twinge of guilt for neglecting my friends for Braden.

Becca glances back down at her fondant. Seemingly satisfied with the color, or maybe she's just given up, she covers it with plastic wrap.

Mom eyes the frosting. "So what are you going for, Becca?"

Becca takes the other bowl, which is filled with batter, and pours it into a greased cake pan. Her fingers are stained green and yellow. "Okay, so you know how Greg is obsessed with *The Office?*" She doesn't wait for an answer. "In one of the first episodes, Jim plays a prank where he puts Dwight's stapler in Jell-O, and I'm basically trying to recreate that, but in cake form." She shows Mom the picture.

"Oh, that's a great idea!" Mom laughs, unself-consciously loud. "What are you going to do about the stapler?"

"I bought a new one that I'm going to wash and set on top, then write *Happy Birthday, Greg!* next to it."

"You guys are so creative."

"Thank you. Nobody else seems to appreciate my vision." Her widened eyes make her look like a sad woodland animal. "They said my frosting looks like urine."

We turn to the frosting.

It still looks like pee.

All four of us burst out laughing.

Mom eyes the group of us with a chuckle. "I'm sure it will come together when it's done."

She puts the lid on the Tupperware, gets off her chair, and puts it back into the fridge. "All right. I have book club. Clean up after yourselves when you're done, okay?" She smooths my hair and presses a kiss onto the top of my head. "Love you."

"Love you too."

Then she does the same thing to Becca and Tyler, partially to make them laugh, but also because it's true. It makes Ty blush, but he doesn't pull away. The sight tugs at my heart. I feel a surge of guilt and gratitude that my mom gets to be here with us.

"Bye, guys!" Mom grabs her purse, fastens her heels, and walks out the door.

※　　※　　※

I'm not sure what wakes me. It's still dark outside. I turn to check the time and notice that my phone is lit up and Braden's name is written across the screen. I roll into my pillow to hide my sleepy smile, sliding my finger to unlock the text.

It was sent six minutes ago: I can't find any rocks.

I read it again. What?

His reply is instant: You know *tap, tap, tap*

For a second, I'm confused, and then I start to connect the dots. My fingers fly: Are you here???

Come outside and see.

My heart starts to hammer in my chest.

He's out of his damn mind.

So am I.

I run to my bathroom and check my reflection in the mirror. I feel like I'm still dreaming. I quickly brush my teeth and run my fingers through my hair. I throw on a pair of shorts over my underwear, settling for the first thing decently clean I can find on the bathroom floor, then go back into my room.

I reach across my desk, pausing briefly with my fingers on the window latch. With a creak, the night opens in front of me. I climb up and plant my feet firmly on the chilly shingles of the roof. The air licks up my exposed legs, across the back of my neck.

I see him.

Here's here. *He's really here.* Moonlight shining off his hair, off his teeth, and he's smiling like a happy fool. A light inside my chest explodes. I reach inside, grab my camera from my desk, and lift it to capture him like that forever.

Evidence that this is real.

I set the camera back and look down at him, raising my hand in silent greeting.

I'm feeling so much, and trying to mask it all is like shoving too many things into a box. Every time I push one feeling down, another jumps out. If my parents find out that this six-foot-something boy is breaking into their house, they'll kill both of us. I know, because I've seen them do it to Remy. She was grounded for more than a month once. But honestly, I want him here so badly that I decide that it's all okay. *What's a month, anyway?*

I whisper down to him, "If you can get yourself up here, I'll hang out with you for, like, ten minutes, max. But if I hear even the tiniest sound that somebody is coming, I'm pushing you off and pretending you were a robber."

We're both beaming like idiots. "Oh, I'm here to steal, that's for sure." He's wearing dark jeans with a hoodie under his jacket, and he looks so good that I almost tell him he can take whatever the hell he wants.

Braden begins assessing the side of the house leading to the roof. "So I was kind of thinking that maybe you'd come down. You know, use a door? Like a human being? But if you want me to come up . . ."

He takes a couple steps backward to get a running start. Then he leaps off the ground and grabs onto something on the side of the house. "Braden. *Shit.* Be careful!" My voice is louder than it should be.

There's a hollow sound of something—some*one*—hitting the drainpipe, and seconds later, he's pulling himself onto the small, flat roof outside my bedroom window. One final pull and he's sitting next to where I'm standing. He breathes a little heavy, rubs his shoulder, and gives me the most self-satisfied look. It's totally obnoxious. I love it.

"I still might push you."

"No, you won't." He's sitting right at the edge.

"You really should have that shoulder looked at, you know."

"You can take a look if you want." He reaches his fingers out to mine.

"That's not what I meant."

"I know. Come here." He pulls me toward him.

Braden moves like he's going to kiss me, with his face only a breath away from mine, but he pauses a fraction of an inch away. Parting his lips slightly, he lowers his gaze to meet my eyes. I feel his breath against my lips. I fight the urge to lick them.

For just a beat, time stops. Looking at him, I marvel at how his simple presence can change the way an entire night feels. How he can turn it into magic.

Then he pulls me in.

A small gasp escapes me as I taste his lips. Warm and cold fuse and slide against each other. He pulls away long enough to whisper, "I thought about this the whole time I walked here."

My heart explodes, and he slams back into me. Kissing Braden is so different from kissing anybody else that I feel like it should have a new name.

"Wait," he says, but I instantly close the space again. He's smiling against my mouth. "Just one second, Hadley." He begins to stand.

"What are you doing?" I start to protest, but he's already walking the few steps toward my bedroom window. Then he's back with my quilted comforter tucked under one arm.

"You had goose bumps," he says by way of explanation.

"I was okay." I try to catch my breath.

"Well, I'm not okay with you freezing." He wraps the blanket around us. "I like your room, by the way."

"It's a mess. I didn't exactly know I was having company."

"You're happy I'm here, though."

I'm fighting back a smirk. "I hate it. It's totally rude. I was *sleeping*, and this is definitely against the rules."

"Oh, it's *rude*, huh? That's your big defense?"

I nod, pursing my lips and looking up at him.

"Come here, rude girl." We're sitting next to each other, but he wraps an arm around me and then another to pull me into his lap, facing him. He readjusts the blanket. Then he looks at me, so much closer now, and slides his hands gently up and down my sides over my tank top. "You're still cold."

"I'm warming up." The words take on a life of their own after I say them, choosing an alternate meaning. Still looking at me, Braden pushes my shirt up a little, and rubs his hands against my bare skin. I'm suddenly very aware of the fact that I'm not wearing anything underneath. But I don't feel shy with him about my body. His fingertips graze the sides of my rib cage, my hip bones, my back. I shiver, but I'm not cold anymore.

I can't stand to look at him while he makes me feel like this, so I lean into his neck, pushing his sweatshirt out of the way with my nose, and breathe in the skin of that delicate place. This close, I can find the fading chlorine. I can't help myself; I plant a kiss there.

He laughs, a deep noise that I can feel as I lean against his chest. "Yeah, I'm convinced. You totally hate I'm here."

I sit up and trace his cheekbones with my fingers, whispering slowly, "I hate everything about you." The words are glittering with a little bit of his magic. And they certainly sound like a declaration, but not the one I made.

I pull his face into mine. He exhales into my mouth, and I take that from him too. I'm a black hole of want. Our speed picks up, and I lean my body into his. He wraps his other arm around me, so we move from vertical to horizontal. One of his hands finds the back of my thigh, and his fingers dig into my skin. He's never touched me there before, not like that, and I'm liquid fire, dripping from the roof, destroying the house, setting the lawn alight. I squeeze my eyes closed and let his arms, his body, hold me up.

I have to stop or I'm going to be lost in this forever.

Maybe I want to be lost in this forever.

I want *more.*

My want scares me.

I force myself to stop.

When I pull away, I swear I can almost see the charge between us, lighting the night air like low-hanging stars.

He's breathing heavy, and his eyes are hooded when they meet mine. I watch his chest rise and fall, averting my gaze from his face, because seeing his reaction to me, to us, almost starts the whole thing all over.

"Hate me, huh?"

"So much," I insist.

"That's too bad." His hands frame my face. "Because I came over here to see if we could make this thing, you know—with us—official."

My stomach flips. "What? You did?"

"Well, no other girl has ever had me climbing houses in the middle of the night. And if you're going to be the death of me, I think you should at least be my girlfriend." Then his expression becomes more serious. "Only if you want."

I can't find any words.

He continues, "I know you said you didn't want to talk about it yet, and if you still feel that way, that's okay. But I just thought I could at least tell you how I felt. So you had all the information. And I want this. You. Us."

I look at him, swollen lips and hopeful eyes, and the idea of telling him no seems impossible. But this thing between us is wild, unwieldy. I don't know how to slow it down. I don't know how to steer.

Still, right now, I want it more than anything else.

I want it more than I'm afraid of it.

So I take a deep breath and tell the truth.

"Okay." I nod, biting back my nervous smile—swallowing it. Inside me, with room to grow, it blooms and explodes like fireworks.

His whole body sags in relief as he laughs. "Thank god."

"Did you think I was going to say no?" I ask, genuinely curious.

He laughs. "Hadley, I had no idea what you were going to do. You keep me on my toes."

He puts his arm around me, and I lean into his shoulder, feeling blissful and alive. The moment is everything I've been afraid of, but here with Braden, that fear falls away now. Instead, with no one but the moon as our witness, I let my heavy eyes close, and revel in the solid warmth of the boy next to me.

after

Senior Year

autumn

CHAPTER 9

The alarm on my phone goes off at six, but I don't remember falling asleep. I groan and reach for it without opening my eyes, knocking it off my nightstand and then pulling it back to me by the charger cord. Before, if I had gotten so few hours of sleep, I would have tried to get Mom to call the school and excuse my absence, at least for first hour. But now I know I just need to tough it out.

My alarm is still playing. I pull open my eyes and silence it. No new messages. Of course not. You'd think I'd be used to that. Every morning since the accident, I wake up hopeful that he will have called, texted, anything. So far, seven mornings of that hope crumbling around me.

I roll out of bed and see two tissues clinging to my bare legs. I throw them into the already overflowing trash next to my nightstand and miss. Without bothering to pick them up, I walk into the bathroom, wearing just my underwear and Braden's T-shirt.

I really need to stop sleeping in this thing.

I turn on the shower and go through the motions of getting ready, feeling like a zombie. I think about shaving my legs, but don't, and wash and sort of dry my hair. So much of it falls out that I have to clean the brush when I'm done. *Don't think about it.*

Pausing for a minute, anticipating the chill in the morning air, I take off my terry-cloth robe and get dressed. I choose a fitted shirt that's soft against my skin and a well-worn pair of skinny jeans. They used to be tight, but like all my clothes these days, they hang more loosely than intended. I put on socks and pull a thin sweater over my shirt, and there's a glitter of light reflected in the mirror as I tuck my necklace under my layered tops. I don't want Becca to see it. I don't want anybody to see it. Straightening up, I look at my reflection. I'm not going to win any beauty contests, but I'm clean and vertical. I'm going to call it a win.

I'm pulled back to reality when Becca's name lights up my phone, and I know it means she's in the driveway. It's 7:02 a.m. I sigh and try to stop myself from wondering how the last half hour passed without me noticing. I keep losing time. I take one last look in the mirror, at the skinny version of me with thunderous eyes and a stiff upper lip, and make my way downstairs.

The kitchen is dark. Before, my parents would have been awake, ready for the day. Lately, they spend more time sleeping. Or maybe just being alone, together. And it's not surprising that Judd is still in bed; none of his classes at the community college start before ten. And Remy's away at Michigan State. Judd was supposed to be there too, but he deferred, choosing to spend his freshman year here with us, taking classes locally. We've all sort of coped differently. At first I clung to Braden, but now, after, I isolate myself.

Navigating through the dark, I walk to the mudroom and swing my school bag over my shoulder, grab my phone off the counter, and make my way outside.

My feet crunch on the leaves as I walk toward Becca's silver Focus, and I'm greeted by her trying-too-hard expression when I open the door. It looks like Becca tied her ponytail too tight and she's smiling through the pain. Except *I'm* the thing that's making her tense. She hasn't given up on me, I guess.

"Good morning, sunshine!" Only Becca could beam and use words like *sunshine* while it's still dark outside. I ignore the absurdity of it, but then I wonder if she's being sarcastic. I used to pay enough attention to notice when she was messing with me.

I used to do a lot of things.

Bec gives me a once-twice-then-three-times-over. She seems pleased. Maybe because I showered? I try not to think of the dirty ponytail I wore for three days before she came over and forced me to wash my hair. I guess the bar is low.

"Morning, Becs," I say, trying to act like a normal seventeen-year-old, one who wasn't up all night replaying every moment with her ex-boyfriend, wondering where it went wrong. One whose room isn't full of bats.

The radio is quietly playing some Broadway something, which isn't surprising but still grates at my nerves. Those big feelings fit perfectly into rhyming lines, neatly concluding at just the right moment.

Becca reaches over to her cup holder and hands me a

steaming to-go mug, then reverses out of my driveway. I watch the gold bracelet, the one that Greg got her for Christmas almost two years ago, slide up and down her arm as she moves. Her eyes don't quite meet mine. "It's cocoa coffee."

Half hot chocolate, half coffee, cocoa coffee is the best of both worlds: the flavor of the chocolate and the wake-up power of the coffee. We came up with it last winter, during one of our many ACT study sessions.

"Thanks, Becca." The warmth feels comforting in my hands, and I take a tentative sip. "It's exactly what I need, actually."

Her high pony sways, like she's proud that she's done something right by me. The total joy in it makes me feel awful. *Exactly how horrible have I been to her lately?*

She doesn't say anything. She's quiet, humming to herself and focusing on the road. I know she's making a conscious effort to not talk to me. I haven't exactly been chatty lately. There are too many dangerous questions, and I don't have any answers.

At first, Becca would say something, or tell me a story, and I wouldn't answer. Or I wouldn't answer right away, or I'd answer with the least possible effort required in order for her not to repeat herself. Now, she just lets me sit in silence. I can feel the fracture in our friendship—and it's me. *I'm the problem.*

I resolve to make an effort. I search for a question to ask her or a way to engage in her life. I work my way out of the dark tunnels in my head and try to find the daylight. It makes my eyes hurt. And I can't think of anything. *When did I run out of things to ask my best friend?*

Stiffly, I turn to her. "So, how are rehearsals going? Has Mrs. Davis had her annual breakdown yet?"

The minute school starts, so do rehearsals for the Holiday Choir Concert. Mrs. Davis, the choir director, is *highly* invested in its success. But that's not really what I want to talk about. It's not what I'm really saying to her at all. What I'm really saying is something like: *I'm so sorry I have been a horrible friend. Please don't hate me, because I hardly recognize myself, and I don't feel like I can defend this person who isn't me. I need you, even though I have been neglecting you.* And a promise: *I'm going to try harder.*

She turns and looks me right in the eye, like she hears what I can't say.

Her body relaxes and she jumps in. "Hads, her freak-out was *epic*. It was seriously the best one yet. Or, I guess, the worst one, if you're Mrs. Davis."

Becca pauses to see if she still has my attention, to see if it's still okay to talk about something like this, and when she sees me looking at her expectantly, she continues, "You know how she sometimes acts like she's kind of hot shit? Like, at the concerts, how she wears those skintight, floor-length skirts with all the sparkle and everything?" She doesn't give me time to reply; she knows that I know exactly what she means. She clarifies, "Not that I'm one to hate on sparkle. *Obviously.* But anyway, this year, she jumped right in. Like, honestly, since the first day of school she's been wearing these super-tight shirts. I mean, Greg and Ty literally haven't stopped talking about her 'blouses.'" She uses finger quotes with both her hands, leaving the steering wheel vacant. I take a shaky breath. She doesn't notice.

"They keep using that word, *blouses*, which, for some reason, is hilarious to me. Maybe because by definition a blouse is supposed to be loose? But whatever." She sneaks a glance at me out of the corner of her eye and adds conspiratorially, "Hads, some of them are *satin*. We're talking *very* little left to the imagination. Like, I know exactly where that woman's belly button is. And she looks good—actually she looks great—but it's not like she's twenty-two. She's got to be in her late fifties, and—" She interrupts herself, "Okay, I know you know that; you don't have to remind me again that you were in freshman choir. Anyway, she's testing the boundaries of her tops, and it's sort of distracting for the class."

I look at her, wondering when she got so good at having one-sided conversations. I nod. "Yeah, got it. She's showing off." *God, that sounds so weak.* But I can't think of anything to add. I try to make my face look encouraging.

She smiles and then immediately looks guilty, like she should have gotten permission or something. A knot forms in my stomach. "So anyway," Becca continues hesitantly, trying to break the awkwardness, "Mrs. Davis is all worked up and wearing one of those *blouses*, and she stopped us during 'Carol of the Bells' because she didn't think we were *e-nun-ci-a-ting* clearly enough. She's, like, shaking her arms around and getting all mad, saying that she needs to hear 'crisp consonants,' and in the middle of a wild arm gesture, the top three buttons of her blouse popped right off her shirt!" Becca bursts out laughing, like there's part of her that's still surprised that this really happened.

I find a bit of amusement. It's dull and distant, but present nonetheless. "No way," I answer. "What did she *do*?"

"Well, she said 'Oh my goodness!', put her hands over her chest—which is not small, I will remind you—and ran out of the room. But not before we all got to see her totally sexy bra. Like, the kind of bra that's superitchy and you only wear *for* somebody. It was red, lacy, and kind of . . ." She pauses for dramatic effect. *"See-through."*

"Oh my god!" I can't help but react to *that*.

"It was dead silent when it happened, and then the room exploded with laughter when she left. Nobody could believe it. Part of me thinks: serves her right for being such a show-off." Becca glances at me from the corner of her eye; her preppy wardrobe doesn't allow for such scandalous pieces. Then she laughs and adds fairly, "But the other part of me kind of thinks: good for her for working that sexy bra! I mean, she's been married *forever.*"

I make a little fist pump to support the Go Girl side as Becca turns left onto our school's street. I kind of love that she subscribes to the If You've Got It, Flaunt It philosophy.

Becca continues, "So she came back a few minutes later with a sweater buttoned up to her chin. It was pretty funny. But really, none of us knew what to do! Just pretend it never happened? She still yelled at us throughout the entire rest of the class, so I guess she wasn't too fazed, but I just kept picturing those flying buttons."

I shake my head. I can feel the grin stretch across my face, foreign but welcome. "I guess she does get pretty into it when she's conducting."

"And, get this—I took it to the next level. The other day, I found online basically the exact same bra she was wearing, and I ordered it." She pauses. "I know, shocking." She continues, "It should be here in the next couple days, and I *cannot wait* to surprise Greg with it. I'm going to try to reenact the whole scene. I have this button-up shirt that's way too small—totally shrunk in the wash; it's pastel purple . . . so I guess it's going to clash, but who cares? He is going to literally *die*!"

She hears it at the same time I do. With that one word, the comfortable bubble we had created bursts. Reality comes pouring in, like water on a sinking ship.

Neither of us speaks.

It's strange how I never realized before how often people, myself included, make light of death in casual conversation. I had never considered the words before. At sixteen, I hadn't really thought about death. But now, it seems to creep around every corner, pawing and pulling at the people I love most.

We're both still frozen with the word *die* hovering around us. It's like a neon, light-up sign pointing right at my head. Except that nobody did die—certainly not me—so I wish it would stop pointing at me like that. I don't want to be a beacon for near-death.

She backpedals. "I'm so sorry. I didn't mean that. I shouldn't have said that."

Everyone is okay. I repeat it in my head to make sure I believe it. My mind flashes an image of Braden, beaten up and bruised. And then I see long, dark strands of hair falling onto a white tile floor. I cast the mental pictures away. I can't let this win.

Becca and I should be able to talk normally again, eventually, and that includes expressions like *I'm going to kill you!* Why can't that start today? It has to start sometime.

I reach over and squeeze her hand. "It's fine, Bec. It's so

funny, and Greg *is* going to die when he sees you in Mrs. Davis's bra." I pause. "Also, that's not a sentence I thought I would *ever* say."

She looks relieved. We both feel it, the lifting of a weight. After months of feeling lost, maybe I'm finally finding my voice again.

❖   ❖   ❖

Becca navigates through the traffic into her assigned parking space, puts the car in park, and turns, looking at me holding my coffee. She goes straight for the elephant in the room. "Hadley, you're going to get through this. I promise."

She's said this to me so many times that I've lost count. I pretty much ignore it, but today, it burrows between my ears. I feel it take root. I can decide to be brave. "I know."

Becca's eyebrows rise to her hairline. She looks like an owl with her hair pulled back so tight, and at the sight of her, I laugh from deep in my gut. I can't believe how surprised she looks about me agreeing that I'm going to literally survive.

And once I start, I can't stop.

I laugh like it's the first laugh the world has ever heard. After she realizes it's okay, she joins me, and our laughter is an earthquake that only the two of us can feel. It's the shifting of the tectonic plates of our friendship; closer, and to their rightful positions.

Becca exhales the weight of the world. "*Oh, thank you, baby Jesus,* I was starting to think I was never going to hear that sound again. Let's go inside. We're going to be late, and it's totally your fault."

Feeling more content than I have in a while, I move to get my stuff together. I'm bracing myself to open the door to start another day, when I decide to get it out of the way.

"Becca, I have to tell you something. But I don't want you to say anything. I don't think I can handle any commentary."

Her face is concerned, but she nods. "Okay. What is it?"

I stare at my lap. "I threw away my portfolio."

I can feel all the things she's fighting not to say.

"I have the raw images. I can make another one. But I missed the early application deadline."

We both know that applying early to Great Lakes could have made a huge difference for me.

I watch Becca swallow her scolding with decided concentration. "I'm not going to say you shouldn't have done that, okay? As much as I really want to." A resolve forms in her eyes. "Tyler's having a party this weekend. The music will be as loud AF. We can yell and dance it out, all right? And then I'll help you put a new one together. Like, immediately."

"Thanks."

"Hadley," she says more seriously, "we've got this. I'm here for you. Everything is going to be okay."

I open the door, feeling a swell of gratitude. "Thanks, Becs."

We move toward the building slowly, soaking up the moment, shoulder to shoulder, resolved to find a new normal.

❖   ❖   ❖

"Hey, Had, how was school?" Judd leans back from the fridge, a long piece of string cheese sticking out of his mouth, as if he were a single-toothed walrus. He takes three big bites, and it disappears. He was supposed to be away at school like Remy, but after this past spring, he decided to defer for a year.

"Not bad." I don't really want to elaborate. I don't want to tell him that today was the first day that nobody passive aggressively asked me about Braden's status, insinuating not so subtly that I was responsible. Today, at least, I didn't hear their whispers: *She dumped him right when he needed her most. And then, well, you know. And he's been unconscious for a week.* They don't know that the last thing I wanted was to break up. Or that I hear Braden's own words echoing constantly: *I love you, Hadley . . . you have to forgive me. I need you.*

But I didn't. I just slammed the door in his face.

Nobody seems to care that I'm angrier with myself than anybody else could possibly be. Or that he broke my heart too. Or that the last conversation we had runs on a loop in my head, keeping me up all hours of the night. Knots start to form in my stomach as I try to forget, and I remind myself that—after almost two weeks of school—today was a decent day.

Today was a decent day, I repeat in my head. I managed to talk to Becca and pay attention in class. And at lunch, Tyler and Greg made me laugh by having a contest to see who could eat three pieces of pizza faster, but they had to stop because Greg started gagging. I even turned in my first English paper of senior year. Am I allowed to feel relieved about those things? Am I allowed to be happy when Braden is stuck?

"Good." Judd pauses and then says under his breath, "Although it really had only one way to go."

"Yeah." I shrug in an attempt to seem nonchalant. I don't

want my family to worry about me; they've done enough of that lately.

My phone buzzes, and I look at the screen: Remy. At my sister's name, frustration simmers in my stomach. Judd watches as I ignore it.

"At least she's trying with you," he says. "She won't answer my calls. She keeps leaving me on read."

"I don't really get it. It's not like she thought you guys were going to be roommates or something."

Judd continues, "The last thing she said to me was that I was trying to be *the good twin*. Like, how does that even make sense? Mom was *pissed* when I deferred."

"Remy probably just feels guilty for leaving."

"I wish she'd get that I was just trying to do what felt right for me. And that it doesn't mean she's wrong." Judd sighs. "Whatever. We'll work it out. I just don't know how to apologize for this."

"Then don't." The words are a little sharper than I intend.

He shakes his head. "Let's talk about something else. Mom's taking a nap. I was thinking I could make some pasta for dinner. Want to help?"

I look at him in disbelief. Judd basically never stops watching cooking shows. He knows his way around a kitchen and *never* asks for assistance.

"All right, so maybe I don't need, like, *actual* help. But I could use some time with my sister."

"Okay." Shoving him affectionately out of the way, I peer into the fridge. "What can I do?"

❂ ❂ ❂

A trip to the grocery store and a couple hours later, Judd and I have put together some semblance of a meal. I'm finishing chopping the veggies for a salad, and Judd's setting the table, when I hear the back door swing open.

"Hey, Dad," I call from the barstool, turning around to see his face.

He looks surprised to see me downstairs, instead of hiding in my room. "Hey, Had—you feeling better today?" For a minute, I think he's going to ask me if I've heard anything about Braden, but instead, he asks about dinner, which is spaghetti with meatballs, and a salad. Which actually smells good. Probably because Judd limited my help to the salad.

Then he's distracted by my bag sitting on the floor by his feet. "And if you are feeling better, would it kill you to put that thing away?"

It's sort of comforting that, in Dad's mind, no amount of personal drama will ever excuse a mess. And that he's no longer walking on eggshells around me. I slide off the stool and grab my book bag off the floor. "Sorry," I say as I go to hang it on its hook in the mudroom.

When I walk back into the kitchen, Dad is opening a can of craft beer with one hand and using his other arm to pull me into a hug. He squeezes me tightly and says, "Want to go check on Mom? See if she's ready to eat?"

❊   ❊   ❊

I pad down the hall to their bedroom door. It's shut. I knock twice quietly, and I think I hear her answer.

Cracking the door open, I peek my head inside. "Hey,

145

Mom, are you up?" She's sitting on the worn-in chair next to her bed, with her pixie haircut ruffled, and reading a paperback. She's wearing black leggings, a dark green sweater, and slippers. Comfortable, but dressed. *She's okay.*

"Hey, hon. Yeah, I'm up." She gestures down at her novel. "I'm deep into this ridiculous love story, but up."

Her smile, once a thoughtless, though pleasant, part of my everyday life, now makes me feel so much that I clam up, embarrassed by how much I need her.

I try to stamp down my emotions, ready to just be *normal.* "Okay, well, Judd and I made dinner." I put my hand up before she can reply and add, "Don't worry. I only chopped."

She laughs. "Your dinners are great." Mom is the eternal optimist. Also, a total liar. Her eyes twinkle as she gets up and puts a gentle arm across my shoulders. She smooths my hair and kisses my head. "Let's eat."

CHAPTER 10

"All right, but just so you know, handing this to me is permission to play what *I* want," I tell Becca as she hands me the aux cord for the speaker in her bedroom. I'm looking up at her from my spot on the floor.

Becca's skirt swings as she walks in a pink bra back to her closet, looking for a top. "Okay, whatever. I need to focus on my outfit anyway."

We both jerk to attention when one of her brothers screams something from the other room. Becca opens the door to yell at them. "Guys! Seriously chill, okay?"

I can't help but appreciate how familiar it feels.

For as long as I can remember, Becca's house has run off pure chaos. The Gomez family has four kids; Becca's the oldest and the only girl. Her younger brothers are in eighth, sixth, and fourth grades, and they always seem to have friends over. When you walk into their house, you almost have to choose which to process first: the noise of TVs, music, video games, and shouting, or the smells of food from the restaurant. It feels like home.

With the door firmly closed again, I hit play on my phone. The music fills Becca's room and almost covers the virtual explosions.

"Do you know what you're going to wear?" Becca asks from inside her closet.

Tonight is the party at Ty's. His dad, Dr. West, is away at some medical conference, so Tyler is using it as an excuse to play music as loud as it will go. Becca and I are convinced he cares more about forcing his playlists on everyone than the actual party.

I look down at my clothes. "I don't know. Just this?"

Becca peeks her head out of her closet. "Okay, this music is more depressing than I was expecting. Do you have any . . . upbeat options?"

I raise my eyebrows. "We couldn't even make it all the way through one song?"

"Sorry," she says, and then turns, sliding her neat hangers carefully back and forth.

I listen quietly for a minute. This song *is* sad. Why didn't I notice that before?

Becca's words are muffled as she pulls yet another option over her face. "What about some Bey? Something fun?" Her head reemerges, and she examines her reflection in the giant full-length mirror.

"Beyoncé reminds me too much of Remy." I try to push away the flood of feeling at the mention of my sister's name.

"Okay, I know you're not in the best place." Becca shifts

her weight onto one leg. "But you can't *ever* hate on the queen. Period." She looks at me more seriously. "And, Had, you really should talk to your sister. This has gone on long enough."

There's an angry mess inside me. "I can't."

"You know she was only looking out for you."

A fire burns in my gut, and I snap, "But *I* wasn't the one who needed looking after. I was the one doing the looking. And if I hadn't listened to her, maybe—"

"Hadley." Becca looks pained. "You don't really think it's her fault?"

I study her face. "Have you been talking to her?"

"What?"

"Have you guys been talking about me?" My skin starts to feel hot.

Her shoulders fall. "We're just worried."

"Well, I'm sorry for worrying you." I sound snotty and sarcastic. I try to steady myself, but emotion is building and tangling in my chest. "And maybe it's not Remy's fault, but then who do you want me to blame?"

"Hadley—"

I interrupt her. "I can't stop thinking about it, Becca." My voice cracks. "Every single day, I find someone new to hate. It's a fucking awful list." I look her right in the eye. "And do you know who's at the top of it?"

"*Hadley.*"

"I am." I swallow the lump in my throat. "*It's me.*"

"It isn't your fault."

Tears run down my cheeks as I nod. "Yes, it is. So . . . yeah, I'm pissed at Remy. But she's not the only one."

Becca sits next to me. "It's *not* your fault, Hadley. That's bullshit, okay? I was *there*, I saw what you did."

"Yeah, you *were* there." I force the words out. "So you know that I *knew* and I didn't *do* anything. And I gave him an impossible choice—"

"What about—"

"Braden is in the hospital!" I look around her room. "And what am *I* doing? I'm getting ready to go to a fucking *party*. And I don't even know if he's going to—"

"You can't stop living your life—"

The thought explodes out of me. "Why not? He did."

Now she looks angry too. "He didn't do that for you. He—"

"Stop. I . . ." I shake my head. "I can't hear it." I can't even think about it.

She swallows what she was going to say, and tries to calm down. "He's going to be okay, Hadley. It's going to be all right."

Incredulous, I brush her off. "Come on, Becca, you don't know that. Nobody does. Not even the doctors."

"The doctors? I thought . . . Did you go over there?"

I don't answer.

"You know what? It doesn't matter." She takes a deep breath. "Hadley, look—I don't want to fight with you. I . . . I hate this, all of it, so much."

"I hate it too."

She squeezes my shoulder. "And if you want to be mad at Remy, that's fine. I'll stay out of it. Because honestly, if you want to be mad at the whole freaking world right now, I don't really blame you."

I twist my rings. "Sometimes it's like it's eating me alive."

She pauses for a minute. "I have an idea."

"What? Becca—" I object.

"No, come on"—she opens her bedroom door—"meet me on the driveway. I'll be right there."

✻ ✻ ✻

Becca's house is on a dead-end street, and as I'm waiting alone in the evening light, too many feelings press on the inside of my skin, looking for a way out. Thankfully, Becca joins me after only a couple minutes. She's got a broom in one hand and a cardboard box sitting on her hip.

She sets the box down, contents clattering. "My parents brought these home from Belavinis last night. They're all the chipped plates that they don't want to use anymore."

Quickly, she picks one up, raises it above her head, and chucks it down onto the concrete. It shatters into a million pieces.

"Becca! What the hell?"

She just looks at me. "Your turn."

"What? I'm not—"

She lifts another. And again, the ceramic explosion packs a satisfying punch, soothing something ugly inside me. I replay it in my head, watching her frame by frame, imagining the photographs I could be taking.

"Aren't your parents going to be pissed?" I ask, but I'm already thinking about picking up a plate.

"I took these from the garbage. And I'll clean everything up." She nods to the broom.

It's enough to convince me. I walk over to the box.

Now, when my anger flares, I let it.

I whip a plate onto the ground. I want to scream, laugh, destroy.

For Remy, who told me to walk away.

I do it again, a furious grunt expelling itself from my throat.

For Braden's parents, who should have known.

Another.

For Coach Jones, who only cared about accolades and records.

I whip them, one after another. And I don't know when I started crying, but a sob fights its way through me.

For the fucking doctors.

Again.

For my camera.

And when I throw one for Braden, I don't even worry if I'm allowed to be mad at him. I just let myself be consumed by the flames. Sharp edges fly through the air, and I'm burning from the inside out.

I pick up two plates at once, sick satisfaction running through my veins. I feel ridiculous, bordering on scary, like I'm going to send Becca running, but instead, she stands next to me, ready with a dish of her own.

Together, we shatter everything until there is only one plate left.

In the sudden silence, she looks to me, and we're both breathing shakily. She takes the final piece from the box and lifts it in my direction.

"Here," she urges.

But the blinding light of fury has subsided in the middle of this broken mess, and suddenly I can't do it. I'm exhausted, and I can't stand the idea of breaking a single other thing. It must be written on my face, because Becca sets down the plate, whole, and wraps her arms around me.

And then, into her shoulder, I finally manage to say the only things that really matter: *thank you* and *I'm so sorry*, over and over.

And, somehow, I think Becca knows I'm not talking just to her.

※　※　※

An hour later, I still feel raw, but I'm lighter. A strange kind of relief courses through me.

"Here, try this one," Becca says as she tosses me a shirt. After we cleaned up, she insisted that we were going to have a fun night, even if it killed us. And neither of us even flinched when she said it.

I try on her top, and Becca stands next to me in the mirror, taking us in.

Her eyes catch on my neck. "Wait. Hadley, you're still wearing that?" She looks sad.

At first I'm confused, and then I follow her gaze. With a jolt of panic, I notice that my silver necklace is completely outside my shirt. I'm so used to seeing it around my neck that I looked right past it. It must have come untucked when I changed.

At the end of the necklace is the silver key to Braden's house.

When he clasped it around my neck during the spring, he said he wanted me to know that I wasn't alone, that he would be there for me anytime I needed. And it didn't take long before I started using it—and Becca knows it. She also knows I definitely shouldn't have it anymore.

And I'm not an idiot. I know I shouldn't be wearing it. For so many reasons, but also because the key makes me feel a mess of emotions. When he first gave it to me, it felt like taking a breath after swimming to the very bottom of the deep end and coming all the way back up again. But after that, I wouldn't have used it, even if I really felt like I needed him. I was afraid of what I might find him doing. Now, it's a temptation. At any time, I could go sit in his bedroom or sleep in his empty bed. I could steal a T-shirt or a bar of his soap. He might not be there, but *I* could be. I could try to find some information about how he's doing. I won't pretend that I haven't considered it.

I look at Becca. "I haven't used it in so long, Becca. I swear. I'm just not—" I stop, unsure how to finish my sentence.

This key has sort of been a symbol for me—of him, of us. It's made me feel less alone. And even if it can open a door, it can't guarantee that anybody will be inside. What good is access to an empty room?

I have to remind myself that I'm *not* alone; I have Becca. And Ty, and Greg too. But then I think of Braden, who *is* all by himself, in that hospital bed. And then I hear the whispers of my classmates and feel a painful tug at my chest, and I just can't stand the idea of abandoning him.

"You're just not what?" Becca asks.

I look at her, willing her to understand. "I'm just not ready to give it up yet."

She searches my face. "You still don't know anything? Even after . . ." She trails off, alluding to my hospital visit.

I shake my head, shoving down the memories that try to overwhelm me: his impossibly slow pulse; those heavy limbs; the countless lies, of omission or otherwise; and finally the harsh truth. It's up to him now—to heal, to reach out, if he chooses. *I had to let him go.*

Unless I ruined everything by letting him go.

"Is it my fault?" The words leave my mouth before I even realize I want to ask.

She puts her hands on my shoulders. "No, Hads. *No.* It's not your fault."

"Okay." I nod, trying hard to believe her. "Is it . . . Do you think it's okay if I keep wearing it, for just a while longer?"

She looks at the key and then back at me. "Yeah. I think it's okay." She pauses. "But I do think you should do something else too."

"Okay," I answer, apprehensive.

"So I'm your best friend, and I only want good things for you, right?"

"Yeah. . . ."

"Okay. Well, I need you to *Perks of Being a Wallflower* this party," she says matter-of-factly.

"What?"

"Tonight. I need you to, you know, *participate.* Keep your eyes open. Talk to people. Actually *be* there. Because you're technically a single woman." She puts her hands up, ready for my counter. "I know it's more complicated than that, and maybe too soon, and I know you're worried about him. But it's his job to get himself better. And it's been a while since he was actually, really, your boyfriend. Not breakup-wise, but, like, behavior-wise."

I take a breath, ready to argue, but the words fizzle in my throat. I'm tired of defending him. There are no easy answers.

She sees my lost eyes and spares me from responding. "I hope the accident was a wake-up call. And that when he gets out of the hospital, he'll get help. That he'll be the guy you want him to be, the one he used to be. I really do."

My chest aches at her words, at how much I wish they would come true. Even if Braden gets better, I think we're broken for good. I think it ended the minute he made his decision. My heart feels like those plates, shattered beyond repair, broken into edges that would only cut me if I tried to put them back together.

Becca continues, "Right now, you need to stop waiting to live your life, Hads. You . . . I'm sorry, but you just can't be the girl whose life revolves around her ex-boyfriend."

I give her a sharp look. How is it that I either feel like the cruel girl who abandoned her boyfriend when he needed her most *or* I'm the pathetic one who can't let go? Is there a third option—someone who made an impossible decision and is hanging on by her freaking fingernails?

She doesn't back down. "A small step forward, okay?"

There really isn't a right answer, but at least this way, I'll be with my friends. And getting out of the house feels . . . healthy, I guess. "If I hate it, I'm calling Judd to pick me up."

Her tone lightens. "If you hate it, *I'll* bring you back, and we can find the box of chipped bowls next. They're smaller, but I'm sure they'd break just the same."

I can't help but smile, just a little. "Okay."

"And I want to see you dance tonight. I'm requesting at

least three shakes of your ass. Some laughter. *Maybe* even look at some guys who don't have a million years of baggage."

I scoff. "Don't push your luck."

"Come on. Let's just have some fun, okay? Ditch the weight of the world."

"I'll do my best."

"Good, 'cause . . . I've missed you, Hads."

"I've missed you too." I smile at her again, bigger this time. "But can we be done with the sentiment now? I'm exhausted. I'll *participate*," I repeat her word sarcastically. "But I need one good pump-up song in the car. Get rid of the feels." I shrug.

Her eyes light up. "Absolutely. I've got the perfect, perfect song!" She grabs her keys off her dresser.

"Nothing from a musical."

"Oh, well, this hardly sounds like—"

"Becca."

"Okay, I have another idea. Let's go."

CHAPTER 11

"Greg, hand it over." It's my fourth, maybe fifth, swig out of this cinnamon whiskey bottle, which I pulled out of Greg's hand when I first sat down on the couch. I'm feeling a little reckless knowing that I'm sleeping over at Becca's tonight and don't have to worry about my parents, and that she's driving.

Greg and I have been passing the bottle back and forth ever since Becca asked him to babysit me while she went to dance. The alcohol burns going down, but it's also working wonders on my mood. The more I drink, the less I seem to care that I'd fit in much better at the hospital than at a party.

Greg laughs. "You all right, Hads? Becca will kill me if I get you wasted."

I look around. Ty's house isn't out of control or anything, but there's a pretty decent crowd. Most of them are feeling very little pain. "I don't think anybody will notice one more tipsy teenager."

"Becca will."

"Ohhhh wellll," I answer as I press the bottle to my lips, feeling looser than I have in ages.

Greg shakes his head. "I'm blaming it on you if she gets mad."

I hand him the bottle. "Obviously. It's not like you're making me drink. I'm a big girl."

Greg's attention shifts to the dance floor. "Speaking of, have you seen my girlfriend? I don't want somebody swooping in, thinking she's available."

I lean over and try to get a better view, but Becca finds me first. She yells my name and waves me over.

Greg sees her, too, and hands me the whiskey. "Here, one more dose of liquid courage."

"Now you're just trying to get me in trouble."

"And get you to leave," he teases. I shove his shoulder. "Watch out for my girl," he adds. Then I press the bottle to my lips one more time.

"No problem."

I move toward the crowd but lose sight of Becca, and Ty catches my eye as I look for her. He's standing behind a table, where he has two laptops and a tangle of cords. His red over-the-top headphones are lopsided. I flash him a grin, and he returns it, nodding.

Closer to the speakers, the music is so loud that the deep vibration throbs against my skin. By the time I make my way through the crowd, the song Greg and I were talking over has ended, and a French rap song starts playing. I watch Tyler mouth some of the words as I approach. *Who knew Ty could rap in French?* I mean, his mom's family is Senegalese, but I didn't know he was *that* good.

"Hiii, Ty!" I laugh at the rhyme. *Okay, maybe I didn't need that last sip.*

He grins and takes off the headphones. "Butler."

"I have a request."

"Oh yeah?"

"Yeah. And I'm sure you have some totally expert song picked out, but the thing is . . ."

"What's the thing?"

"Well, mostly that I haven't felt like dancing in ages. And I'm dying to hear that last song from your playlist."

He looks me over appraisingly. "Do you really think I'm the kind of guy who would deny your request?"

"Yeah." I nod. "I think you're exactly that kind of guy."

"Well, true, I guess I am. I have a flow going. But for you, I can make an exception."

A raspy voice fills the air, and I squeal in delight, a sound I haven't heard myself make in a very long time.

"Yes! *Thankyouthankyou!* You're my favorite." Blowing Tyler an exaggerated kiss over my shoulder, I dance away. He pretends to catch it and slams it into his chest. He takes two steps backward, like the force propelled him away from me. I feel the bubbling happiness come from deep in my belly.

As I look around for Becca, all the individual movements of the crowd—arms, legs, pulses, shimmies, and shuffles—transform into one big wave flowing to the music. Controlled chaos, with Ty conducting.

Then the crowd moves in just the right way, and I spot her. She's in the middle of the makeshift dance floor, which is just the regular carpeting with the couches and coffee table moved up against the wall. The glow from the TV shines multicolored light onto her skin as it plays the video for the song. I pause to wonder how Ty figured out how to do that.

When Becca sees me, she throws her arms into the air.

I shake my hips in her direction.

She places one hand on her heart and the other becomes a microphone fist. When Becca gives me a turn at the mic, I feel like I'm exactly where I'm supposed to be.

Greg joins us, pulling Becca into him, and I fall into my own world long enough that somehow, I wander away from my friends. The beat picks up again, and I don't care that I'm dancing alone. The music is blasting; it's like I swallowed the speaker and it's playing from inside me. I'm throwing as much as I can at the walls, onto the floor, at anything that will stick. Song after song, some type of release. And all at once I'm so grateful for Ty; this music is like its own version of shattering dishes.

I walk-dance up to him. Ty looks up from his computer and leans closer so I can hear him over the music. "I'm a reasonable guy and everything, but I'm not going to grant you *two* requests in one night."

"Hey, I just came to compliment the DJ." When he meets my eye, he suddenly looks alone, standing behind his computer. The guy who's hosting this amazing party isn't even getting to enjoy it. "Take a break and dance with me! I'm sure you have the next few songs picked out."

He pauses, just for a second, before saying, "All right, but try to keep up, Butler."

I swat his shoulder before pulling him around his table. He hits a key on a keyboard before letting me lead him away.

A fast song starts, and Tyler gives me a knowing look. I throw my hair back and forth, giggling like a fool.

Backing away, and making my eyes purposely heavy, I point at him dramatically. He answers with a goofy expression, and his voice is deep as he sings. The song is really high energy, whatever it is, and we jump up and down next to each other, throwing our hands into the air. I feel it with my whole body.

When the chorus hits, Ty moves right with the beat. He has the smallest sounds memorized, and his robot arms are bending and stopping, legs sliding and freezing, all at the perfect moment. It's dorky and awesome, and I can't stop grinning. When the song hits its last note, we're laughing and gasping for air.

The next song starts, and it's still got a good beat to dance to, but it's slower. Tyler takes a few steps forward, moving closer, and he surprises me by placing a tentative hand my hip. When I look up at him, his amber eyes are on my face. I can't totally read his expression, but in this moment, something about him is easier to see, more exposed.

Ty mouths the lyrics and slowly rocks to the thump of the bass. The words echo in my ears: *Might be better off without you. There's too many people all around you.*

I've never heard this song before.

He pauses and then slowly sways me; I didn't realize I wasn't moving. Before I can wonder why I feel a little nervous, the next lyric cuts me off short. He moves his mouth along with the words, looking at me: *You're so gorgeous.*

It doesn't feel like he's just singing along.

The rhythm picks up, and our bodies have twisted together. Somehow, we're pressed close now; I have a leg between his, and he has one between mine. My heart rate starts to accelerate; it's a beat of its own.

Tyler and I have danced together plenty of times, but never like this. Something is different. Maybe it's him, maybe it's me, or maybe it's both of us. I try not to worry about it; I just dance. I hear Becca's voice in my mind: *participate*.

I'm lost to the music, lost in this moment. Ty's swaying me back and forth, and my hands find his neck to help keep my balance. A jolt moves up my spine, but I don't think about it. My brain has left, and I'm all body and heart. I'm laughter, and fun, and whiskey in my bloodstream. And something else. I haven't been this girl in so long. And just for tonight, I let myself hold on to her by tightening my grip on him.

Tyler's other arm wraps around me, and I lean in to his body. His hands move to the small of my back. Our faces are closer than they were before, maybe closer than they ever have been.

Ty lifts a hand and brushes my hair away from my face.

My heart thumps faster.

And the world continues to move around us, but the music fades, and now it's just my heartbeat keeping time. He's asking me a question with his eyes.

And, somewhere deep in the back of my mind, I know the answer.

I don't think.

I kiss him.

I feel the air go out of him when my lips touch his. There's the slightest pause before he reacts, and then his hand moves behind my head and pulls me closer. *Closer.* We stop dancing.

Too soon, the song ends. And in the brief moment of silence, my thoughts come rushing in: *What in the hell do you think you're doing? You can't just make out with Tyler!* Because there was a naked truth in that moment, something I had been trying not to see.

And what about Braden?

Holy effing shit.

I pull away, breathing hard. I look at him, his mouth.

The next song starts, and it thumps around us as Tyler and I stare at each other in disbelief. We're the only still point in the wave of dancers.

"Whoa," Tyler says.

I can't stop looking at him. He risks a smile.

Whoa.

But then I see Greg marching toward us, eyes on us like a hawk stalking prey. When he reaches us, he grabs me by the arm. He pulls me away from Tyler, through the crowd, and into an office, where we were hanging out before. Over my shoulder, I watch Tyler standing with his arms slack at his sides, looking like you could knock him over with a feather.

"What the hell, Hadley?"

Some small voice in the back of my mind objects, saying that Becca told me to do this, to participate. But I know that's not true. She didn't mean Tyler. I just royally, royally messed up.

"What the *hell* do you think you're doing!"

I find some words. "We were just dancing! I don't know—"

He cuts me off. "Well, you better figure it out!" He looks down at his feet. "God, you're going to get me into *so much shit.*"

"How is this going to get *you* into any shit? It has nothing to do with you! Jesus, Greg, it was just a kiss!"

His voice is firm. "No. It was *not* just a kiss. That was *Tyler.* You two can't have *just a kiss.* God, Hadley, you fucking know better." I've never seen Greg so angry.

He's right, and it makes my stomach turn. I knew there may have been something there, between me and Ty, at least at one point. But I didn't know there was so much behind it. And I definitely didn't know I would match some of it. Tears start to gather in my eyes, but I force them back. Feeling like the worst person in the world, I lash out, "Can you just *back off?*"

Greg presses his lips together. Then he exhales. "Had, you've been getting all kinds of free passes because of . . . everything. But this isn't one of those times. You cannot mess with Tyler." He looks at me. "Anybody but Tyler, okay? You're not in the right place to start something, and it will mess everything up. For him, and for the four of us."

My chest is tight.

"Look, I get it. But you *have* to make it right. Even just for yourself, you need a friend like Ty right now." He pauses, listening. "I'm going to check on him. Are you okay?"

Greg is still looking at me, waiting for me to answer. But I can't yet. My thoughts take over. *I betrayed my friend. How could I risk hurting him?*

And now Braden isn't the last person I kissed. The thought stings.

If I speak, I'm going to totally lose control, so I just nod at Greg and leave the room. As soon as I'm out of sight, I run up the stairs, my heart like a ticking bomb.

during

Junior Year

spring

CHAPTER 12

"Yes! Go Braden!" I'm on my feet the second he dives off the starting block. It takes only moments before he glides ahead of the other swimmers, and he doesn't come up for air until almost halfway across the pool. "Yes!" I shout again as he finally breaks the surface.

Greg is yelling to be heard over the cheering crowd. "So they really just go back and forth? I thought they might step it up after their little break. I mean, at least the divers looked cool."

This is my friends' first meet, and Greg said this same thing at the start of each race. I thought he got it out of his system during the first half, but apparently not. My guess is that he didn't love his girlfriend's wide eyes when she first saw the team in their uniforms.

Becca interjects, "Well, I think it looks impressive as hell. I don't even like to get my hair wet."

"Thanks, Bec." I redirect my attention to Greg, a little annoyed he needs to object quite so often. "And yes, for the *millionth* time, they swim back and forth. I'd like to see you try it. Especially fly—it's by far the hardest."

"This is fly?" Ty asks.

I elaborate without moving my eyes from the swimmers. "Yes, this is the butterfly. The race he won earlier was freestyle. Which is easier, but Braden's times are superfast. And not every swimmer has two strokes."

Ty teases, "Oh, so you're hip to the lingo now?"

"When your boyfriend holds the school record for the hardest stroke, you remember what it's called," I retort.

"I'm real tempted to make a joke about all of Braden's *stroking*," Greg says.

Ty chokes on his laughter, and I shoot Greg a sharp look.

Greg puts his hands up. "I won't." Then he starts to ramble, "But you can't just keep repeating the words *hard* and *stroke* and expect nobody to pick up on it." Becca puts a hand on his arm. He takes the hint and stops talking.

Becca wisely changes the subject. "Ty, I'm still thinking about that third equation on the math section. Do you remember what your answer was? Because I think I marked *A*, but now I'm doubting myself."

We took the ACT last week, and Becca has been reliving it ever since. Unsurprisingly, we're all starting to lose our patience.

Ty sighs. "Becca, my answer is the same as the last ten times you asked me: I don't remember. There were a lot of questions."

"Okay, I know. But the average U of M student got a thirty-one on their ACT, and I swear to god if that one equation stops me, I'm going to lose my mind."

"Are you sure you haven't already started?" Ty asks innocently.

Greg tries not to laugh, but then turns to soothe her. "Becca, I'm sure you got it right. You're the smartest person I know."

She ignores him and talks to Ty. "Okay, I'm doing that thing that I do, I know, but I can't help it, okay? And I think I remember the equation, so maybe I could write it down and we can see—"

"Becca, I love you." Ty looks at Greg. "Platonically, of course."

"Of course." Greg nods approvingly.

Ty continues, "But if you don't stop asking me about this, I'm going to be forced to push you into the pool."

"You guys, can you argue about this when my boyfriend isn't in the middle of a race?" Braden finishes the first fifty yards, half a pool length ahead of his competition.

Becca mumbles an apology.

Braden moves even faster. I let out another whooping cheer and then Becca is on her feet, too, standing next to me, cheering just as loudly as I am.

Thank god something got her out of her head.

Two more lengths to go until the end of the race. I watch Brade's muscular arms and shoulders move in and out of the water, propelling him farther and farther ahead of the other swimmers. My chest bursts with pride.

But then, at the last turn, when Braden makes contact with the wall and moves to push off, he jerks abruptly to the right. He comes to a near stop, and the other swimmers start to catch up.

I feel my face fall.

"Wait, what just happened?" Becca asks, full of concern.

"I don't know." I can't look away from Braden. He's lost his lead now, moving slowly. "Something's wrong." I've never seen him do anything but win.

Braden forces himself to the other side of the pool by what looks like sheer will, and he struggles out of the water, clutching his shoulder. Face twisted in pain, he approaches his coach. I watch their exchange as a couple of swimmers celebrate an unheard-of victory against Braden Roberts. It makes my stomach turn.

"I'm going to go see if he's okay."

❋ ❋ ❋

I weave through the crowd, down to where the team is gathered. I hear Braden explaining, "Yeah, when I pushed off. It's the same spot." I know he's been battling tendinitis, but I thought the steroid shots he gets were keeping it under control. "But I don't know." He grimaces.

"Braden," I call, and he turns to look at me. "Hey, are you okay?"

His face is twisted in pain, but he nods. "I'm fine. I'm sure it's fine." It looks more like he's saying *It has to be fine.*

"Braden?" Coach's voice breaks our gaze. "That was your last race today. Why don't you go get it checked out?"

My worry spikes. "What? You think it's that bad?"

"That's what we need to find out. Braden said his parents couldn't make it today. Do you have a car here, Hadley? Can you take him to the doctor? I hate to ask, but I've got to stay for the rest of the meet."

"Yeah, um, of course. No problem." Ty actually drove me, but I'm sure he'll help out. "I could take him to urgent care? My friend's dad works at one close by."

"Sure, better safe than sorry," Coach answers.

I catch Tyler's eye from the stands and wave him down. Becca and Greg follow.

Braden turns to me. "I'm going to put some clothes on." And I know he's hurting, because there's no teasing in his eyes as he says it.

Coach looks back at Braden. "Roberts. You do what you need to, to get back in the pool." The two of them hold a meaningful look, and then Braden nods.

As Braden makes his way to the locker room, Tyler finds his way over to me, and I explain what happened.

"Would you mind taking us? Is your dad working?"

"Yeah, I think he is, actually. What happened? Is he all right?" Ty nods in the direction of the locker room.

"I think so. But he's not sure."

"My dad will help."

I turn to my other friends. "Becca, will you and Greg be okay if we go? Can you get a ride?"

Greg answers me. "We'll figure it out. No worries."

Becca puts a hand on my elbow. "You okay?"

"Yeah, no, I'm good," I answer, distracted. "He's fine. I'm sure he's fine."

❊ ❊ ❊

173

An hour later, my knees are anxiously bouncing up and down in a waiting room chair. Ty takes a hand and presses it into my knee. "Butler, relax."

"Sorry." I force my legs to still, and Tyler moves his hand. But it's like the energy just transferred from my legs to my fingers, because now I can't help from clicking my rings together.

"It's just an X-ray, Hads."

"Yeah, I know. You're right." I don't know what I'm all worked up about. Braden was quiet in the car, but clearly in no immediate danger.

Dr. West, Ty's dad, approaches us wearing a white coat, a stethoscope around his neck, and a clipboard in his hands. "All right, guys. I was just talking with Dr. Wilseck, who's working with Braden. It looks like he has a small tear in his rotator cuff. They're discussing options now, but he's just fine."

Tyler gives me a *told ya so* look.

I release a bit of my concern. "Is he going to be able to keep swimming?"

"He'll have to take a break, rest up, but he should be back in the pool soon enough." *Even a break is going to devastate him.*

"Thank you." I look between the two Wests. "Both of you. For your help."

Dr. West nods. "Anytime. I have to get back, but Dr. Wilseck should be able to answer any other questions." I mumble another thanks as he turns to go down the hallway.

I turn to my friend. "Seriously, Ty. Thank you."

"Don't get ahead of yourself. I'm going to cash in on a *major* favor for this."

"Oh yeah? Like what?" I can't even imagine what Ty would want from Braden.

"I'll think of something."

"Okay, well, I'm sure you guys will sort it out."

"Wait." Ty laughs. "Oh, no. Not Braden. *You* owe me."

"What? This isn't my favor!"

"Oh please. I didn't do it for Roberts."

"Fine. *I* owe you."

"That's right. Don't forget it."

I force a smile, because I know he's only trying to make me laugh. Ty doesn't really care about a favor. And he knows I'd always help him if he needed it anyway.

"Hey. Thanks for waiting." At Braden's voice, my head shoots up. His arm is in a sling and he looks shattered.

I stand up and wrap my arms around his waist. "Are you okay? What did the doctor say?" I ask, looking up at him.

I can tell he's mad but trying to keep it under control. "It's a *fucking* tear."

"I'm so sorry."

"I can either have surgery or rest and do physical therapy."

"Surgery?" I feel my eyebrows meet above my nose.

"I'm fine. It's fine." He has a determined look in his eye. "I'm not going to do the surgery. Not in the middle of the season, right when I have scouts in the stands." Braden is hoping for a swimming scholarship, and before today, there was no reason why he shouldn't get a great one. "If it still hasn't healed by summer, I can take time off club and get the surgery then."

Club swimming isn't technically part of the school sport—it takes place during the summer, hosted by the local public pool—but most of the team participates. They have meets too, but they're less formal, more of a way to stay in shape than to truly compete.

"Okay." I try to process everything he's just said. "Yeah, that makes sense. So the physical therapy, then? How long do you have to rest? How long do you need that thing?" I gesture to the sling.

"They said a month, but there's no way I'm waiting that long. Spring break is coming up, so if I go three weeks, I'll miss only an invitational." Invitationals don't count against season rankings, I remind myself.

"Braden, you should probably do what the doctor says," I answer, worried.

"I've got this, Hadley. I have a plan, and the season's almost over. It'll be like it never happened."

Tyler eyes us and claps his hands, trying to cut through the tension. "All right, well, if you're all set, let's get out of here, huh?"

I look back at Ty. "Right." I try to dismiss my concerns. "Okay. Let's go?"

Braden nods, and with his uninjured arm, he takes my hand, giving it a little squeeze—a silent peace offering. Then he says, "Hey, West. Do you mind if we make a pit stop on the way back? I've got to fill a prescription."

Tyler gives me a satisfied look. I can almost hear him thinking, *Another favor.* "Yeah, no problem, man. Let's get out of here."

CHAPTER 13

"I'm scared." The words leave my mouth before I even realize they were tiptoeing across my brain.

No longer needing his sling, Braden pushes himself up from his elbows to his hands, palms flat against his navy sheets. His face hovers above mine, blocking out the light from his bedroom window. A piece of hair falls into his eyes, and without thinking, I reach up and slide some of it back through my fingers.

His voice is soft. "That's okay, Had. We don't have to." He slides his weight from on top of me to next to me, and props his head up on his elbow.

The space between us pulls at me. He's still touching me; he's still close. But not close enough.

We've been talking about this for so long. I even told Mom about it, and she got me a doctor's appointment right away. I've been prepared, taking the pill for months. And god, I want him.

I close my eyes and then open them again. "No, I mean,

I want to. I do. I'm just scared anyway," I admit. I press my hand into the familiar muscle on his chest—not to push him away, but to feel his heartbeat. It's moving fast, but not as fast as mine. "Are you? Scared, I mean," I ask in a small voice.

He grimaces, and I realize I must have irritated his shoulder. "Shit, I'm so sorry. Are you okay?" With Braden trying to get back into the pool, the last thing I want to do is cause him more pain. I move my hand. "Is it still hurting? Even with the painkillers?"

"Only a little bit. Honestly, the medicine works well. I think swimming is going to be fine."

I sit up, not convinced. "Maybe we should wait. I don't want to make it worse."

"You're not going to hurt me, Hadley."

"No?"

He shakes his head. "No." His expression finds some mischief. "But if it helps, with the nerves, you should probably know that my expectations are already ruined. I basically expected to seduce you with one look, rip your clothes off with my teeth, and then listen to you scream my name for . . . I don't know. However long a long time is." The corner of his mouth twists, teasing. "So it's really only downhill from here."

The laugh comes from deep in my stomach, and I roll over to him, wiggling my body against him. I look up to his face. "You're such an ass." But even the insult sounds like a term of endearment when I say it to him.

He continues as if I didn't speak, folding his hands under his head, "Yeah, I hate to tell you, Had. But everything about this is sort of a bummer. Two working parents on the last day of spring break. And I'm naked in bed with the girl I'm, like, stupid in love with. It's only fair you know that before anything happens. That I'm totally, completely disappointed."

I laugh again, and he moves so he can see my face better.

Then he says, "Hey, speaking of parents, my mom wants you to come to dinner at the house this weekend. My grandma is going to be in town, and she wants to show you off, I think."

"That's what you want to talk about right now?"

"Nope. Actually. Not at all." He smirks and then looks at me more seriously for a moment. He kisses me gently. "It's just me, Hadley. So nothing to be nervous about there. And you know I've never done this before either." The light shining from his eyes is so bright that it melts hazel into gold. "Did I mention that I love you?"

"Yeah, I know. I love you too."

"And I promise that's not going to change. And I promise to stop if you want, if it hurts or anything." He looks at my hands; he's lacing my fingers with his.

I'm not afraid of it hurting. I don't have language for what I'm afraid of.

"But if you don't want to," he continues, "we have plenty of time. I'm not going anywhere."

I look at his face. I've kissed every inch of it. He's seen this much of me before. Honestly, it's a decision I made a while ago. I want to be with him, in every way you can be with somebody. The idea of not doing it, about not having this experience with him, is so much worse than the nerves I feel about going through with it. I wet my lips and nod, just slightly. "I want to."

He kisses me for a moment before I feel something change. He laughs into my mouth. "Shit, Had."

"What's wrong?"

"Now I'm kind of scared."

"We don't have to."

"No, no. It's okay." His voice is a whisper. "I don't mind being scared with you." And then he pulls my face to his.

It's slow at first. I'm so aware of every movement that my trembling hands make. And that his make too. I think of all the times before, when we forced ourselves apart, breathing heavy and electrified. This time, we don't stop.

I pull him on top of me, heart hammering.

And we get as close as two people can be.

At first, there's a deep pressure, but it passes. And then, it's right. We move together, both unsure of what we're supposed to do. He whispers into my ear, asks me if I'm okay. I can only nod. I ask him, too, a beat later, and he kisses me in response. After I few minutes, I give in to it. I close my eyes, and I let myself simply feel.

The thought fills my mind before I can stop it: for as long as I live, Braden and I will have this moment. And we love each other, and what could be more important than that?

❀   ❀   ❀

After he comes back from the bathroom in his boxers and gets back into bed, he bites the corner of his lips. "Was it like you thought?"

I bury my head into his chest, too embarrassed to answer. A moment later, I lift my face, resting my chin on a curve of a muscle that doesn't belong to me. "I don't know. I don't know what I thought. But it wasn't . . . not what I thought."

He sounds tentative. "Can I say something corny?" He plays with the end of my hair. "You can't make fun of me."

I trace a finger across my chest, making an X. *Cross my heart.*

"I kind of feel like . . ." His hazel eyes, steady and earnest, find mine. "I feel like . . . well, it means a lot to me. To share that with you."

Every corridor of my heart blows wide open.

I don't trust my voice. So I look at him, and I hope that the emotion on my face tells him what I cannot. He gives me a secret smile in return.

I can't find any words to describe how I'm feeling. I guess I could say I feel like, somehow, we're more together than we were before and there's nothing that makes me happier, or feel safer. I could tell him while there are plenty of technicalities we will work out in the future, today was perfect anyway. He was perfect. I could say that I love him in a way I didn't know was possible. But I don't say anything. He knows. So instead, I carefully move on top of him, as his arms wrap around me, and let our hearts beat against each other.

Eventually, Braden kisses the side of my head and sits up, bringing me with him. "Hey, Hads, did you, maybe, work up an appetite?"

I burst out laughing.

"Because I'm starving. Have you had lunch? Want to go get a burger?"

And after another fit of laughter, we get dressed, gathering the clothes from the floor and exchanging items across the bed.

❄   ❄   ❄

Thirty minutes later, Becca slaps two burgers down in front of us at my favorite booth at Belavinis. "Here you go, lovebirds." Since we're on spring break, and some of the few still in town, she's filling in for one of the daytime girls who had a baby-sitting issue.

"Thanks, Becs," Braden says as he takes the lid off the ketchup bottle.

While Braden tries to figure out a way to get ketchup onto his plate, I take advantage of his distraction and give Becca a look. She twists her head microscopically: *What?* I shift my gaze to Braden, who has a knife clinking into the bottle, and nod. She focuses on me, and then she looks between the two of us in a final, confirming question. I nod again, and she opens her mouth into a soundless, happy screech. Then she looks at Braden struggling and grabs a full bottle of ketchup from the table next to us.

"Here, bud. Try this one," she says before she walks away.

My phone lights up seconds later. I hope he had more luck with you than he's having with the ketchup.

The laugh that moves through me is weightless. Braden looks up at the sound. He furrows his eyebrows. "Why do I feel like I missed something?"

"You did. But it doesn't matter." I take a fry and dip it into the ketchup on his plate. "Eat. I seem to remember you work-ing up an appetite."

He answers me by taking a savage bite of his burger. And I feel it; feel the click as my mind captures it. This moment—silly, sweet, and completely perfect—leaves a permanent im-print on my heart.

* * *

I come home in a happy daze. I set my purse down, remove my phone, and take off my shoes. Braden is already texting me: **Come back.** I smile at the screen.

My family is sitting down for dinner. Remy and Judd just got back from Florida this afternoon, where a group of them rented a house on the beach. Even with how different they are, their friends get along weirdly well. I pull my chair out and sit in my usual spot. Dad sets the final tray down onto the table, and I look up from my phone once we're all seated. Then I notice the expression on Mom's face. Something's wrong.

"Guys, Dad and I have to talk to you about something."

And then the world cracks and breaks beneath my feet.

CHAPTER 14

For the next few weeks, I stare into space so often that focusing my eyes starts to feel like work. I move through school in a stupor, and I don't get out of bed unless I have to.

I ignore everyone. I ignore everything. I snap at my friends. I know I'm doing it, but I can't stop. I stop everything else, though. I get my ACT score, which is higher than I hoped, but I feel no sense of accomplishment. It doesn't feel important anymore. I stop doing homework. I know I need to keep my grades up, but I can't seem to find the energy to care. I stop going to work. I don't quit or call. I just stop going. Mom has to take a leave of absence, so I might as well take one too. Becca must have explained what's going on, because after I miss four shifts, the restaurant stops calling.

I sit in silence with Braden, who inexplicably keeps showing up. Braden, who after Mom told us, rushed over and held me in his car as I shattered into a million pieces.

My body echoes hers.

Mom doesn't sleep; I don't sleep.

Mom doesn't eat; I don't eat.

I didn't know so much of me was made of her. I don't tell her. I don't know if I want her to know.

I whisper the word *cancer* in the shower until it loses its meaning. I obsessively check my chest for lumps, pressing frantic fingers into doughy flesh, hard enough that it hurts. Salt water mixes with fresh as it runs down my face. I am made of her.

I'm scared. And I'm the kind of angry that rattles my bones. I don't even know what I believe in, but I'm furious with God.

Mom is mine; you can't have her. I tell him, her, them, whoever-whatever-might-listen. She doesn't deserve this. But I still pray.

I pray like I never have before. I pray she will live. I pray that her cancer is localized, that it hasn't spread. I pray that they caught it early. I pray it won't take her softness, her kind-ness. I pray simply: *Please.*

I lie awake at night, seeing malicious cells dividing, taking over.

She's only forty-four.

It doesn't feel real. This happens to other people, not us. Except that's not true. Because this isn't even the first time it's happened to us. And I'm so angry it's not true.

I pray for Dad. That he has the strength to see her in pain. That he can accept this powerlessness. I wonder sometimes if this is even harder for him, to watch her suffer. I hate myself for wondering that. She certainly has it the hardest.

I pray for Remy and Judd. That they have someone to listen. That they don't feel alone. And I hate myself for not being that person for them. I hate myself for not having the strength to reach out to them. I pray they reach out to each other.

I hate that I can't say any of this out loud. I hate that I can't fight it and I can't run fast enough.

So for a while, I hide.

CHAPTER 15

"Hads, Remy, you girls ready?" Mom calls up the stairs to my bedroom.

"Yeah, coming." My voice is sharp, even to my own ears. I grab the nail polish, the shade of breast cancer awareness that I ordered online earlier this week, telling Mom that during her surgery, at least her nails could tell cancer to go to hell. A pink-painted middle finger.

It's been a month since she was diagnosed, and the surgery is tomorrow. The doctors are going to do a lumpectomy to remove the tumor in her breast, along with the lymph nodes under her arms. After the surgery, they'll confirm the stage of her cancer: zero to four. Four being the worst. With that information, they'll figure out the rest of her treatment plan. It's all so clinical, except for the fact that we're talking about Mom's life. I swallow the emotion in my throat. I need to be strong for her. I steady myself and head downstairs.

In the kitchen, Mom's standing with her shoes on and her purse around her shoulder. My heart hitches. It's jarring;

looking at her yoga figure, her glow-y olive skin, and her shiny hair—she's a vision of health. Except she isn't.

There's this hopeful part of me that keeps thinking that none of this is real, and it's that false hope, again and again, that knocks me over. It's unrelenting, and it almost makes me want to stop looking at her seemingly healthy outside. But how could I ever do that? So I just let my heart break a little bit every time instead. It's not much compared to what she's about to do.

I shake the thoughts away and slip on my shoes before we walk out the door.

❅　❅　❅

I can't stop the what-ifs. They run along the bottom of every thought, scrolling like the evening news updates. They move faster and faster, torturing me with horrible possibilities. I roll over in bed, and the sheets tangle around my legs. I throw them violently to the floor. Then I sit up and close my eyes, trying to breathe. I'm not sure if I've fallen asleep. Not sure if these thoughts ever shifted into nightmares. It's still dark outside, but I can't be in this room anymore. I descend the staircase without turning the lights on, using my phone as a flashlight.

Mom's sitting in the dark at the kitchen table.

At the noise, she turns. "Hadley," she says, surprised.

She can't sleep either. Of course not. *She's the one who has surgery today. She's the one who has cancer.* I'm the healthy one. I have no right to be so scared. "You okay, Mom?" My voice is raspy from lack of use.

"Yeah. Can't sleep. I was just thinking . . ." She trails off.

"Me too." I try to shrug away the flood of emotions.

"I think you guys should go to school today."

"What? *No.* We're coming with you."

She shakes her head. "There's no sense in missing school. This surgery isn't dangerous, and I get to come home right afterward. And if we start pulling you out for every little thing—"

"Every little thing? Are you kidding? Mom, you're having surgery! That's not little." Mom used to call me out of school a couple times a year just so we could go to lunch at her favorite Chinese restaurant.

She's quiet for a moment before she answers in a heavy voice, "Hadley, please. I'll just worry about you." And when she looks up at me, her eyes are full of tears. We're both fighting this so hard; it pains me to see her lose control. She *never* loses control.

I wrap my arms around her. "Okay. All right. I'll go." I bite the inside of my cheek. "I get it."

And I do. She's always taking care of everybody else, and today she needs to focus on herself. I can get through the day. I will do anything that will help her do the same.

"Do you want a glass of water?" Moonlight shines through the window, illuminating my pink fingernails against the dark cabinet as I pull two glasses from the cupboard.

"I can't have anything to eat or drink until after the surgery."

Shit. How could I forget that? "Oh, right." I put the second glass away.

"You should go back to bed, honey. It's barely five in the

morning. Do you have a ride to school? Or should I remind Judd to wait for you?"

"I'll ask him." Normally, I like to ride with Braden, but if I can't be with Mom, I'd like to be with my siblings. I drink all my water in a few gulps, and set the glass down into the sink. I pad back over to Mom.

"You're sure you don't want us to come?"

She nods.

"Okay." I pull her into a hug one more time. "Love you." I squeeze too tight.

"Love you too, hon. I'll see you tonight."

"Okay," I answer, and move quickly up the stairs.

❋   ❋   ❋

"Any bets on what this is?" Judd and I are standing in front of the fridge with the door open, staring at the stacks of Tupperware. It feels like everyone Mom has ever met has dropped off a meal. Which is so thoughtful, but I have to admit, none of them look all that appetizing. Judd's got one in his hands, with the lid sitting abandoned on the island counter, next to where Braden and Remy are sitting.

"I don't know. Smell it," I suggest.

Judd pulls the dish away from his face. "I'm not smelling some mystery meal!"

Remy reaches toward us. "I will."

I take it from Judd, walk over, and hand Remy the Tupperware. It's sort of a brown, lumpy mush. "Maybe it's sloppy joe?" she suggests.

Remy passes it over to Braden. "What do you think?"

He jerks his head back to attention. "What?"

I study him. "Where'd you go, Brade?"

He shakes his head. "Sorry." He takes the container from Remy, leans into it, and grimaces.

I wrinkle my nose, moving to pass the food back to Judd, who returns to rummaging through the Tupperware in the fridge.

"How about we order Chinese?" I remember thinking of Mom's favorite restaurant early this morning. "I bet they'll deliver it if they know it's for Mom. But if they won't, Braden and I can pick it up." His eyes are still unfocused. "Right, Braden?"

"Yeah," he confirms, a second later. "For sure."

Judd ignores our little exchange but takes my suggestion. "Chinese is a good idea." He pulls his cell from his pocket and dials the number from memory.

While Judd's on the phone, I put the food away and move to Braden, leaning into him as he wraps a heavy arm around me. "You okay?"

"Yeah, I'm good. These new meds are just taking a little getting used to." Braden's injury, now more than a month old, is still not healed. The doctor recently changed up his prescription—same type of thing, just a little stronger. I feel my face reflect my concern, but he brushes me off. "It's all good, Hads. Totally normal side effects."

"Are you sure?"

He nods. "I'm the last thing you need to be worrying about right now."

191

I squeeze Braden's hand as Judd orders enough for ten people, instead of five, and I hear him thank the owner as she offers to have it delivered.

❋　❋　❋

It doesn't take too long for the food to arrive. I unpack it, removing the cartons one by one, and set them out like a buffet on the counter. Judd pulls out plates and silverware, while Braden gets some water bottles from the garage. Remy puts on some music. The familiar routine is comforting, but I'm still nervous. My parents walk in as we're finishing getting everything ready. My entire body starts at the noise.

"Mom!" I exclaim too loudly as she walks slowly into the kitchen. I pull her into a hug, and she flinches. "Oh shit. God, I didn't even . . . I'm so sorry." I jerk away and take her hands instead. "How are you feeling?" My own body is nauseous and relieved.

"Good." I study her. "I'm fine, Hadley. I promise." I look down at our intertwined hands and notice that her nails are bare. "What—" I start to ask, before Judd moves me out of the way.

"Quit hogging her, Had." Judd wraps Mom into a tight hug, and again she flinches. "Sorry," he says sheepishly, but looks relieved to see her.

Remy opts to only squeeze her hands. "Glad to have you home."

Dad watches us for a moment, curls wild atop his head, before his eyes land on Braden. "Hey, guys. Mom's tired." Dad wraps an arm around her. Leading her to their bedroom gingerly, Dad says to her, "I'll get your meds from the car after we get you situated."

"I don't want those pills. I'm okay."

Dad objects, "Mia, the doctor said—"

"Just get me into bed, please?"

"Wait. We got you your favorite, Mom." I gesture to the Chinese feast.

"Oh, thank you, honey, but I'm just not hungry right now."

I nod as my parents disappear into their bedroom.

"Well, I am," Judd says as he fixes himself a plate and heads into the living room.

"Me too." Remy joins him.

Braden moves to my side. "She looks good." He kisses the top of my head and takes my hands in his. "Are you?"

I lean into his chest.

"It's me, Had. You can say whatever you want."

"They took her nail polish off. We just got manicures yesterday. I was trying to cheer her up. And she doesn't want the food either."

He presses his lips together. "Hadley. You're doing everything you can. She knows that. It's not about the nails or the food, not really. She knows how much you love her."

My stomach turns. "Okay."

He tightens his arms around me, looking down at my face, "But if you're all right, I'm going to go. I don't think your dad wants me here. This feels . . . like a family thing."

Braden doesn't feel any less like family than anybody else in this house, not to me, but I didn't miss that look from Dad either. It doesn't seem fair, since my parents and the twins both have one another, but I know that Braden's probably right. "Yeah. Okay. Thank you for being here."

"Always. Everything is going to be okay, I promise. I'll have my phone with me, all night." He kisses me, fingertips brushing my cheek, and walks out the back door.

But then I'm alone in the kitchen, hanging on to a promise from a boy who has no way of keeping it. I want to join my siblings, but when I look at the cartons of food on the counter, the fried smell fills me with a wave of nausea. My mouth floods with thin, unpleasant moisture, and I run to the bathroom and hurl into the toilet.

Three days later, the results are in: Mom has stage three breast cancer. She's going to need six rounds of chemo, followed by four weeks of daily radiation.

I pray some more.

CHAPTER 16

"What? I thought it looked sort of edible today." Tyler defends the lunch special, chicken tenders with mashed potatoes, which I'm eyeing doubtfully. "Not all of us can get by on an apple and a Coke, you know."

It's just the two of us at the lunch table. Braden is having his shoulder checked out again, and Becca and Greg are in the later lunch hour today. This afternoon, the caf is full of that wild, end-of-the-year energy. I can't believe we have only a few weeks left of junior year.

"Yeah." I look at my meager lunch. "I just haven't been superhungry. . . ."

He meets my eye and nods just slightly. "I remember that feeling. Sucks."

I look down at my hands. "Yeah, it does."

"It's easier if you try things that actually taste good." He takes the cookie from his tray. "Here. Have this."

"I'm not taking your cookie, Ty. That's the only thing you have that looks halfway decent."

He smirks. "That's the point, Butler. Eat it. I can get another one."

I unwrap it and take a bite. It's chewy and chocolatey, but most notably, it doesn't turn to ash in my mouth. "Thanks."

He pulls at his sleeve. "How's she doing after the surgery? Is it okay to ask?"

My stomach tightens. "She's hanging in there."

"And how are you?"

My body tenses.

"What, I can't ask about you?"

"I'm fine."

"You don't have to be so tough, Hads. I'm sort of . . . worried about you. You seem far away. Are you talking to anybody?" He looks down at his tray. "How's Roberts been with everything?"

"I'm fine, Ty. He's been great."

He gives me a look.

"You don't think Braden could be great about this?"

"Not really."

"Ty!"

He shakes his head. "That's not what I meant. I just meant that you, I don't know, you don't seem fine. And if I'm being honest, no, I don't really think Mr. Perfect All-American *could* get this."

Reflexively, I object, "He doesn't have a perfect life; his parents are basically never around. I've only met them, like, a handful of times—" Then I stop short, because his parents are just working. They aren't gone like Tyler's mom. "I'm sorry, I didn't mean . . ."

"It's fine."

I exhale loudly. "Honestly, I don't know how to talk about this with you, Ty."

"What? Why?"

"*Because*," I say meaningfully, hoping he'll fill in the blanks.

I watch understanding cross his face. "Because I lost my mom?"

"Well, yeah. Because *of course* I know you'd understand how I'm feeling, probably better than anyone, but I can't complain about my mom being sick when . . ."

"When . . . ?"

"When I'm sure you'd love to have that problem."

He takes a deep breath. "I'm not comparing your situation to mine, Hadley. I'm just trying to be here for you. We're friends. Friends don't keep score. Not about the things that matter anyway."

"Well . . . maybe I am a shitty friend. Maybe I do keep score."

He frowns.

I sigh. "Sorry."

"Hadley, I would never expect you to just be okay with all this, just because something different happened to me."

"Something harder. Worse."

Amusement fills his eyes. "Maybe you are a shitty friend." Then his face goes more serious. "Hads, I'm sorry. I really wasn't trying to take a dig at your boyfriend. I just want you to know that I'm here. That I'm having seventh-grade-nurse-Trisha flashbacks." His tone is light. "And if you want to talk to somebody who might, I don't know, understand how this shit takes over your life, I'm here. But no pressure."

I look at his face, earnest and kind, and suddenly feel like maybe he has a point.

"There actually is something"—I lean in—"I feel . . . helpless. I keep trying to *do something*, but everything I try either makes no difference or kind of makes it worse."

"Yeah. I know what you mean. The other day my dad caught me trying to set up a dating profile for him, and he was . . . not thrilled."

I can't help but let out a little laugh before continuing, "She's starting chemo this week, and not everybody loses their hair, but I think if she does, I'm going to shave mine too."

His eyes light up. "Really?"

"It wouldn't help anything, not really. But I feel like it would show her that she's not alone, you know?" I pause. "Do you think that's stupid?"

"Are you kidding? I think that's so badass."

For the first time in what feels like forever, my smile starts from a deeply content place in my chest—something close to pride. "Don't tell anybody. I don't want Becca or Braden to try to talk me out of it."

"You think Braden would try to talk you out of it?"

"Oh, come on, Ty. No guy wants their girlfriend to shave her head."

"But your hair is always hiding your face."

I look at him, surprised, and we're quiet for a moment. "Just don't tell anybody. I might chicken out, anyway."

"You definitely don't have to do it. But if you did, it would be cool."

"Becca would freak."

"Yeah, you'd definitely have to let me be there when she saw."

I laugh.

"Either way, Hads, whatever you do might not actually cure cancer—which, by the way, is the only thing that would directly help—but it wouldn't go unnoticed."

"You think my mom notices?"

"Are you kidding? Definitely."

With him looking at me like that, I feel understood in a way that's different from anybody else. It isn't really what he's saying, but that he isn't afraid of talking about the uncomfortable details. He's not flinching or insisting everything will be okay; he's just here.

"Thanks, Ty." I clear my throat. "And . . . maybe this is weird to say right now, but I'm sorry that you lost your mom."

"Hadley—"

"Just let me. I haven't really said it since seventh grade. And I'm sorry for that too. I don't think I knew how to talk about it . . . how to bring it up. Other than on birthdays and anniversaries and stuff, I mean, because then I know you're already thinking about it. But I didn't want to upset you or make you go there if you were having a good day or something." His light brown eyes look especially golden today. "But I do. Think about it. I never forget, even if I don't say anything. Even if I can't totally understand."

The words fall so far short of what I want to say. But there really aren't words for the ache in my stomach, knowing my friend had to hurt like that. And I *am* sorry, because I've envisioned what it would be like to live a motherless life a million times, and just the thought of it paralyzes me. He's lived with that reality for almost four years.

"Thanks, Hads. I know, though."

"Good. It's important to me." I pause. "Can I ask you a question about it?"

His brows come together. "Of course."

"When did you . . ." I'm not sure how to phrase it. "When did you feel like you got through it? Like, did you have a moment when you felt like things could be normal again?"

He moves his fork around in the mashed potatoes. "I still kind of feel like I am . . . getting through it. It doesn't really have a finish line, you know?"

I nod.

"Sorry. That's probably not the answer you were looking for."

"No, it's the truth. That's all I wanted."

He shrugs. "You can ask me anything. But we don't have to talk about all this right now. I just wanted to offer up my shoulder, or whatever."

"It's a good shoulder," I answer, and he smiles. "Thank you, Tyler."

"Anytime." He looks up at my face. "Don't go telling Greg or anything, but you're kind of my best friend. Got to look out for you."

"You can have more than one best friend. There isn't a limit or anything."

"Maybe." His eyes meet mine. "Hey, I've been meaning to ask. Didn't Great Lakes release the portfolio theme? For the application, I mean."

I feel another sharp pang of guilt. *He really is a way better friend than I am.* "Yeah, actually. It's something like 'Choose twenty images on a theme that has deeply impacted your life.' "

"Got any ideas?"

"Not yet. Thank god I have until September for the early deadline."

"I'm sure you'll think of something great."

"Yeah, 'cause I'm feeling *real* creative lately."

"I wouldn't bet against you, Butler. I think sometimes the best art comes out of difficult times."

"Yeah?"

"Definitely. Basically all my favorite music is about people going through shitty situations. Maybe because something like that reminds you what's important. Don't get me wrong, it just plain sucks most of the time. But occasionally . . . I don't know. You get perspective. For me, loss reminds me that I need to . . . What's that expression? The Latin version of YOLO?"

"Carpe diem?"

"Yeah, exactly. That kind of thing. Seize the day and all that." He looks at me for a beat before he adds, "I guess what I mean is, look for the good. You'll find some. Nothing is a hundred percent bad, not even the worst thing. And maybe you can use that."

Knowing that he speaks from experience, I can't help but take comfort in Tyler's words. "Okay. Maybe I can."

CHAPTER 17

I wake up to my phone buzzing. Groggy, I reach for it. But it's not my alarm.

"Braden? What time is it?" My voice is raspy, the only sound in the silent house.

"Hadley. I need your help."

When I sit up, sleep slides right off me. "What? What's wrong? Where are you?"

"Outside." He hangs up before I can ask anything else.

Outside? I wonder. *Like outside my house? What the hell is going on?*

Heart racing, I shoot out of bed, throw a robe over my pajamas, and quickly pad down the stairs. The spring air is mild, but fear strips my skin of warmth, making me shiver— until I turn and see Braden's car, parked crookedly across my parents' driveway, and I go numb to everything but him.

In the moonlight, his hair and skin glow a faint blue, and he paces back and forth. His face is tense, his body hunched.

"Braden?" I whisper.

He jumps. "Hadley."

"Are you all right? What's going on?"

He rushes over and wraps himself tightly around me. His shirt beneath his jacket is damp. "I didn't know what to do."

"Have you been drinking?" There's no denying that smell.

He takes a step backward, anger flashing across his face. "That's what you're worried about right now?"

"What?" I look at him incredulously. "Yeah, of course I care if you were drinking before you drove here. Something could have happened, and nobody would have even known where you—"

"Shit." He shoves a frustrated hand through his hair. "I know. You're right. I'm sorry. That was so stupid."

"Braden, you're scaring me. What happened?"

He starts to pace again. "I'm out of meds. And my shoulder is killing me. And I—I don't know. I thought a drink might help, but it didn't do shit. And I can't sleep. I feel . . ." He turns and puts a hand on his chest, his face twisting in pain. "I don't know."

"When did you run out?"

He moves up and down the driveway, talking quickly. "Yesterday morning. And it was supposed to be okay. Slight discomfort, they said. And I have an appointment with a sports medicine doctor tomorrow. A specialist. But I—I don't think I'm fine, Hadley." He looks scared as he moves toward me. "And the only thing that made me feel like I wasn't going to rip my skin off was being with you." He's looking at me like he's desperate for my understanding. When he takes hold of my arms, his fingers are trembling. "Can I, please . . . can I just come inside?"

It's basically the worst time to be sneaking him into the house. Mom did her first round of chemo this week, and she's exhausted and scared. We all are. But face to face with the fear in Braden's eyes, I find it hard to be reasonable.

I nod to the door. "Of course. But we have to be super-quiet, okay?"

For the first time since he got here, his body relaxes. "Thank you."

❋ ❋ ❋

Thump.

We're barely two steps inside before Braden trips over one of Judd's sneakers. The shoes clunk together, and his hand knocks against the wall as he catches himself. I give him a sharp look, and he mouths *Sorry.*

We freeze, listening for anyone stirring.

A handful of heartbeats later, we seem to be in the clear.

I take Braden's hand and carefully lead him into the basement. When the door clicks closed, I exhale in relief. We descend the stairs in silence.

Only half-finished and decorated with the most beat-up furniture in the house, the basement isn't exactly the ideal place to hang out. "Didn't want to go to your room?" Braden asks quietly, looking around.

"This is farther away from all the bedrooms, and I don't want to wake anyone up. Plus, I thought it would be easier, when you have to leave. Remy sneaks in and out of that window every summer."

Braden collapses into the couch, looking exhausted. "I'm so sorry, Hadley."

"It's all right." I sit next to him. "But I don't understand what happened. I know those meds were making you feel a little weird, but I guess I didn't realize . . ."

He runs his hands roughly through his hair. "The second prescription was stronger. And it didn't really happen until I ran out, and then it hit me hard."

"What exactly is wrong?"

Braden leans forward, elbows on his knees. His voice is strained. "I feel sick. And like I can't sit still. Like everything's racing."

"What can I do?" I ask, rubbing circles on his back.

He shakes his head without looking up. And then I feel his breath catch. And another hesitant, jerky inhale.

Then I realize, he's crying. I've never seen him cry before.

Everything in me jumps to attention. "Oh, Brade, it's going be okay. It's *all* going to be okay." I move my hand back and forth. "You'll go see that doctor, and they'll sort it out. Just tell them what happened. And I can go with you, if you want." He said the only thing he wanted was to be with me, but I have no idea how to fix this.

He sits up and angrily rubs at his face. Then he turns to me. "I'm scared, Hadley." Emotion catches in his throat. I know it cost him something to admit it. "Swimming . . . It's the only thing I've ever really *done*. The only thing I'm any good at. And the medicine, it's *helping*."

I scoot closer. "That's a good thing, isn't it?"

His brows knit together. "I thought so. But I don't know."

He pauses, looking at his hands. "I think it might be, like, fucking me up. I don't think it's supposed to be so hard. Going off it."

"They said it would be uncomfortable."

"Yeah . . ." He shakes his head. "But I'm *used* to uncomfortable, Had. You know that. I push through every practice, every meet. None of that is a big deal. But this . . . this is worse."

"Maybe it's different for different people. Or maybe they were downplaying it? Trying not to freak you out?"

In the semidarkness, his face looks ghostly white. "Well, it didn't work."

I open my mouth to say something placating, but he shakes his head again and stands.

"You don't get it." He moves back and forth in front of the couch, tension tying him in knots. "Tonight, not having my meds . . . It's not just my shoulder that hurts, it's *my whole body*." He can hardly get it out quickly enough, the words climbing on top of one another. "And I try to breathe deeply, like in the pool, but *nothing works*, and I want to go *fucking apeshit*. But I can't. And I can't sit still either. And before I knew it, I was here."

He sits back down. His throat bobs as he takes my face in his hands, rubbing his thumbs across my cheeks. "I'm supposed to be a rock for *you* right now." The words stumble over his emotion. "And I'm fucking it all up."

"Braden, *no*." And that's when I realize I might be able to help. "Look at me." We sit up, and I wipe at his face. "You feel like that right now? The way you described?"

He nods.

"And when's your appointment again?"

"Tomorrow."

"So you just have to make it through tonight?"

"I know, it sounds soon. But it doesn't *feel*—"

"No, I get it. I have an idea. I'll be right back."

As quickly and quietly as I can, I move through the house to the kitchen. When I spot the orange tube—in the corner cabinet in the kitchen, exactly where Dad left it—I snap a quick picture of the label. I unscrew the bottle and slip a single pill into my pocket. Then I think of Braden's pale, tear-soaked face and take a couple more. A little prickle of guilt runs through me, but Mom did say she wasn't going to take them.

Less than five minutes later, I'm safely back in the basement.

I hand him my phone. "Is this what the doctor gave you?"

"What? What is that?"

"My mom's."

"What? Hadley, *no*. I'm not taking that."

"Well, she isn't either. You heard her yourself the other day. She doesn't want it." I tell myself as much as him. "I thought maybe it was the same thing you had."

"How did you even get that?"

"They're literally sitting untouched."

He gives me a questioning look and then studies the picture again. "It is the same. Hers is just a higher dose."

"Well, do you think it would help? Just for tonight, a Band-Aid. And then you can get everything sorted out at your appointment tomorrow."

"Yeah, I mean, it would help, but are you sure that's okay?"

"I keep trying to help my mom, and I can't seem to get it right." I take a pill from my pocket and look down at it on my palm. It's such a small thing. "But if I can, I'd really like to be able to help you."

He must see the emotion in my face, see how much I mean it, because he nods and takes it from me. "Okay."

"Here, I grabbed a couple more, just in case." I hand them to him and then realize . . . "Shit, sorry, I forgot to get you some water."

He tosses a single pill into his mouth and swallows it dry. "I've gotten used to it." The rest go into his pocket.

We settle back into the couch.

"Hadley?"

"Yeah?"

"Thank you."

"You're welcome." And I try to stifle it, but a yawn fights its way through me.

For the first time tonight, Braden almost smiles. "Come here."

We lie side by side on the couch, and Braden tucks his arm around me. I rest my head on his chest, close my eyes, and listen as his heart *thumpthumpthumps*.

A few quiet moments pass. The pauses between thumps lengthen.

Half asleep, I whisper, "Any better?"

"I think so, because I just noticed that you're wearing a robe."

I open my eyes to find his on me. "Well, you did show up in the middle of the night."

He laughs. "I did, didn't I? Bad habit." And with gentle

fingers, he lifts my chin and presses his lips to mine. "I knew you'd save me. You always do." His eyes look a little unfocused, but now in a sleepy, happy way. I'd choose that over terror every time. But even as I think it, a small whisper of doubt moves through me.

I try to be present in the moment. "I'd do worse for you," I tell him, running a finger along a seam on his shirt.

"Me too," he echoes.

The night starts to feel like a heavy blanket, coaxing me to sleep. But I fight it, letting Braden drift off first. His breathing finds a deeper, steady rhythm.

Just before he fades away, a sleepy voice murmurs in the dark, "Hadley?"

"Yeah?"

"I like seeing you in your jammies."

I smile at his closed eyes, and a few minutes later, I follow him and drift away.

※　※　※

I'm floating in space, surrounded by small, twinkling lights, and my body glides weightlessly through the indigo sky. I reach out, trying to catch them like fireflies, but just before I close my fingers around a light, it extinguishes. It starts a chain reaction, and one by one they wink out, and the purple fades to black, and then I realize that the air isn't air at all. I'm not floating; I'm submerged. I don't know which way is up or down, and I can't find the surface. My lungs ache as I realize I'm drowning, I'm drowning, I'm—

I jerk awake. For a brief moment, I'm disoriented. And then: *Braden, basement.*

Shit. I shake my head. *What time is it?*

Braden's arm is thrown heavily around me. "Brade?" I whisper.

He grumbles but doesn't move. His breath holds steady.

"Braden?" I try to get out from under his weight. "Come on."

For a brief moment, I'm trapped. I manage to break free by sliding right off the couch and then pull my phone out of my robe pocket. It's four-fifteen. Two hours until my family wakes up. *Thank god.*

"Braden?" I press my hand to his uninjured shoulder. *Is he always such a deep sleeper?*

I try again.

Nothing.

Again.

My mind floods with fear.

The pill. And he was drinking.

I forgot he was drinking! Is it dangerous to mix those things? The doctors would have told him that, right? But what if they didn't because he's underage?

Stop, I command my racing thoughts. I need to be rational. He's breathing. I can clearly see that. *He's just asleep, right?*

Holy shit. What did I do?

Without pausing to second-guess myself, I click a number on my recent calls and wait for it to ring.

"Hadley?" He clears his throat. "Is everything okay?"

"Ty. I'm freaking out. I think I messed up."

His sheets rustle. "What happened?"

I tell him as quickly as I can and then explain, "And I'm sorry that I'm calling in the middle of the night. I thought

210

because your dad's a doctor . . . I don't know. Now that I'm saying it, it makes no sense. But I don't know what to do."

"It's all right. And you said he seems okay now?"

"As far as I can tell. I just can't get him to wake up."

Ty sounds calm. "I've seen Greg like that a couple times after drinking too much. He's always all right. But we should make sure. Hold on. Let me get my laptop."

I take the deepest breath I can manage. "Thank you." And then it hits me. "Oh my god, Ty, I'm such an idiot. I could have just googled this myself."

"It's no big deal. You were scared. I get it."

I'm probably freaking out over nothing, right?

His typing clicks and then stops. "Okay, so it's good that we're looking, because that combination you described can be, um, bad."

Panic strikes like lightning. "How bad?"

"Hold on. You said he's breathing normally? Not too slowly?"

I watch Braden's chest rise and fall at a steady pace. "Yeah, it looks normal."

"Okay, that's a big one. That's good news."

But I don't feel any better. "Ty, what did I do?"

"I just want to go over a couple things. Check our boxes, okay?"

Even though he can't see me, I nod.

"Can you find his heartbeat?"

"Um, yeah, one second." Holding my phone with my chin, I press my fingers to Braden's neck. I have no idea what I'm doing, but I manage to find his pulse. *Is it fast? Slow? Normal?* I take my own to compare.

211

"You're looking to make sure it isn't too slow," Ty clarifies.

"It's slow compared to mine, but I think that makes sense. I'm kind of freaking out over here."

"Okay. But not too slow?"

"I don't think so."

Ty pauses. "Does he feel cold?"

I shake my head. "No. Not noticeably."

"Do you know how much he had to drink?"

"He said he had *a* drink, but I don't know what that means. He probably took a pull off something from his parents' liquor cabinet."

"And just the one pill?"

The question makes me feel sick, but I force myself to answer honestly, "Yeah, but he did say it was stronger than what he was used to." *And he has several more in his pocket. Maybe I should take them back?* I push Braden's hair away from his face. "I can't believe I did this, Ty."

"Well, from everything I can find, it looks like he's going to be okay. Watch his breathing, and as long as nothing changes, give him another hour. He'll sleep it off, and I'm sure everything will be back to normal in the morning."

"What if something changes?"

"Then you need to call nine-one-one."

I feel like I got kicked in the gut. "Nine-one-one? Seriously?"

"Yeah, I don't want to freak you out, but this shit is kind of serious. Like, people die when they take too much of that, especially if they start mixing it with stuff."

"Oh my god. I thought I was helping."

"You didn't know. And he's all right. Just for future reference."

"Future reference?"

"Yeah, I don't know." He pauses. "Hadley?"

"Yeah?"

"Are *you* okay?"

My chest constricts. "I'm scared."

"I could . . . We don't have to hang up. If that would help. While you watch to make sure nothing changes."

"You said I should do that for an hour."

"Well, I'm already up."

I sigh into the phone. "You're a way better friend than I am."

"I told you we don't do that."

In response, I find myself smiling, and I realize that even in these difficult moments, I still have things to be grateful for. It reminds me of what Ty said recently, to look for the good. That I'd find it.

We talk about small things, sit in comfortable quiet, or I listen as he strums on his acoustic guitar. Time passes in a blur, and at half after five, Ty and I are still on the phone.

My voice is raspy as I finish telling him a story about Remy and Judd and how they used to hide food in their bedroom, and the day Mom found all of it. "She still can't eat peanut butter."

Tyler's laugh is low.

It's followed by a rustling, closer.

"Oh my god," I say breathlessly.

"What?" Tyler asks.

"Hadley?" Braden mumbles.

"He's awake," I say into the phone. "I've got to go, Ty. Thank you for everything. Seriously. I can't tell you enough." When he says goodbye, I move quickly to the couch.

"Braden, you scared the shit out of me."

"What, why? What time is it?"

"I couldn't wake you up. I thought . . ."

"I was just sleeping, Hads." He kisses my head and then spots my cell on the rug. "Were you on the phone?"

"Yeah, Ty was helping me make sure you were okay."

"You told Tyler?"

"I'm sorry. I didn't know what to do. *Are* you okay? How are you feeling?"

He frowns. "Hadley, I know you share a lot with your friends—" And when he uses an arm to sit up, he's distracted. He moves his injured shoulder gingerly.

"How does it feel?"

"Better. Like, way better."

I exhale a million pounds. "I'm so glad."

"Me too."

"But, Braden, tonight . . . I can't stop thinking that this is a lot more serious than I realized."

He runs a thumb along my cheek. "It's just my shoulder, Hadley. It's really okay."

"Will you just hear me out?"

He nods. "Of course."

"It's just . . . you're almost done with swim season, right?"

"Yeah," he confirms.

"Well, I know this is already the plan, but will you just promise me that if it's still hurting when you finish, you'll

214

have the surgery?" I keep talking, hoping he won't interrupt. "I know you, and you're not going to want to miss club. But if you do, you can go back to swimming senior year with it healed. It's just . . . this was scary, Brade. It seems like those pills are intense. I don't want them hurting you again."

He studies my face, taking in the concern. "You know, I think you might be the only person who cares more about *me* than my times in the pool."

I roll my eyes. "Braden, come on. Your parents, obviously."

He shrugs. His face is made of sharp edges, but his eyes are soft. "Okay, Hadley. I promise I'll do the surgery over the summer, if it hasn't healed."

Relief courses through me. "Thank you."

"Is everybody still sleeping?" he asks.

"I think so, but we're cutting it kind of close." I look at him. "Please don't scare me like that ever again."

"But what fun would that be?"

"Braden."

"I'm just kidding. Hads, I'm sorry. I know. Tonight was a low point, okay? Up from here." He wraps his arms around me. "But I think I should get out of here before everybody wakes up."

"Are you all right to drive?"

"I'm fine." He puts on his coat and shoes. "Is this Remy's escape window?"

I nod. "Yeah."

He kisses me. "Thank you."

But he disappears before I can answer, and I'm left alone in the dark.

CHAPTER 18

Three days later, I'm standing in the kitchen, preoccupied with worry. Braden's been quiet since his appointment, and I'm not sure what to make of it. My siblings, on the other hand, are blissfully ignorant.

It's Sunday morning, and Judd's giving a pancake tutorial to Remy and me. "The trick is to flip them when they are cooked enough to not fall apart, but not so much that they're burnt at the bottom. I like a golden brown, myself."

Remy tries to flip one, but it isn't ready, and the dough splatters. "Shit!" she exclaims, trying to make sure it didn't get onto her new T-shirt.

Dad's drinking coffee at his computer while we cook. I don't hear Mom when she comes into the kitchen, but something still makes me look up. She's in her bathrobe with soaking-wet hair, standing at the threshold of the room with a vacant expression on her face and an invisible, heavy weight on her shoulders.

"Mia?" Dad asks gently.

She leans against the wall, and her face crumples in her hands.

The doctors warned us that the side effects would probably start after two or three chemo treatments, and it's as if all of us realize it at the same time: her hair. Probably while she was washing it.

Dad immediately stands and moves toward her, enveloping her in his arms. "Did . . ." he trails off, unable to finish his question.

Mom nods, eyes squeezed closed, her hand tightening on his shirt.

Dad rubs her back in loose, repeating strokes. "It's okay. I won't let it be anything but okay," he murmurs.

Mom lets out a sob that rocks the room.

Dad pulls away, holding her by her elbows and urgently looking her in the eye. Her face is a gargoyle of itself, sculpted by fear. "Your hair doesn't matter, Mia. It isn't what makes you beautiful. I know you, who you are. *That's* what makes you beautiful. Okay?" His gaze is unbreaking, forcing Mom to nod before he will continue. When she does, he pulls her tightly back into him and whispers, "I love you no matter what."

I'm frozen in place, a strange mix of admiration and dread filling my veins, realizing that my parents are scared and don't know what to do either, other than hold on to each other. I feel tears fall down my face.

Dad's voice is breaking. "You can't leave me, okay? I need you." He glances back at me and my siblings. "They need you. We just have to get through this part. One step at a time."

A hissing sound comes from the stove, and Judd jumps to tend to the pancakes, black and burnt.

I ignore our ruined breakfast and move toward my parents, wrapping my arms around them both. I hang on to the love between them like a lifeline. I can't say anything, do anything, to fix it. So I just stand there squeezing my parents together with all my might. Remy and Judd join me, and we do our best to hold one another up above the fear.

❆ ❆ ❆

A couple hours later, Mom is sitting on a chair in her bathroom. I'm standing behind her, pulling her ponytail through my fingers. "Are you sure?" I ask tentatively. But when heavy strands tangle in my hand and fall freely from her head, I know that it's time.

Mom hands me the scissors. "Let's just get it over with." I look to Judd and Dad, each sitting on an edge of the bathtub. They seem as uneasy as I feel. But Remy nods at me, and it makes me feel steadier.

"Okay. I'm just going to . . . do it. I guess." I press the scissors just above her hair tie. "Um. Okay. Here we go." The first cut makes a sharp, crisp noise, and Dad sucks in a breath. I do it again. Again. Until her ponytail falls into my hand. *Shit, shit, shit.* Mom and I look at each other.

Her hair is now cut in a jagged bob, and surprisingly, it looks kind of cute. "We could just stop here?"

"Hadley," Remy says.

"Okay. You're right. Um, here." I hand Mom the ponytail; she moves it in her hands and then quickly drops it into the small garbage can at her feet. She doesn't want to look at it either.

Judd attempts to lighten the mood. "Hey, Mom, what are you doing throwing that away? You could have, like, the world's nicest duster. Or you could sell it! Don't girls pay tons of money to glue other people's hair on their heads?" Judd leans over and plucks it out of the garbage. The smile on his face doesn't reach his eyes. He's been wearing that expression a lot lately.

"You're so right," Remy answers. "People look at this cancer stuff all wrong. We're going to get rich off hair. I know I'd buy it." She tries for levity, but it falls flat, her voice breaking. Judd moves toward her and puts his arm over her shoulders. She relaxes into him, visibly fighting the lump in her throat.

Dad takes the ponytail and gingerly runs his fingers through it.

"Keep going, Hads. Before I lose my nerve," Mom tells me. I gather more pieces together and cut them short. Over and over. Dark hair falls to the white tile of the bathroom floor. Mom's chest rises and falls in a forced, steady rhythm.

"Okay, Mom. First step is done." Her entire head is covered in uneven dark sprouts.

She squares her shoulders and meets her own eyes in the mirror. "Hadley, will you do me a favor?"

"Of course, what is it?"

"Will you take my picture?"

"What? Right now?"

Her eyes don't waver. "Yes."

I grab my camera, adjust the settings, and lift the lens. The motion is comforting, familiar.

Without looking away from her own eyes, Mom nods. I click the shutter, letting everything but her face and fierce eyes fall to the background. If this image had a name, it would be *Courage*. I snap a couple more, trying to ensure a good shot from my unsteady hands. I want to show the love in the room, the strength of Mom, and the power in taking ownership of your fate. I think of Tyler; I want to remember the good in a sea of heartache.

Taking a step back, I also capture the fragmented pieces of her on the floor—the pieces we had to cut away to keep the rest.

When I put the camera down and plug in Dad's electric razor, an uneasy energy fills the cramped bathroom.

With a quick look at me, Judd gives Remy a squeeze before he takes over. He picks up the razor and moves it from hand to hand nervously. "What number are you thinking, Mom? A one? A two?" He adjusts the settings on the clippers. They both pretend to laugh a little, but then he steadies himself and turns it on. The razor buzzes. "Here goes nothing."

He puts it to her head, leaving a trail of dark fuzz in its wake. Halfway through, he turns to Remy. She nods and steps forward. When they're done, Mom opens a drawer to get a new blade for her razor—the last step. It's Dad's turn now. He turns the handle on the sink and waits for the water to get warm. Swallowing, he slowly lathers her head with his shaving cream and picks up the razor.

"Wait," Mom says breathlessly. Her hair has been replaced with a thick white foam, and she has a determined look in her eye. "I want to do it."

Dad looks a little relieved. "All right."

I hear the last of her hair quietly snap away as she slides the razor across her scalp. None of us speak. She moves it again and again, shaving as much as she can reach. She's a force, and I capture the moment again with my camera.

Eventually, she looks to Dad. "Marc?"

And then Dad carefully shaves the places she couldn't reach, uncovering more and more skin. Her scalp looks as vulnerable as a newborn, but she glows with rebellious courage.

The whole thing doesn't take more than thirty minutes.

Dad gently pats her head with a towel, and she faces her reflection: her head is smooth, round, and smaller than I expected. Various lengths of Mom's hair surround us on the floor. She looks like a cancer patient now. I try to unthink it, but I can't deny the truth. There is another truth here, too, though; harder to find but present, nonetheless: in this moment, she's strong and she's brave.

I try to be those things as well, as I take a final image. I don't want her to do this alone. If she can do it, so can I.

Buying time, I walk into her closet and take a few deep breaths before coming back with an ornate box in my hands, a fancy designer scarf from a friend at book club. One of many gifts after she was diagnosed. I take it out of the box, and the material is smooth on my hands.

I nervously run the silk through my fingers as I speak. "Mom? I want to go next." My heart hammers.

"Yeah," Judd jumps in, running a hand through his dark, unruly curls. "Me too, Had. I'm in."

Remy freezes.

Mom looks up at me and her face is resolved. "No." She takes my hand and squeezes before she pulls the scarf from me. "Thank you, but no."

Remy exhales.

"That's it? The lawyer doesn't have an argument? Just no?" I ask. But the truth is, I'm relieved too.

"That's right, honey. Just no."

And after weeks of building myself up to the task, it only takes that one word for me to back down. I feel a tiny, rotten flower of shame bloom in my stomach.

Mom lifts the scarf to tie it around her head, but when the material touches her scalp, she jumps. "Oh my gosh, it's so cold!" A sound escapes her, a sound that I would call a laugh in any other circumstance. "Do we have anything cotton?"

All five of us do laugh then—just a little.

Dad disappears for a minute and comes back with a worn-looking T-shirt decorated with an obscure band's logo, something he wears a lot on the weekends. Mom raises her eyebrows as he lays it flat onto the counter, takes the discarded scissors, and slices through it without hesitation. When he's finished, he stands behind her, and judiciously ties the piece of cotton around Mom's head.

She speaks in a voice meant only for him. "That was your favorite."

He only shrugs. "You're my favorite."

CHAPTER 19

Later that night, I can't stop thinking about webs of hair tangled between fingers. I feel like I'm caught in one of those webs, thrashing. I pull at strands on my own head, wondering if mine will start to fall out. My body keeps following her symptoms. No doubt from stress, but it feels like an echo of her illness. *I am made of her.*

I can't believe I chickened out. I shouldn't have let her do it alone. I wonder if Remy feels that way too. I wish I could get myself to talk to her about it. I let out a shaky breath. The fear is building inside me, worry stacking atop worry, growing to heights I'm afraid to climb. I need *something*, someone, to make me feel better.

I won't bother my family. It feels too selfish. I think about calling Becca or Ty, asking them to come over. My parents wouldn't want Braden here in the middle of the night, but they would understand me needing a friend. I can't be alone anymore.

Then I remember the key around my neck. The one Braden gave me shortly after the diagnosis.

Screw the rules. What do rules matter when the world might be taking away Mom? I already broke them anyway, when Braden showed up the other night. And I've been so distracted with Mom that I still haven't pressed Braden on how his appointment went. *Why does everything have to fall apart at the same time?*

Are you awake?

I wait a few seconds. No sign of typing, no response. When I call, he doesn't pick up.

Forget it. I don't care. I'll wake him up when I get there.

I switch my pajama pants for jeans, grab my camera, and pass through the dark house. And then I step right out the unalarmed back door. I don't even care about being caught.

I just need to see him.

I move purposefully, quickly, and for a long time, watching the dewy grass leave moisture on my shoes. I take pictures of trees in the distance to pass the time, observing as they get closer and closer, then find new ones to focus on. Braden only lives a couple miles away, but I've never walked there before. I have no idea how long it takes me. But eventually, I'm outside the basement door.

❋   ❋   ❋

I pull the key from the chain around my neck and unlock the door. I take off my shoes once I step inside, holding them between my fingers. Something inside me warns: *You don't belong here. What about his parents?* But I ignore the feeling and pull my phone from my pocket to light the path ahead of me. Braden's room is in the basement, so I just need to walk down the hallway to get to him. My socked feet sink into the carpet as my footsteps get faster.

I twist the handle and open his door, and he doesn't stir, even when I go to sit on the bed. "Braden?" I slide my fingers gently through his hair. "Brade?"

He still doesn't move, and it strikes an unexpected fear through me. Not again. I shake him harder and call his name for a third time.

Slowly, Braden turns over in his bed and flutters his eyes. My body sags in relief. "Hadley?" he asks in a voice thick with sleep.

He sits up, and the plaid duvet slides down his chest. He moves a hand to brush his messy hair from his face. I unzip my jacket and set it in a pile next to my shoes.

"Hadley," he murmurs sleepily, as if he answered his own question. "Come here."

As his voice moves on my skin, the urgent energy inside me takes over. I climb into his bed and onto his lap. My hands tremble when I hold either side of his face, but my mouth is sure on his. I don't want to talk. I can't find anything to say.

I run my hands down the length of his rib cage, across the broad space of his shoulders, along the muscles of his back. My fingers, my body, my brain, my heart—they're all begging to feel something that doesn't hurt. I pull him closer, and the love I feel for him starts to fill me up. Love so strong it nearly matches the fear, the two emotions boiling together under the surface of my skin. For once, I don't try to push them away.

I feel it all. I let the tears fall from my face to his. He doesn't pull away, and my gratitude is so deep it aches.

Love is a risk. I know that, even more so lately. Anything loved can be lost. But right now, I don't care. This love makes me feel alive, and I need that. I need the pressure of his body. I need to feel him move, to hear his heart, to watch him breathe. I want all the proof I can get my hands on. He's wearing only his boxers, and I pull my layers off to match. I want his skin on mine. *Healthy, young, healthy, young, alive, safe.*

He pulls away, for just a second, to look me in the eye. Even in the darkness, I can see his thoughts brewing. I stare back. After a moment, he nods and pulls me back into him.

Hands tangle in my hair as he meets my intensity, no words necessary. I press myself into him, as if I can take some of his strength in this mysterious world of night. He gives me everything, and I take it without reservation.

❊　❊　❊

Afterward, his thumbs move along my cheekbones, my jaw line, and across my neck. He holds me tightly with our bodies pressed together, rubbing my back. I try not to compare the moment to my parents, earlier, in the kitchen. I am not sick.

Neither of us says anything. There aren't any words. And in this quiet, safe space of his arms, I cry. The real release my body needed.

I don't know how long I sob into his chest, but eventually, I lift my head. My body is spent, bone-tired, but my mind is finally clear. The panic has left.

He clears his throat. "Did something happen?"

I whisper, "Her hair."

He nods, understanding. "I'm sorry."

"It just feels . . . so real, now."

He sits up, leans against the headboard. I grab one of his T-shirts from the other side of the bed and slip it on. It smells like him, faint chlorine and pine. When I sit back down, I lean my head into his left shoulder. "Sorry." I move to readjust, but he puts an arm around me.

"No, it's okay. It's feeling way better."

"Do you want to talk about it?"

"I'm fine."

I look at him. "My mom isn't the only one I'm worried about, you know." He doesn't say anything. "Did you tell them about what happened?"

"I really am fine, Hads. The specialist gave me some new stuff, same kind of thing, but they work better. And no big deal, but I broke a record at our meet yesterday."

He looks so happy and relieved that I am confused by the nagging voice in the back of my head. "But if it's the same, won't the same thing happen when you stop again? Shouldn't you talk to them about the surgery?"

"I'm still doing physical therapy." He frowns. "I thought you'd be psyched for me. I'm doing exactly what the doctor said."

"But did you tell her—"

"I've got this, Hadley." His tone is steel, leaving no room for argument. Then he exhales some of the tension away. "I just want you to be able to focus on your mom, okay? I already got in the way last week, and I don't want to do that to you again."

"Are you sure? I—"

"God, trust me, okay? You can even ask Coach. He's giddy that I'm back to myself."

I can't let go of the concern all at once, but I manage a distracted apology. "I'm sorry I wasn't there." It was an away meet, and Mom was feeling sick, but I still feel a pang of guilt that I opted to stay home instead.

"You've got a lot going on, Hads. And you never said you'd be there. It's all good. Plus, nobody's surprised I'm breaking records."

I brush aside his bigheadedness. "So you like the new doctor?"

"I do." He leans toward me and tucks a stray piece of hair behind my ear. "And can we talk about how freaking *great* the timing is, because the Richmond meet is this week—last one of the year—and we're going to freaking *annihilate* them," he says. "I've got this."

I make a sound somewhere between a sigh and a laugh, wanting so badly to believe him. "All right, well, I'm glad you're happy, Varsity." I can't help the smirk on my face.

He returns it. "I thought that dumb nickname was James's thing."

"Nope, I love dumb nicknames," I tease. Then I put my hands to my neck and pull the chain out from under Braden's shirt. "Hey, and thank you for being here tonight, for this. I was . . ." I don't know what to call the state I was in. "It wasn't great."

He furrows his brow. "Don't. I'm here. I want to be." He looks up from his lap. "It's what you do when you love somebody."

"Let them sneak into your bedroom for a middle-of-the-night booty call?"

"Literally anytime. My body is at your disposal." He puts his hands behind his head. "I'm happy to serve."

"Gross."

"You love it."

I shake my head, but he isn't totally wrong. Not about the stupid comment, but the way I feel right now. I relax against him and embrace feeling normal and safe. I press my body into his, and he tucks me close. I try to soak up every second, but I feel the clock *tick-tick-tick*ing, and I know that I can't stay here forever. I have to get home. I'm being reckless, even if it saved me.

"Brade, will you do one more thing for me?"

"Probably. What is it?"

"Would you drive me home?"

His eyes twinkle. "Hadley, I'd drive you to Mexico if you asked nicely." His eyes snag on my bare legs. "But you have to put some pants on. So your dad doesn't murder me if we get caught."

"Braden Roberts get caught? Never."

He smiles. "Just a precaution. Can't go risking you."

"Deal. But can I wear your shirt?"

He squeezes my hand. "It's yours."

I untangle myself from the blankets and retrieve my clothes from the floor. As I fasten my jeans, I notice several orange pill bottles sitting on Braden's dresser. I take a step toward them, curious about the new prescription, when Braden's arm finds its way around my hip. He pulls me toward him and kisses the top of my head. He's fully dressed now.

"I told you not to worry about it."

"I just—"

"Please, Hadley, let me deal with it, okay? Let me take something off your plate."

I trust him, don't I? I have to stop looking for problems. "Okay."

"Are you ready to Bonnie and Clyde out of here?"

"Yeah." I shove my own shirt into my coat pocket. "Let's go."

We go out the way I came in. Quietly, Braden opens the driver's side door, puts the car in neutral, and starts to push it to the street. At first he uses both arms, but then he pulls the injured one back, continuing one-handed. I join him, and together, we push. It's not nearly as hard as I thought it would be. Once he's determined we're far enough away from the house, he gestures to the car with his head, and we both get in.

Inside, he turns the key and shoots me a self-satisfied smile. "All right, Bonnie. Let's get you home."

❉   ❉   ❉

The next day, when I open my eyes, the first thing I see is Braden's T-shirt. Then I'm assaulted by memories of Mom's bald head. I picture her fingertips pressing against the bare skin, and my heart splinters.

The whole morning is like a lingering bad dream, but somehow I make it to school, and to my locker, in one piece. The only thought I can keep in my head as I try to remember what books I need is that the hallway is way too loud. The end-of-the-year excitement is radiating in the halls. They're full of people laughing and yelling, guys slapping one another's lockers. Each time they slam closed, I jump. *What class do I have first hour today? Does it matter?* I know I should be worried about finals, but I just can't muster it. I've been dodging Becca's texts inviting me to study with her. I let my eyes shift out of focus when I feel someone approaching me.

I look up.

"Oh my god." The words leave my mouth the minute I see Braden's face, which is no longer surrounded by his signature long hair. He buzzed it so short that he and Mom are nearly matching. He looks nervous, but he's smiling a little. "Oh my god," I repeat. "When did you even have time to do that?"

"This morning." He runs a hand along the buzzed tips. "Is it that bad?" He's more uncomfortable than he's letting on. I know he takes solace in certain things: his clothes, his shoes, his athleticism. His hair is high on that list.

"You wouldn't even buzz it for the team."

"I'm the fastest no matter what my hair looks like," he says.

"I love it," I answer, shaking my head in disbelief. It makes his cheekbones stand out, makes his lips look fuller. *I can't believe he did this for me, for Mom.*

"Yeah?"

"Yeah."

He did for her what I couldn't. And he didn't even know about my promise to myself. I stand on my toes and throw my arms around his neck. The words come from a broken place in my chest. "Thank you, Braden."

"Always, Hads." But when he looks at me, something about his expression looks different. Dazed. I pull away and try to get a better look, but he averts his eyes.

"Hey, Brade, everything okay with you?"

"Yeah, I told you I'm good—"

"Roberts!" a tall, lanky guy calls. His hair and eyes are dark, especially against his pale skin.

"Logan." Braden nods at him. "You remember my girl-friend, Hadley?"

"Of course, man. Hey, Hadley."

"Hi." I try to sound friendly. I think he's on the swim team too.

Logan looks at Braden. "So, Roberts, I forgot to tell you at practice this morning, but I found that—"

"Hey, you know what, Logan, not to be a dick or anything, but I'm going to walk my girl to class. Is that cool?" He doesn't wait for an answer. "I'll find you at lunch, all right?"

And then Braden puts an arm around my shoulders and leads us away just fast enough to make me wonder whether something strange is going on.

CHAPTER 20

Standing on Braden's front porch, I ring the doorbell. Normally, I'd just let myself in through the garage, but tonight, not only are his parents home, they're also hosting an end-of-the-season dinner for the swim team, so I want to be on my best behavior. I rock back and forth on my Keds, Remy's borrowed sundress swishing gently around my knees. Nervous butterflies flutter in my stomach. I haven't spent a ton of time with Braden's parents before, and things with Braden and me have felt a little off lately.

Seconds later, the door swings open, and I'm greeted by his fresh buzz cut, the sharp lines of his face, and that megawatt smile. There's a kitchen towel thrown carelessly over his shoulder, and he's wearing a fitted, short-sleeve button-up and dark jeans. Braden's eyes light up when they meet mine, and he pulls me tightly into him.

"Thank god you're here." He takes a step back, rests his thumb under my jaw, and kisses me softly.

Suddenly my concerns feel silly, like maybe they were only in my head.

"It's not going well?" I ask, knowing Braden was nervous about his parents inviting Coach Jones.

"No, it's fine. Just better with you." He looks around the entryway, and, finding it empty, puts two hands on my hips and gently pushes me outside.

"Don't you have a house full of people?"

He takes another couple steps forward, leaning me against the brick wall of the porch. He's grinning so big.

"Yes, I do," he says, "which is why *we* are so smartly outside." And then he wraps a hand behind my head and kisses me deeply.

My body relaxes, leaning against him, and I make an embarrassingly satisfied noise. He nips my lip in response.

"Braden—"

Without pulling away, he shakes his head. "Very busy right now," he mutters against my mouth. Then he presses a thigh between my legs, pushing me more solidly against the brick. Then the front door bursts open.

"Jesus Christ, Varsity," a familiar voice says. Then he looks at me. "And, Hadley—you know, I expect better from you."

"Sorry, James." I grin at Braden's best friend, not feeling sorry at all.

I try to wiggle free from Braden's grasp, but he doesn't budge. "Hashi, can a guy not enjoy two private minutes with his"—he turns to me—"very beautiful girlfriend without you barging in?"

"Sorry, man, but your mom isn't messing around with

234

this dinner. She wants you in the kitchen." He looks at us, at Braden running his fingers through my hair. "All right, whatever, I'm telling her I tried." And then James goes back inside.

Alone again, I shift my attention to Braden. "You're in a good mood."

He nods. "Well, I just killed my last meet of the season—broke my own record in the fly—and scouts were there from a couple Ivies. And now I have you here too. So, yeah, I'm in a good-ass mood."

"Braden! That's awesome!" I steal a quick kiss and then pull away before he can sweep me up again. "I can't believe I missed that. I'm so sorry I wasn't there."

"No, it's okay. I knew you couldn't make it. And I'm obviously not going to an Ivy. They don't do athletic scholarships. But it's still cool."

I feel myself relax a little. It's still a year away, but thinking about Braden moving to the East Coast makes my stomach sink.

"Definitely," I say. "Things still going well with U of M?"

University of Michigan is still Braden's first choice. They have a top-ten swimming program, offer scholarships to athletes, and have shown some solid interest. Plus, we would be in the same state. Not that we're really talking about that—not yet, anyways.

"So far," he says. "But I guess we won't know for sure until the fall." He takes my hand. "Come on, let's go inside. I want to show you off."

* * *

As we approach the kitchen, the smell of sweet roasting carrots and rosemary chicken fills the air. A Hall & Oates song is playing, an oldie I recognize from Dad, who sometimes sings to it on Sunday mornings.

Braden's hand is resting on the small of my back. He leans in and whispers, "I forgot to warn you, my mom is on her third glass of wine."

"Hadley!" Mrs. Roberts exclaims when she sees us. Her blond hair is tousled in an attractive way, and her white collared shirt is perfectly pressed, sleeves rolled up. She's wearing layers of necklaces, skinny jeans, and her heels are loud on the hardwood.

"Hi, Mrs. Roberts," I say as she hugs me, wineglass in hand, enveloping me in her floral perfume.

She takes my hands in her empty one and lowers her voice. "How's your mom?" But before I can answer she continues, "Braden told us about her hair. I just think it's so sweet that he cut his too. You know, he doesn't—"

"*Mom,*" Braden scolds her.

I look at him, fighting the urge to run my fingers along the soft ends of his buzz. "Me too. And she's all right. Hanging in there. Thanks for asking."

"Of course, honey."

I look around the room, taking it in for the first time. James is peering into the oven, a towel now over his shoulder too. Mrs. Roberts must be recruiting the boys to help. And Coach Jones is standing near the table wearing a Lakebook polo, his bald head shining under the kitchen lights, with Mr. Roberts next to him, husky and dark, and in his usual sport coat. They're speaking in an urgent, serious way, each with a bottle of beer in their hands.

Logan approaches us, a little underdressed, and the echo of something uncomfortable moves in my gut. "Hey, guys."

But then Mrs. Roberts draws our attention.

"Okay, everyone," she says, turning down the music. "I just want to say congratulations on a fantastic season. I know that we've missed some meets this year—catering always seems to happen *right* in the middle of everything—but we wanted to take a minute to appreciate your hard work and let you know it did not go unnoticed. So thank you, Coach Jones, for helping Braden through that little injury to finish strong." She pulls a cold bottle of champagne out of the fridge and then pops the cork, looking proud.

James lets out a whooping cheer.

A beat later, she's passing out flutes. She hands a glass to everyone—even me and the rest of the underage crew—each with a splash inside. She winks at me. "Just a taste."

"Hold on just one more second, Molly," Mr. Roberts says to his wife. His voice is deep and authoritative. Everybody looks at him.

"Braden," Mr. Roberts continues, "Coach said you didn't hit your numbers." But his expression doesn't match his words. He's grinning, and it reaches all the way up to his eyes.

Braden stands up taller. "What are you talking about, Dad?"

Coach clears his throat. "Not your times, Roberts. Your ACT score. I was talking to some scouts tonight, and they want to see you up a few points before—" Coach has that same strange energy.

"Oh, the Ivies?" Braden interrupts, clearly confused. "I'm not going there anyway."

Coach looks pleased with himself. "No, not them. Somebody else. They called me earlier." He pauses. "Stanford."

Braden sets down his champagne. "What?"

"Oh my god." James looks impressed, which is a rare sight.

Logan says, "That's the number one program in the country."

"Well, *no shit*, dude," James replies.

Braden takes a deep, steadying breath. Then he rubs his face. A sure sign he's trying to keep his excitement tempered. "A few points on the ACT? How many is a few?" He knows that I worked all winter to get my math score up a single point.

"Three. They want to see you go up three. But they're happy with your times in the pool; you'd just have to keep it up." Coach is all but beaming. "Probably means you can't take that break this summer, for the shoulder surgery. You'll have to do club this summer to keep in shape. But what do you think? Can you push through for Stanford?"

"Until November, for signing." It's not quite a question.

At the suggestion, my stomach sinks. Braden needs to get off those pills, not delay the solution.

"Signing starts in November, yeah," Coach confirms, "and there are four opportunities to retake the ACT between now and then. Two over the summer and two in the fall."

"Holy shit." The expression on his face opens up, all teeth. "Holy shit, holy mother of all—oh *my god*."

Mrs. Roberts, looking almost as thrilled as her son, tries to give him a warning look for his language.

"Hadley, *oh my god*." He picks me up, plants a smacking

kiss on my cheek, and spins me in a circle. He's so happy—experiencing such unbridled joy—that I can't bring myself to voice my concerns. Not right now.

"Congratulations," I manage, truly feeling pride behind my worry. Everybody is looking at us, all wearing matching grins.

Then Mrs. Roberts raises her glass. "To Stanford!"

And the whole room clinks, drinks, laughs. My mouth is bubbling with champagne, but it tastes sour, like dread.

Braden's dad claps him on the shoulder, a surprising show of affection, and Braden's smiling like he just won the lottery.

Except he didn't. He worked for it. And sacrificed.

And I can't stop wondering, *How much?*

※　　※　　※

Throughout dinner, the room is jovial. Candles burn low, the music remains upbeat, and food is passed around with gusto. The boys continue to joke around, playfully picking on one another, and it's all fun and games except for one uncomfortable moment when Logan lays into James a bit too hard.

Braden's arm rests comfortably across the back of my chair, and I lean against him, grateful he's happy, and try hard not to focus on anything else. But the worries are persistent, pressing themselves to the front of my mind every few minutes.

And then, three hours after I arrrived, everybody is getting ready to go. Braden walks Logan to his car, who said he wanted to show him something, and James and I are standing alone on the front porch. Braden's parents are inside, showing Coach some pictures from their son's early swim days.

James turns to me, looking a little lost in thought. "Hey,

Hadley. Um, this might be . . . I don't know, but what do you think of Logan?"

I bite the inside of my cheek. *Did I give myself away? I don't have a good reason to feel weird about him.* "What? He's fine. Why?"

James shrugs. "I don't know. Braden's been hanging out with him a lot lately. Just seems kind of random."

Even though I agree, and I got a weird vibe from him, too, I find myself defending Braden. "Well, they are on the same team. They kind of *have* to spend a lot of a time together."

He sighs. "Yeah. You're probably right."

"Did he upset you, earlier? That jab about JV?"

"No, that's not a big deal. I don't know; it's probably nothing." He shakes his head. "Anyway, I'm going to get out of here. I'll see you later, okay?"

He gives me a one-armed hug and walks down the steps, just as Braden is walking back. They slap each other's shoulders in parting.

"Hey," Braden says, still on a high from the Stanford news as he wraps an arm around my hips.

"Hey," I answer, feeling conflicted.

"What's wrong?" He cocks his head. "'Cause if you ask me, that was a seriously great night."

"No, it was. I mean, it is."

"Then what is it?"

"I just . . . I mean, I thought you were going to have that surgery this summer." *You promised.*

He lets his head fall. "I know. I'm sorry. I did say that. But, like, how can I not try? And it's just a couple months' difference. As soon as I sign, I can take care of everything. It's just

240

the final push, you know? I've basically been training for this my whole life." His hands move up and down along my arms, and his face is so openly satisfied, so proud of himself, that I'm finding it difficult to protest.

I nod, trying my best to be happy for him.

"You're worried, huh?"

"I am. I'm sorry. I want to be the supportive girlfriend. I just can't help—"

He interrupts, "You've had a hard year, Hadley. I understand why you'd worry. But I'm okay. I really am. Not everything is going to turn into the worst-case scenario."

And suddenly this conversation feels familiar. It's like when Braden and I first met, and I was afraid of my feelings for him. But if I hadn't tried, I would have missed all of this. So I decide to be brave. I decide to try to be happy for him. "Okay. You're right."

And by the time I get into my car to drive home, I almost believe it.

CHAPTER 21

I'm sitting next to Dad at Remy and Judd's graduation ceremony. I can't believe the school year is over. Between my concerns for Mom and Braden, I feel like I've only been halfway present for the last couple months. The ceremony is long, loud, and honestly, pretty boring. But since Mom felt too sick to attend, I'm trying to make up for her absence, cheering as loudly as I can when my siblings accept their diplomas.

When we're finally back home, the only thing I want to do is take a nap, but the plan is to continue the celebration with Mom. At least here, if she feels too sick, she can go lie down.

The five of us are sitting in the living room with the windows open to the late-afternoon breeze, trying to learn how to play one of Judd's favorite board games. The new graduates are both still wearing their caps and gowns.

"So the goal is to accumulate four cones, but in order to do that, you have to build a civilization." Judd looks up at our faces to see if we're with him. "Okay, and I guess we need to talk about the Spirit cards too." He looks down at the stack. "Or maybe, first, we should talk about the players. What do you think, Rem?"

"Your call," Remy answers, watching as Judd references a homemade set of instructions. She looks like her head is spinning as much as mine. We all know how badly Judd wants this to work, but I'm losing hope by the second.

He says decidedly, "Let's go with the players. There are, um, kind of a lot." He lists them on his fingers. "Two wizards, a maverick, the Arbiter—"

"Judd," I interrupt, trying not to let the forced cheerfulness collapse around us. "I don't know if we're going to be able to figure out how to play this game."

"No, it's *totally* doable."

"Judd." Remy backs me up. Her tassel sways as she shakes her head. There's a tension between them, and I'm not sure why. I've been debating asking all day, but they both seem to be pretending everything is fine. Our family doesn't usually do the whole politely friendly and overly optimistic thing, but we've all been trying, because these days, it feels like optimism *means* something.

Mom's face is pale, but she presses her lips together, trying not to laugh, as she gingerly adjusts Dad's old T-shirt around her head, her arms still moving a little stiffly after the surgery. I think Mom secretly finds it kind of amusing, watching us on our best behaviors.

"What TV show is this from again?" Dad asks.

Judd and I answer at the same time: "*Parks and Rec.*" Judd says it with his mouth full of crackers and hummus from the spread of food sitting next to the game.

"That one the kids have been having me watch, with Amy Poehler?" Mom tells Dad. "It's pretty funny."

We've been trying to keep Mom's spirits up in every way we can think of. Remy loves to entertain her with endless fashion shows, presenting options for any and every occasion. I've been documenting the process, capturing silver-lining moments. And Judd tries to make her laugh with comedy marathons on Netflix and—his favorite option—every board game *ever*. Including homemade varieties, like this one, that he and his gamer friends work on for fun.

I speak as nicely as I can, "Judd, this game is literally described as 'punishingly intricate.' And they never even fully reveal the instructions! It would be basically impossible to figure out. Let's just play Exploding Kittens again. That one is easy."

Judd's true personality finds its way through our wholesome fun-for-the-whole-family facade. "If you're going to suggest *literally* the most basic game we own—"

"I like Exploding Kittens!" I object.

Dad looks through the pile of games sitting on the floor and picks one up at random. "We haven't played this one."

Remy chimes in, "What if we play a different kind of game. We could do a pretend ceremony? Hadley could call out our names, take pictures? Dad, you can pretend to be the principal, and we can reenact it all, for Mom."

"Remy," Judd scoffs. "Come on, I'm not pretending—"

"Hey. Kids." Dad's voice is suddenly serious.

When I look up, Mom's face is agonized.

My heart rate kicks up. "Mom? You okay?"

"Yeah." She takes a short breath. "But, Judd, would you

244

mind moving the food? I just . . . the garlic smell." And then she puts a hand to her mouth, quickly stands, and moves to the bathroom. My heart sinks. She tries to keep us from seeing the chemo-induced nausea, but she can't always fight it.

"One second, guys." Dad follows to check on her.

Judd freezes, a pained look on his face. "It's not your fault," I tell him quietly.

"I should have thought of it. I shouldn't have been eating in front of her."

Even Remy shakes her head. "No, it's okay."

At that exact moment, my phone rings. Braden's calling. I ignore it, reminding myself to call him back later. We keep missing each other; he's so busy trying to impress Stanford.

"I'll put it away." I pick up the snacks, and I'm closing the fridge when Dad comes into the kitchen.

"Shit," he mutters, looking at his phone. And then I notice the empty orange bottle on the counter.

How is it empty? Dread moves in like a fog. "What's wrong?"

Dad frowns. "Mom ran out of her medicine this morning. I can't figure out how. I must have counted wrong. So I've been waiting for a call from the pharmacist all day. I had a voice mail, but it's not them."

My heart races, beating even faster. "What do you mean?"

"Hold on, Hadley. I'm going to call again."

Before I can ask any other questions, Dad has his cell to his ear. He explains the problem and then listens carefully. "No . . . yes, I *understand* that's a schedule-two drug, but my wife is fighting *cancer*." He sounds like he's struggling to keep his patience. "Yes, I'd like to know when I can pick up a refill." He waits. "Okay, all right. Yes, I understand. Thank you."

A schedule-two drug?

My mind races, flashing back to my hands, opening that same bottle. Taking one, then taking more. Braden waiting in pain in the basement. "What's going on, Dad?"

He exhales slowly. "Mom's still hurting from the surgery. Her medicine . . . Some people have a problem with it since it can be addictive." He looks at me levelly. "Not your mom, though, honey. The pharmacist just needed to make sure it was okay. I'm going to go pick it up for her."

I feel sick. "Right now?" is the only question I can manage.

He looks at me, his face a little lost. "The sooner I get back, the sooner she'll feel better."

Nausea rolls.

"You'll keep your siblings from fighting too much?"

Somehow, I manage a nod. But when the door slams, I feel like the worst daughter in the entire world.

CHAPTER 22

A few hours later, my eyes hurt from staring at the computer screen. *A schedule-two drug has high potential for abuse, which might lead to severe dependence—both psychological and physical.*

My whole room spins around me. *Symptoms of withdrawal include: anxiety, difficulty focusing, insomnia, perspiration, body aches, nausea . . .*

I shake my head, reliving the night Braden showed up at my parents' house.

If an overdose is suspected, immediately administer a dose of naloxone, to avoid fatality. Due to a dramatic increase in opioid abuse, naloxone is now available over the counter in many states.

I pick up my phone, and he answers on the second ring. "Hey, Hads. How was graduation? Sorry I missed it; I've been swamped."

"Well, I'm pretty sure my mom missed it because I stole her meds and gave them to you." Guilt and fear riot in my gut. "Did you know that shit you're on is a schedule-two drug?"

"What are you talking about?"

"Did you hear me?"

"Um, yeah, I heard you. But I don't know what that is." Except he sounds uneasy.

"My dad had to go refill my mom's prescription. He thinks he counted wrong because she ran out too soon."

"Shit."

"Yeah, *shit*. She's in pain because of *me*."

"I'm sorry, Had—"

"I can't believe I did that to her. She's just sitting in her room, waiting for my dad to get back so she can stop hurting. And he's mad at himself because he thinks he messed it up." Hot tears threaten to take over. "I won't do that again, Braden."

"Okay, yeah, of course not."

"And I heard him talking to the pharmacist. They didn't want to give her any more of it, apparently, because it's really addictive."

"Did they?"

"Yeah, it's on her file or something that she can have a refill. So it's fine. But that's not the point. Did you know all that when I gave it to you? Is that why you told me not to worry about it? Is that why you've been kind of distant? Are you in trouble?"

He takes a deep breath. "Okay, I get it. You feel bad, and we shouldn't have taken that from her, and I'm sorry."

"No, I'm—"

"Just hold on, okay? Let's think this through. Are you asking your mom if she's in trouble?"

"What? No—"

"Right. And why not?"

"*I don't know*. Because she has cancer! And the doctor prescribed them."

"Just like the doctor did for me. And she went through a bottle, just like I did."

"But—" It comes out choked.

"Hadley, I promise you, I've got this under control, okay? I took a couple pills that weren't mine, and I mean, honestly, you're the one who gave them to me." My stomach sinks even deeper. "I don't want to fight, so I'm just going to pretend you never accused me of anything, okay? We can be done with this, because I get it. This stuff with your mom . . . It's hard."

There are so many objections rising up inside me, but maybe he's right. He has been stretched pretty thin, between studying to retake the ACT, work, and swim club starting. Maybe I am too upset to look at this logically. I can't think of an actual reason why what he's doing is any different from what Mom is. And just because he's been busy lately doesn't mean he's hiding something.

But Mom didn't have a night that looked a lot like withdrawal.

Unless she did have a moment like that, and she didn't let me see it. Maybe Dad has been there for Mom, during these uncomfortable times that I have no idea about.

Am I being totally unfair? Maybe I'm just scared that since this one awful thing happened, every other bad thing will follow.

So, unsure of anything at all, I just nod, even though he

can't see me. "Okay. All right. I'm sorry." But not long after we hang up, I find myself looking up the name of that overdose medicine.

Naloxone.

First thing the next morning, before I can think myself out of it, I buy a package. An insurance policy. *I'll never need it*, I whisper to myself, and slip it into my purse.

during

Junior Year

summer

CHAPTER 23

"Hadley, it's nice to see that you still have teeth and everything, but you're hogging the Hunan chicken. I want some too." Judd points his chopsticks at me.

It's the day we've been waiting for, and Judd's right, I *am* smiling. With teeth and everything. I can't seem to stop, actually. Which is kind of weird, because my family is sitting at our dinner table, and there's no question: we have looked better.

Dad is across from me, and these three cancer-ridden months have aged him. Lines that used to only tease his face are now deeper, well-traveled roads. The twins have matching sunken eyes surrounded by dark circles. And Mom's face is smooth and pale, unhindered by eyebrows or eyelashes, with bluish circles that give the twins a run for their money. She's still wearing the remnants of Dad's favorite T-shirt around her head, something that's become a bit of a signature look. The idea almost makes me laugh. And I don't need a mirror to know that I look terrible. My hair hasn't been washed in days, and my clothes hang too loose on my frame.

All of us, frankly, look like shit.

But no family in the history of the world has ever been happier to look this awful.

Even Judd and Remy seem to have forgotten their weird tension from graduation day, at least for now. And every single one of us is smiling a real smile, the kind that reaches our eyes. Because we made it. For now, we have won.

Mom is done with chemo.

It's not over, of course; she still has to do radiation. Which will be difficult—a new challenge in the world of cancer. She has to go every single day, for weeks. And it requires so much precision that she has to get these small, freckle-like tattoos in the exact places where the machine lines up. But right now, Mom, our family, gets a whole month without cancer treatment. We get a break. We get to breathe. And hopefully, she will never need to put an IV full of those awful drugs into her veins again. Her hair will start to grow back. Her appetite will return. Her body will slowly become her own again.

So tonight, we're celebrating with a feast of takeout. It's the first time we've sat at the dinner table as a family since she told us about her diagnosis. I'm glad I didn't know then what these months would bring. But sitting here, so much closer to the other side, I feel a kind of hope I worried might have been lost to me.

I blink away my thoughts and pick up the plastic container, handing it to Judd. "Sorry, here you go. Hunan is all yours."

Judd grabs the takeout container from me and piles chicken onto his plate with his chopsticks. "Thanks."

I sit up taller in my seat, looking for the pork and hoisin sauce, when the teakettle sounds. Dad wanted to do a celebratory toast, but since alcohol isn't really an option, he made Mom's favorite anti-nausea tea. It's sort of a send-off. Hopefully, she won't need it again for a while.

Dad gets up to get mugs, and I flip my phone back over to see if Braden texted. I haven't heard from him all day, which is kind of weird, especially since he knows we're celebrating. *It's fine. He's at work.* Dad brings the mugs over, two by two, and sits back down in his seat. We pick them up and look to him.

"To your mom. To Mia"—emotion makes Dad's voice crack—"who has been so brave. Who has fought and endured so much so she can be here with us." He clears his throat. "We love you."

Mom gently places her hand over Dad's and squeezes it. After a moment, she redirects her attention, her eyes dancing. She raises her glass higher and declares, "But most importantly, good fucking riddance to chemo."

We laugh, all of us, and echo, "Good fucking riddance."

"Kids, don't curse." Her eyes sparkle as she sips her tea.

CHAPTER 24

I dial the number from memory and pace the house as I wait for someone to pick up.

I've been nervous all day, wondering how my parents are doing in Chicago. There's a radiation oncologist they wanted to meet in the city before Mom starts her new treatment; he's supposed to be the best. Mom can't fly for a while, because the chemo is so hard on her immune system, but it's only a four-and-a-half-hour drive, and they were able to get an appointment on Saturday morning, so they left this afternoon.

Remy and Abigail dragged Judd to some outlet mall, and I haven't exactly been enjoying the alone time. I keep worrying that the doctor will find more bad news.

I just wish Braden would get here.

"Pieces and Pies, Alice speaking. How may I help you?"

After all this time, Braden's coworker, Alice—aka the lovesick hostess from our first date—and I have settled into an uneasy, almost-friendly acquaintanceship. "Hey, Alice, it's Hadley."

"Oh. Hey."

"I, um, wanted to order delivery?"

"All right. What do you want?"

I tell her my order. "So basically just Braden's usual, then?" she asks when I finish.

"Yeah," I admit.

I tell her we're going to pay in cash, but before I hang up, she says, "We're a little short-staffed today, so it will be longer than usual. Maybe an hour or so?"

"Oh, okay. No problem. But do you know if they're going to call Braden in? The pizza is for us, so I could just come in and eat it there, if you think they're going to."

She doesn't answer me for so long that I'd think she hung up if it weren't for the fact I could hear the noises from the restaurant in the background. Finally, she says, "Hadley, Braden got fired. Like over a month ago."

"What?"

"I can't believe he didn't tell you." She sounds almost smug. "He was late a bunch of times and missed a couple shifts. Mona, the owner . . . She didn't want to fire him, but he didn't really give her a choice." I hear her tap her long finger-nails on the hostess stand. "I mean, *Braden* couldn't even talk his way out of it."

My blood thins, and the lie comes out quickly, "Oh, you know what? He did tell me. I'm sorry, I've got a lot going on at home. He's been with me tons, helping and everything. I guess it slipped my mind." I can't believe I just played the cancer card. "I'm sure that's why he was messing up his shifts. Anyway, thanks for taking the order. I'll have the cash ready. Have a good night." I hang up the phone before she can answer.

❊   ❊   ❊

When the food arrives, an hour and ten minutes later, Braden still isn't here. I watch the unopened box, imagining the pizza getting cold, going bad, rotting. He was supposed to be here at six, and it's closer to eight. I've called three times, and all three calls went directly to voice mail. I don't even want to count how many texts I've sent him.

Braden's never blown me off before, and I'm starting to worry. My mind is going to that familiar worst-case-scenario place. I try to ignore it. I try to be logical.

At ten to nine, the front door is thrown open dramatically, and I hear it slam against the doorstop. A loud, confident voice singing. *Singing.*

"*Ohhhhhh! Darling, please believe me!*" The door slams shut, and I'm frozen in the kitchen. I have been sitting in nervous silence for hours, and Braden's voice sounds startlingly loud. He's positively cheerful. Wait, actually . . . drunk?

His raspy voice, mimicking the Beatles and singing with gusto, is getting closer. He's still making his way through the house. I don't move.

He struts into the kitchen and falls onto his knees in front of me as I sit on a bar stool at the island. "*If you leave me, I'll never make it alooone!*"

"What the hell are you doing?" I ask in a flat voice.

"Please forgive me?" He isn't really singing anymore; more like talking to a beat and changing the lyrics to suit his needs.

He notices my expression. "Shit, you're really mad. I'm sorry. That's what I was doing. It was a stupid way to apologize. I was trying to make you laugh. Do you forgive your shit boyfriend?"

"For what? Being three hours late or for not telling me that you got fired *a month ago?*" I ask.

Something moves behind his eyes. "Fuck. I'm sorry. I didn't want to give you any more bad news. Don't be a drama queen about it, okay?"

A drama queen? "What happened? I thought you liked that job."

He moves from kneeling to standing. "Yeah, I do. I did. Mona was just being a bitch. I got my schedule mixed up, and she was, like, *so pissed.* It was ridiculous. Honestly, it was more like I quit. I'll get another job. No worries." He waves a hand in dismissal, and his lips curve. "And about tonight. I was going to go to the gym, but I ran into Logan when I walked in, and we decided to blow off some steam instead. Anyway, my phone died, and I felt terrible." He corrects himself, "Feel. I feel terrible. I just lost track of time."

Something about what he's saying feels . . . off. I can smell alcohol on his breath and a faint trace of smoke. And something lingering beneath his words. "You smell like whiskey."

"Just had a taste. No meds today." He lets his gaze linger on me. "I could share—come here."

I don't move. Instead, I rub my hands against my head,

trying to ease the dull pain forming there. "Did you drive here like that?"

"God, Hadley. I'm not drunk; I'm just messing around. And no, I didn't. We talked about that, remember? I'd be fine to drive, by the way. I just didn't want to upset you. Logan dropped me off."

I exhale, frustrated. I take a minute to look him over. He suddenly feels so distant. "Braden, seriously, what's going on with you?"

"I just told you."

I shake my head. "I don't think you really did."

He frowns. "What do you mean?"

"Something's up, and I want to know what it is." I'm afraid I already know, and I desperately want him to prove me wrong.

He meets my eye, anger just below the surface. "Honestly?"

"*Obviously* honestly. You keep saying that you—"

He cuts me off, "*Honestly*, I am just *so sick* of this conversation. You know what I did tonight, Hadley? I had some fun. Is that a crime? Does everything really have to be the end of the freaking world?"

"No, of course not—"

"It has been *so long* since I could just . . . I don't know, *relax*. I've been swimming and studying nonstop and"—he looks down—"and, like, obviously I want to be there for you. But it can be . . . well, it can be hard to see you upset all the time. Especially when I have such limited free time."

"Oh, it's hard for *you*?" My own anger rises.

His voice is cold. "Don't look at me like that. You told me to tell the truth."

I swallow my frustration and let him finish.

"Hadley, come on. You know that shit has not been easy lately, with all this Stanford stuff. So I needed to let loose a little. Do we have to fight about it?"

"So, what? I'm not allowed to be mad at you for lying because *I'm* hard to be around, because my mom is sick?" I can't stop myself from snapping. "And what the hell were you doing all those times you told me you were at work?"

"*Jesus!* Hadley, I needed a fucking hour to myself, okay? I needed some time when I wasn't under a freaking microscope. Coach literally monitors me down to fractions of seconds in the pool, and then out of the pool, you're studying me, like, *trying* to find something wrong! Is it really so hard to understand that I need a break?" His jaw is clenched, face tense.

And suddenly it hits me square in the chest that I might actually be close to losing him. I think of his calls that I've ignored while I was spending time with my family. I think of all the meets I've missed and how I've been suspicious and accusatory, and looking for problems that maybe weren't there. I *have* been doing the things he's saying, and I want to take it back. I want to rewind, because the fear of losing him makes everything else seem insignificant.

His shoulders fall, and he meets my eye. "You're not the only one having a hard time, okay?" His face relaxes. "You mean the world to me, Hadley, but I do have other shit going on. Hard shit. And I'm just trying to get through it."

I pause, full of guilt. Taking the ACT four times—twice already and two more to go—sounds really stressful. Not to mention all the other things he described. He just has to deal with this overloaded schedule for a couple more months.

261

"You're right." I nod. "I'm sorry. Stanford is a huge deal." And he still hasn't hit those three extra test points.

"We should blow off some steam." It's a desperate invitation.

"Yeah?" he asks, tentative.

It feels like a lifeline. "Yeah. When . . . when was the last time you swam just for fun?"

"It's been a while."

"Do you think you can? Like, would it make it worse? Your shoulder."

"Depends what you have in mind."

"How about we sneak over to Pebblebridge. Just you and me?" I love night swimming. There's something about the moon and the stars, and the cool, still water. It makes me feel electric, just like he does. And the only thing I want is some normalcy between us again, to hit reset. This feels like the perfect way to do it.

Braden smiles. "Okay. Yeah, I'm in."

"Great." *Thank god*, I think, but my head still throbs. "Just one second." I move to open the cabinet, grabbing myself a Tylenol, but I falter when I see Mom's prescription bottles, lined up at the front, ready for her. A reminder of the tension between Braden and me.

I can feel his eyes. Something slimy moves inside me. I grab what I need and slam the door closed, trying not to show my body sag in relief. I pretend I didn't block them from his view.

I swallow the pill dry. "Okay, just let me grab my suit and some towels."

He raises an eyebrow, a challenge. "Just towels. It wouldn't be fair. Since I don't have a suit."

The familiarity of it comforts me. "You're on. Let's go."

❋ ❋ ❋

I take in the summer night as we walk to my car. My group text is buzzing; Becca and Ty making plans, asking where I am, but I put my phone back into my purse, saving my attention for this moment. Stars are everywhere, and the moon is hanging low and bright. I lift my camera to snap a picture of him. While I'm distracted, Braden snatches the keys from my hands. I remember the smell of whiskey. "Hey, Brade, no. Let me."

"Do you think I'd drive my girl if I were impaired? I told you, I just had a taste. I got you. Always got you."

"Come on. Give them back. I don't want—"

"Hadley, what happened to loosening up a little?"

This doesn't feel like loosening up. It feels dangerous. Precarious. I fix him with the sternest look I can manage. "Promise me it was just a sip."

"Promise. It was nothing." He kisses me thoroughly before walking to the driver's side, and I find myself assessing how strongly his mouth tastes like alcohol. I cling to the fact that it was faint.

After we get settled in our seats, Braden pulls his Ray-Bans out of my cup holder, left from sometime last week, and dramatically slides them onto his face.

"Really, Brade? It's dark." *Whiskey* and *sunglasses.*

"Dark, shmark. I need to show my girlfriend how good I look in these shades." He turns toward me, lowers them with one hand, and winks.

My worry slides into irritation. "I've seen you in those a million times."

"And it never gets old, does it?" When he starts the engine, with his phone plugged into the aux cord, "Oh! Darling" is pounding through my car's speakers.

I give Braden another pointed look, and he slides the sunglasses up, letting them sit on the top of his head. Then he turns the music down.

I let my breath out, feeling a little better that he's taking me seriously.

Without breaking eye contact, he rolls the windows down, his facial expression a question: *Is this okay?*

This time, it's easier to agree.

Finally comfortable, I stop monitoring Braden and review the image on my camera screen, looking at the picture I just took. The way I feel about him is so obvious in my photograph that I'm almost embarrassed. I can see it in the way I let the moonlight cradle his face, and the way I focus on his eyes. The way everything around him blurs.

When the sunroof opens, Braden brings me back to the present moment. "I'm taking the dirt roads tonight. Get ready to fly, Hads."

He goes out the back exit of my subdivision and reaches the less developed part of town, full of newer streets that are infrequently traveled. I usually love it out here because it's full of fireflies lighting the road like living twinkle lights.

I look at Braden, debating. Flying is what we call standing

out of the sunroof while the other person drives. He promised he was okay, and I don't think he'd knowingly put me in any danger. And I remember my fear at the idea of losing him; I remember all the times he's made me feel wild and free. *I want that back.*

So despite a quiet protest at the back of my mind, I agree.

We've gotten this down to a routine. He nods and slows the car down to a near stop. Carefully unbuckling my seat belt, I start to stand, one foot on his seat, one on mine, and I lift my head and torso through the sunroof and into the summer night. My stomach flutters in anticipation as the air caresses my bare shoulders under my spaghetti straps.

"Ready?" Braden asks.

"Ready," I answer.

He counts "One, two . . . ," and then he hits the gas.

I'm prepared; he never waits until three.

My body pushes against the back of the opening of the sunroof, and the wind immediately pulls my long hair from my face and neck. It's exhilarating, bordering on scary. But it's impossible to think about anything except for right now, this moment. *I'm alive.*

"Thirty, forty . . ." He shouts how fast he's going so I can hear above the wind.

I yell into the night air, spreading my arms wide.

"Fifty!"

"Shit!" The road is a blur around me.

"Don't be a wimp."

"Okay! Okay! Fast enough!" I shout from above him and grip on to the sides of the sunroof.

"Sixty!"

I plead, "Come on! Stop!"

"Seventy!"

"Braden!"

Four pounding heartbeats later, he slows down.

I carefully lower myself back into the car, with messy hair and pounding adrenaline. "Braden, that was way too fast, oh my god."

He leans over and kisses my cheek. "You love it."

I used to, I think. But I don't answer out loud.

❊ ❊ ❊

We pull up in front of the still lake, and he puts the car into park, even though we both know we're not supposed to leave it here. "We'll be fast," he assures me, answering my unvoiced concern. We jump out of the car, and he grabs the towels before locking it. As he starts to jog, I follow, filled with nervous, wild energy. He's singing again.

He's contagious. Dangerously so.

When we get to the dock's edge, we look at each other. And then he starts stripping. He moves quickly again, throwing his shirt over his head and dropping his shorts. And now we're both in our underwear. He takes my camera from me and tries to take a picture of the two of us, but I dodge him and take it back. I snap one of him, sunglasses still on top of his head, black boxer briefs, and sun-kissed skin.

"Well, are we doing this or what?" I ask.

In response, he drops his boxer briefs. Then he leaps into the air, yelling like Tarzan and tumbling into the dark water. This is the boy I fell in love with.

He breaks the surface of the water, whipping his head as if to move the hair out of his face. It's grown enough that the short strands shake. Then he lifts his hand and slides his Ray-Bans back on. "Scared, Hads?"

I carefully set my camera down in response, wrapping it in my jeans. Hesitating for just a second, I unclasp my bra and drop my underwear. And then I leap into the cold water, naked and distracted by what might linger beneath the surface.

CHAPTER 25

The next morning, I'm sitting in the back seat of Becca's car, and we're on our way to pick up Braden. It's a perfect day for the beach. The sun is shining unobstructed, leaving my skin pleasantly warm, and this summer's megahit is blasting through the speakers. All four of us—me, Becca, Greg, and even Ty—are belting out the cheesy lyrics.

As it comes to a close, Becca's perfect alto keeps right on singing. She laughs loudly. "Shit, I always do that!"

"Hard to know it's ending when the whole song hits the same three notes over and over." Ty, sitting next to me in the backseat of the car, laughs with her.

"Becca, did you text me the address?" Greg asks, adjusting his baseball cap. "I can't exactly navigate without it."

"Greg, did you even look before you asked? I texted it to you before we left."

I turn to Ty, ignoring the conversation in the front of the car, and nudge him with my shoulder. "I just saw you sing *every single word* to that song you hate so much."

He smirks. "I have an ear for music."

"Mm-hmm."

"I can't help it if I remember *some* lyrics," he says, grinning widely.

"Right. Just like Becca definitely had an *accidental* solo."

"Hey! I heard that," Becca chastises us.

I put my hands up in surrender. "Sorry! You just . . . you know, don't exactly shy away from the spotlight."

She sweeps her hair dramatically off her shoulder. "No offense taken. I was *made* for the stage."

"Yeah you were, baby," Greg says.

Ty and I exchange a look, trying not to laugh.

Being with my friends makes my whole body feel light. I've been looking forward to our mini–road trip all week. We're heading about an hour away to a huge park that's known for biking trails, hiking, and most of all, a giant crystal lake and sandy beach. Lakes are pretty much the best thing about Michigan, and getting away, hanging out, it just feels so *normal*. I love it.

Greg is rifling around the car. "Wait, Becca." He stops searching, face concerned, and declares: "We made a huge mistake."

"That sounds . . . serious," she replies, amused.

"It is. All our snacks are packed."

"I know," Becca answers, trying to follow. "Hadley and I loaded the cooler this morning."

"Yeah. Which is great. And Ty and I appreciate it."

Ty, leaning against the car door to face me, nods dramatically.

"But, Becs, we don't have anything *for the ride*," Greg finishes.

"No car snacks," Ty adds quietly, "the gravest of road trip errors."

When I laugh too loudly, everybody looks at me.

"Hadley," Greg says, "only monsters go on road trips without snacks."

"Yeah, Butler. Only monsters," Ty says.

"Thank you!" Greg exclaims.

I shake my head at Ty, who's loving this way too much. "Greg," I say, "I would never, *ever* dream of standing in the way of snacks."

A few minutes later, we're pulling out of a gas station. Becca's tank is full, Greg is loaded down with all the snacks, Ty is sipping an Arnold Palmer, and I'm admiring how golden the world looks through a new pair of five-dollar sunglasses.

"Had, I hope your boyfriend is ready to go. If we leave right away, we'll get there around noon." Greg's reviewing the navigation on his phone.

"He said he'd be outside. I talked to him when I dropped him off last night," I tell Greg. I text him to let him know we're two minutes away; just a little late.

"Do you have a schedule you're trying to keep, Greg?" Becca teases, eyeing his three different bags of chips.

"As a matter of fact, yes, I plan on *maximum* relaxation. And the more time we have, the more chill I get."

I look down at my camera, strapped around my neck, and, on the seat between us, the books Tyler and I brought and Becca's headphones. I wonder if Greg actually has anything to entertain himself. Despite what he just said, a bored Greg is not chill. Or quiet.

Ty notices and casts me a glance. His voice is low. "I was thinking the same thing."

I laugh, nodding to Becca. "You guys can share custody."

Ty snorts.

"Why do you guys keep whispering back there? What's going on?" Greg asks.

Ty and I share a look. *Were we whispering?*

He sits up straighter in his seat. "No, man. Nothing."

And I'm saved from answering, because then we're in Braden's driveway. But Braden isn't.

"So much for waiting outside," Greg mutters.

I check my phone. He hasn't replied. I click to call him, but after a series of rings, I'm sent to his voice mail. *Maybe he's in the bathroom?* I wait a few seconds, not hearing my friends or the radio, and try again.

The third time I call, dread spreads through me like a thick fog.

There are so many rational explanations, I tell myself, but my body understands something my mind doesn't.

"Hadley?" Ty asks.

"He's not picking up." I sound far away. "I'll go . . . I'll go get him."

I throw the car door open before anyone can respond.

❋   ❋   ❋

I'm barely a step into his house. "Braden?" My voice tremors through the empty kitchen. "Brade, are you ready to go?"

Silence.

He probably just overslept, I repeat in my head. But I don't believe it.

I call his name again.

The hairs on my arms stand.

I start moving faster, searching the kitchen and living room, then race down the stairs.

I call for him again and again as I approach his room.

I see his blond hair first. On the floor.

He's next to his bed, spread across the carpet. An empty orange bottle is on the nightstand next to him. Written across it, clear as day, is Logan's name.

"Braden!" He doesn't stir. I throw myself onto the floor and shake his shoulders. *"Braden, please."*

Nothing.

I remember my call with Ty. *Check if he's breathing.* I study his chest, but my eyes have filled with tears and I can't see clearly enough. My heart pounds as I press trembling fingers into his neck.

And wait.

"Please, Brade, *please.*"

Thump.

I exhale a sob.

My purse and camera are still looped around me, and I rip them off, abandoning my camera as I furiously dig through my bag.

You're supposed to use it, even if you aren't sure.

There's so much fucking stuff in here, I want to scream in frustration as I dump it all onto the carpet.

There.

I tear the packaging open.

"Hadley?" a muffled voice calls from upstairs. Tyler. I ignore him.

My hands tremble as I lift Braden's head and press the naloxone applicator into his nose. "Come *on*, Brade," I pray.

Someone moves behind me. "Had? Oh my god, *shit*." Ty kneels on the floor. "Do you know what you're doing with that?" He helps me support Braden's head.

Without taking my eyes off him, I nod. The day before I bought it, I read the instructions online, over and over again.

"Help me move him to his side."

Together, we turn Braden's body. "You found him like that?"

"Yeah." We both know what it means: we don't know how long he's been out. I try to regain control of my thoughts. "We have to watch him. If he doesn't wake up in two minutes, I have to give him another dose. What time is it?" I frantically look through my pile of things. "Where's my phone? Do you see my phone? *I need my phone.*" I'm starting to feel hysterical.

"I've got mine. Two minutes?"

"Yeah." I take a trembling breath.

"Where are you guy— Oh! Becca, I found them." Greg's cheerful voice grates against my bones. "Wait. What are you doing?"

"Is everything okay?" Becca asks from down the hall.

"No," I snap at my friends. I hear them move behind me.

"Oh my god," Becca says from the doorway. "What happened?"

"Call nine-one-one," I tell her.

"What?" I've never heard Becca sound so lost. "What do I say?"

Tyler answers for me. "Tell them it's an opioid overdose. And we used naloxone."

"What?" Greg asks.

Becca repeats it back and then asks, "What's the address?"

Ty's phone chimes. "That's two."

Fear and fury are a storm in my chest. I lash out at Becca, *"Figure it out."*

I rip open the second package from the box.

Greg grabs Becca. "Come on. We'll go look at the front of the house."

I nod at Ty, and he tilts Braden's head back while I administer the second dose.

This time, after we turn him, Braden stirs.

The weight of the world falls off me. I imagine throwing myself on top of Braden, sobbing into his body. But I can't move. I can't cry. I'm frozen, crouched on the floor, watching his breaths deepen, his limbs shift.

A group of footsteps pound upstairs.

Ty's brow furrows, like he's thinking the same thing I am: that was fast, even for an ambulance.

"Braden Maxwell Roberts!" Mrs. Roberts's voice booms into the basement. "What the hell is going on?"

And then she's in his room.

When her eyes find her son, the wind goes out of her. We're all still, staring at him barely conscious. Greg and Becca hover at the doorway.

And then she's a flurry of motion, pushing past me.

"Braden?" She strokes his face, and I wish my fingers were hers. His eyelids flutter. She looks at me. "What happened?"

I take a halting breath. "He was like this when we got here. I think he . . ." I can't bring myself to use the word *overdose*. "I think he took too much of the medication."

"That's ridiculous. He sees the best sports medicine doctor in the state. He probably just practiced too hard and didn't eat enough. It's happened before." She turns to him. "Braden?"

His weight shifts. "Mom?" a groggy voice asks.

The fist around my heart loosens. *He spoke.*

"You're okay, honey," Mrs. Roberts soothes. Then she continues, looking at me, "Hadley, I don't understand. Braden would never do anything to risk his scholarships. He's never . . . he's never done anything like this before."

I clench my jaw, trying desperately to focus my wild emotions. "He has."

"What?"

"You're right, he *would* do anything to keep swimming," I say. "Even take those horrible pills for way too long." Saying it out loud feels like betrayal and relief tangled together.

Something in her expression cracks. She glances at Braden, who is still deeply out of it.

"I wish it wasn't true. *So bad.* I tried to—" I nearly choke. "He's taking more than he's supposed to. He has been."

She shakes her head. "No."

I glance at Ty. His eyes are steady. I wish any part of me felt steady. I hold on to a simple fact: Braden needs help. He needs his parents. *How can I make her understand?*

And then it hits me.

I give her the ugly truth, unmistakable: "He is. And I know, because I gave it to him."

Everyone except for Tyler gapes at me.

I wipe at a tear falling down my cheek. "My mom had the same medication. Braden came over, and he was in a lot of pain. I shouldn't have. I didn't understand—" Emotion gets the better of me, and I'm unable to finish the thought. "I don't think I'm the only one, but I may have started it."

Sirens wail in the distance.

Mrs. Roberts's words are barely contained rage. "Get out. Get out of my house—right now."

"You have to tell them what happened. And that we gave him naloxone," I tell her.

"Now. Or I'm calling the police."

I steal a glance at my boyfriend. His eyes are open, but he looks lost. Scared. Leaving him in that room nearly tears my heart in two, but I do it.

❈　❈　❈

When I get home, Remy's waiting for me in the driveway. I slam Becca's car door closed. She must have told my sister what happened, but she pulls the car away before I can say anything.

"Hadley," Remy starts, "are you okay?"

"I can't do this right now."

"Becca said something about an OD. Calling nine-one-one? What the hell happened?"

I try to sidestep her to get into the house, but she blocks me. My chest tightens. "Let me through, Rem."

"No. Not until you talk to me. How can Braden possibly be this bad and I know *nothing* about it?"

"Remy, I'm not doing this." My insides are churning.

She scowls. "You don't have a choice! You can't let—"

"'Let'?" I'm furious. "What part of this do you think I have control over?"

"I'm not saying you have control over it—"

"Obviously not! So what the hell am I supposed to do? What does my *big sister* suggest?" I sound so awful, and it's satisfying.

"I'm saying, you control *you*," Remy says, trying hard to be calm. "You tell somebody. You make him get help. Or you walk away, Hadley. You have to. If he won't get help, you have to leave. He could pull you into this mess, too. . . . He'll hurt you, even if he doesn't want to."

"Really? You think this might hurt?" I shake my head, swallowing the lump in my throat. "And how would you know? Do you have experience with this?" I narrow my eyes. "I guess you *have* dated every asshole in town."

"Hadley, come on."

"You literally have no room to talk."

"Maybe not. But I'm smart enough to know when something isn't healthy anymore."

"Oh really? Because I thought it was totally cool—*superhealthy*—walking into my boyfriend's bedroom after he OD'd. I just thought that was all perfectly normal!" A sob fights its way through me. "Jesus, Remy. *I'm* the one who is constantly picking you back up when some random jerk fucks up. So can you give me just *one minute* to deal with this before you climb down my throat?"

The back door opens to the driveway, and Judd steps outside. "What the hell is going on? I can hear you two from the kitchen."

Remy sighs and turns to our brother. "I can't deal with you right now too. Just go back inside, Judd."

"*Jesus*, Remy, can you let it go?"

Remy's face flushes. "*No!* No, I can't let it go that you're just *not* going away to school."

"What?" I ask.

"He's deferring from Michigan State, going to take all his freshman classes right down the street. He doesn't want to leave Mom before she finishes radiation. So now I'm the only asshole leaving." Remy looks between me and Judd. "You know, I don't know what the hell is going on with the two of you. When did everybody get so secretive?"

"Remy, believe it or not, not everything is actually about you!" Judd is frustrated; they've clearly had this argument before.

I can't cope with this news right now; my head's spinning and I'm starting to feel sick. "If the two of you want to fight, can you at least let me go inside?"

"You're not going anywhere, Hadley," Remy says.

"You can't tell her what to do, Remy."

I move past her, and Remy says, "I might not choose perfect guys, Hadley, but I've never dated anybody who did what Braden did today."

I turn to her. "No, the guys you date do totally wholesome things like cheat."

"*Jesus*, Hadley. This is serious. You can't just walk away

from me and pretend everything is okay. He needs help. And you need to figure out what *you're* going to do."

Suddenly I can't take her criticizing him anymore, and I'm yelling, "He's trying to get a scholarship! His coach, his parents, they all expect—" I know I'm making excuses, but it doesn't make any of it less true. "He's doing his best. It's not his fault—"

Remy's quiet. "Do you even hear yourself?"

"Hear *what?*"

She shakes her head. "You sound like one of the people Mom works with. Those women who let men walk all over them."

"Remy!" Judd says.

Her words nearly knock me over.

This is nothing like that.

I can't listen to her for another second. "Fuck you, Remy."

Then I turn, open the door, and in private, crumble into a million pieces.

CHAPTER 26

*R*_{ing}

Braden's name appears on my screen. It's been two days of
worrying myself sick. I'm so desperate to answer that I nearly
drop my phone. "Braden?"

"Hadley, I'm in your driveway. Will you come out?"

"I'll be right there."

As quickly as I can, I make my way outside, concrete warm
on my bare feet. When I see him standing there next to his
car, looking healthy and whole, my heart fuses itself back together. I throw myself onto him, around him, pulling him as
close as I can. He clasps his arms around me.

"You're okay," I say around the lump in my throat.

"I'm so sorry," he replies.

"I called you a million times."

"I know." He's touching my face. "My mom just gave me
back my phone. I'm not supposed to be here, but—"

"I'm so glad you are."

His eyes fill. "You saved my life, Hadley."

"No, I—"

"You did." He presses his fingers behind my ear, pulling my forehead to his. Our tears are a salty mess on each other's faces. "I'm so sorry. I didn't mean to. I honestly didn't think—"

"It's okay," I manage.

"No, it isn't."

I nod, tears falling freely now. "You're right. . . . It isn't. Braden, you scared me so bad."

"I scared myself too."

"Did they take you to the hospital? How long were you there?" I can't stop touching him, making sure he's okay.

"Overnight. I'm okay. I really am."

"You had to stay overnight?" My heart fractures again.

"Just for observation."

I take a shaky breath. "*God.* I'm so mad at you, Braden. I'm so mad that I don't even know what to—"

He pulls me into him. "I don't blame you."

For a while, I just take in his solid weight. His arms, strong and sturdy around me, the familiar way I have to stand on my toes to reach around his shoulders, the way he rubs my back, in looping, comforting circles.

"I'm so sorry about Stanford."

He pulls away. "What?"

"Well, I mean . . . you're getting the surgery now, right? You obviously can't stay on those pills."

He takes a step backward. "Hadley—"

Memories of that morning flash through my mind. "I saw the bottle, Brade. Logan's."

He bites his lip. "I'm sorry. I know I shouldn't have taken it."

"This isn't okay. I thought you were—" I swallow the words: *going to die.*

Braden shakes his head. "I really didn't think those meds were a big deal. They were just left over from Logan getting his wisdom teeth out. He was trying to help, because I ran out and my times would have bombed."

"The same way I was trying to help?"

He looks at me like he's being torn open.

And suddenly my feelings are tied in knots. I'm overcome with relief he's okay, but I can't forget how many lies he's told, can't forget how angry I am that he got himself into this mess. How angry I am at myself.

"You can't keep putting people in this position, Braden."

He tenses. "What? I never asked anybody—"

"I know." I rub at my face. "Honestly, that's not even the point. I just can't believe how bad it's gotten. I've been making myself sick over the stuff I gave you. And your mom. Oh my god, your mom. She's so mad. She kicked me out of your house."

"I'll deal with my mom." He pulls me into him again, and I slide my hands all the way around his body.

Something crinkles in his pocket.

He jerks away, but not fast enough.

And then I'm holding a bag of pills in my hand.

"I can explain—" he objects.

I look down at the bag. "Did you just stand there apologizing to me while you had these in your fucking *pocket*?"

"Hadley—"

"I had to call nine-one-one *two days ago*, Braden! How can—"

"It was just in case of an emergency. You don't know what it feels like, getting off those—"

"Are you on that shit right now?" I can hardly speak quickly enough. "How did you even get this?"

His eyes focus on something off in the distance. "It was just sitting in my room."

"What? The pills?" But I know that's not what he means. Dread engulfs me, tangible as the weather.

He steps closer, urgency taking over. "I lost my job, you know? And I . . . I needed money. But I'm going to get you a better one! I am. I'm going to get a new job, and I already looked up the model. Here . . ." He reaches for his phone, but I ignore it.

I take in a shaking breath. "You sold my camera?"

"I'm so sorry, this is—"

The truth hits me right between the eyes. "You sold my camera." I search him over, wondering how such a familiar face could hide such horrible secrets. "You sold my camera for drug money." The words weigh a million pounds, so heavy I'm afraid they're going to fall through the concrete and drag me down with them.

"No. Hadley. *Please*. No, don't say it like that."

"It's what you did, though, isn't it? You sold my camera." Anger rips through me. Everything we had, this hope inside me, it feels like it's crumbling to pieces. "You *know* what that camera means to me. How could you—" My voice breaks. He reaches for me, but I rip away. "*No*. Don't touch me."

He drops his arms and keeps the space between us. "I love you. *Hadley*. And I'm *so fucking sorry*. I don't even know . . ." His eyes are full of tears. "You have to forgive me. You have to. *I need you.*"

"I want to be there for you, Braden. I do. But I can't do this if you don't stop. I don't know how to live like this." The air feels too thin to bring into my lungs. "It's almost killing you—it feels like it's almost killing me too. I don't know—"

He reaches for me, but again, I step out of his grasp.

I continue, "Tell me you're having the surgery. Tell me you're getting off the painkillers. Tell me you're not going to keep putting your life at risk for a college scholarship."

"It's just three more months, Hadley. I can't give up now. I've worked my *whole life*. I need you to understand. And I know my limits. I know what I did wrong. I'm not going to—"

A sob breaks free. "I can't do this. I can't." And then I find myself saying, "You have to choose."

He looks like I punched him in the gut. "What?"

I'm starting to panic. "You have so many options. You don't need to go to Stanford. Just get the surgery, recover, keep trying for Michigan. Or take a break from swimming altogether. Anything, Braden, anything but this. You're going to . . . I can't do this."

His expression is agonized. "Do you even understand what you're asking? Give up the best program in the country, right as I'm about to get it? How can you ask that? You know how hard I work."

I look at him. At his hazel eyes, cropped hair, full lips. At the face I love most in the world. And then I picture him lifeless on the floor. "Braden, how can I not ask?"

And then I'm crying in earnest, because I know him—through and through—and I know what he's going to do. Braden Roberts wants to stand on the top podium at the Olympics. He can't walk away from a challenge, no matter what. Not even if it kills him.

"Hadley . . ." It's there, that single-minded drive, written all over his face. "Please don't make me do this."

"*God, Braden.* Please don't make *me.*"

It's only a few seconds. Two people, standing so close, but somehow too far to reach each other.

And then he says, "I have to try for Stanford, Hadley. *I have to.* But I promise, I'll be so careful. I won't let anything happen, not like that. I won't—"

And then it's real. He made his choice.

And it isn't me.

It's a stab in the heart.

I force myself to say, "Then I need you to go."

His eyes harden. "No. Hadley—"

I feel so betrayed, I can't think straight. "I can't keep having this fight. I won't watch you destroy yourself."

It's quiet for a beat. "If I leave, it's over," he says.

"I know," I manage.

I want to beg him to change his mind. I want to pull him into me and keep him there, safe, forever. But I can't. And I can't wonder every time I talk to him if he's lying, or every time he misses my call, if he's in trouble. I can't live like this. And if it's not what he wants, I can't make him want it.

"Hadley, this is a mistake. You're making a horrible mistake."

I can hardly speak, emotion thick in my throat. "Maybe."

He grabs my hands. "So take it back. Just change your mind."

I force myself to say the hard truth. "I can't." I look at him. "Can you?"

He sighs, halting and heavy. And then he shakes his head. "Then you need to go."

"Hadley—"

But I don't have anything left to say, and I'm afraid I'll lose all resolve if I keep looking at him. So I walk into the house, shut the door behind me, and lock it.

❄   ❄   ❄

My heart rate is still elevated an hour later when my phone rings. This time, Mrs. Roberts's name lights up my screen.

Why is she calling me? "Hello?"

Her voice is tight. "Hadley?"

"Yeah?"

I hear her exhale. "Oh, god. I don't know how to tell you this. . . ."

My heart skips a beat.

"Braden was in an accident."

"What?" The floor falls out from under me.

"He ran a light on a left turn. He"—she pauses to regain herself—"flipped the car."

"Oh my god." A nauseous wave fills my gut. I choke out the words "Is he okay?"

"It's serious. We're waiting in the emergency room."

My thoughts start to spiral.

I force myself to speak. "I'm so sorry. I should have . . . Oh my god. What's going to happen?"

"We're still finding out. But he broke some ribs and pierced one of his lungs."

"I'll be right there."

"Actually, Hadley . . . I'm sorry. But I don't think that's a good idea." Her voice is resolved. "I wanted you to hear it from us, but Braden won't be having any visitors. He's not conscious, but even if he were, we need to work this out as a family. Get it under control. Please respect our wishes. Braden doesn't need any outside influences right now. I'll let you know if anything changes."

And the line goes dead.

after

Senior Year

autumn

CHAPTER 27

I can still hear the muffled music coming from the party downstairs, and I try to ignore my pounding heart long enough to think. I have to get away from the noise. Greg's scolding words echo in my head.

I kissed Tyler. I can't believe I kissed Tyler. My stomach turns. *What about Braden?* I fumble into Dr. West's bedroom, still feeling too exposed, and move past the bed and into his large bathroom. *What the hell was I thinking?*

Sliding onto the floor, I tuck my legs tight into my chest, and let my heart pound against my knees. A wave of nausea rolls through me. I open the lid to the toilet and expel the cinnamon whiskey. It burns even worse coming back up. I wish I could fold into myself until I disappear.

"Had?"

Great. Wonderful.

"Yeah." I lean back into the wall, feeling empty. I answer his question before he can ask it. "I'm fine." When I'm finally brave enough to look up and see Tyler's face, his eyes are full of concern.

"You don't look fine."

The truth is that my head's spinning. My throat is burning. And I'm still drunk. Drunker than I realized when I was dancing. Making out with one of my best friends. He glances at the toilet. "It wasn't that bad, was it? The kiss."

The sound I make is pitiful and amused.

He finds his way to the wall opposite me and then slides down to the floor too.

The words leave my mouth before I can think myself out of them. "You called me gorgeous." It sort of sounds like a question. Or maybe an accusation.

He looks at his shoes. "Oh. Well . . ." He pauses. "Yeah, I guess I did. But to be honest with you, Butler. Right at this *specific* moment, you're looking kind of a mess."

My laughter echoes in the bathroom. "Yeah. No kidding."

"Like, you're a little boney these days, and you've got makeup under your eyes—"

"You really don't need to give me details."

His nose wrinkles. "And this entire room smells like puke."

"Sorry," I answer sheepishly.

He shrugs. "I wasn't talking about how you look, anyway. But on a normal day, yeah. That too."

"But mostly the puke smell, right?"

"Yeah, mostly."

I study Tyler, thoughts and emotions all tangled together. In the last year, it feels like he's the only person who understands me. The only one who sees me clearly. And I don't think I've been repaying the favor.

"Ty?" I manage.

His face goes serious. "Yeah?"

"Do you have any mouthwash?"

He laughs and lifts himself up from the floor. He hands me a bottle of neon blue liquid from the cabinet below the sink. "Here."

"Thanks." I take a swig, swishing it around, enjoying the minty relief.

Ty looks at me as I sit back on the floor. "Do you want to talk about . . . the other thing that happened?"

My heart rate spikes again, and my fingers pull at the threads of the white rug next to me. "I'm sorry, Ty." I risk a glance up at his face. "I shouldn't have—"

His gaze is steady. "Don't be. I'm not. And you might have been the one who actually, you know, kissed me. But I sort of started it."

My brow furrows. "I'm the one who asked you to dance."

"But I didn't dance with you like a friend would."

"And I didn't kiss you like one."

"Well, yeah. Okay. I don't really know how friends would kiss." He moves, sitting up straighter and leans toward me. "That did surprise me. It was . . ."

"Yeah," I agree, because whatever he was going to say, he's right. I laugh to try to dispel some of the awkwardness. "It was really good."

His eyebrows lift.

"You didn't think so?" Then I laugh even harder, feeling

mildly deranged. I let my head fall heavy against the wall behind me.

He puts a hand out. "No. I agree." His voice is firm. "I just
didn't expect you to say it."

"Well, I did." I gather my resolve and sit back up. "But—"

Ty sighs, and as if by a switch, the light behind his eyes
goes out. "I know. I get it. You don't have to say anything. I
understand."

"How do you know what I'm going to say? *I* barely know
what I'm going to say."

"I just . . . I assumed you were going to say it was a mistake.
Weren't you?"

I'm suddenly aware of how close we are. I remember his
hands in my hair and the surprised sound he made when I
kissed him.

I shake my head. "I don't know. I probably should, but . . ."

"But?" His expression is hopeful. I don't know what to
say, so I just watch him. "We don't have to figure it out right
now—" He pauses for so long that I wonder if he's going to
continue the thought. Finally, he says, "I have an idea."

The air in the room charges. I curse myself for noticing it.

"An idea?"

I look at his eyes. They're alert, present, assessing me carefully. I'm so close I can see his lashes, short and curly. "Maybe
we could try one more time before we decide anything?"

"Try?" My body feels light, nervous. "Like an experiment?"

"Just to see. Like, if it was a fluke. No pressure if you don't
want to."

I can't help myself. I have to clarify: "So you want to kiss me?
In a bathroom that smells like puke that I'm responsible for?"

"Yeah," he says with a laugh. "I kind of do."

For a beat, we're both still, and I realize I have to be the one to do it. He's not going to close the space between us. Especially not now, not after drinking, and not when I'm so confused. So I move toward him, palms steady and knees sliding on the cool tile.

He's against the opposite wall, watching me approach him. Aside from his chest rising and falling, he doesn't move at all, not until our faces are just inches apart. I tilt my head into him.

Slowly, he sits up straighter and then barely presses his mouth against my lower lip. I suck in air, surprised at the current of feeling between us. He stops at the sound, pulling away to look at me.

Do we stop now?

I'm frozen. Then I dip my chin, very slightly, and he lets go of whatever had been holding him back. His fingers press gently on the sides of my neck as our lips meet with greater intensity. He lets go of whatever has been holding him back as he wraps an arm around my waist and pulls me closer. My brain leaves entirely.

I haven't been touched like this, feeling safe and wanted, in longer than I realized. It's filling a void I didn't know existed, but now that I've noticed it, it's endlessly deep.

His body shifts, pressing against me, and I feel a pull from deep in my stomach. He moves his lips to my neck, his teeth brushing the thin skin over my thumping pulse. I barely remember to breathe as his mouth works its way back to mine.

Without thinking, I grab the ends of his shirt. Tugging it over his head, I rip our mouths temporarily apart for the chance to touch more skin. See more skin. I look at him and feel my heartbeat pound.

He follows my lead, lifts my shirt and discards it. He stops for a moment, eyes tracing my body.

The word *beautiful* leaves his lips, and I catch it. His hands wrap around my exposed back. I press my teeth gently into his bottom lip, and his fingers dig into my hips, low. My heart is beating so fast—

"Had? You in there?" It's Becca's voice.

Tyler and I open our eyes at the same time. I pull away from him and jump up off the floor. "Yeah, hey," I say in a shrill voice as I look for my shirt—actually, it's Becca's shirt—and pull it hastily back on. When I look down, Braden's key is hanging in the middle of my chest.

I might be sick again.

I hear her walk into the bedroom, making her way toward us through the open door. "Oh, *hi*, Hadley. I've been looking everywhere for you!"

She knows.

"I'm sorry. It's my fault." Tyler's shirt is on backward. Oh my god. *Oh my GOD, what have I done?* I thought I messed up downstairs, but now I've really done it. And it's definitely not his fault.

She's leaning in the doorway. "You're big kids. You can do whatever you want." Becca's really trying to play it cool, but there's something uneasy under her actual words. "But I'm leaving. You still want a ride, Hads?"

"Yeah, I'll be right there." My voice is tight. Becca takes the hint and leaves the bathroom.

Tyler and I are both standing now, facing each other in

the small space of the doorframe. His mouth is swollen from kissing me, and his shirt is all rumpled, but tight around his biceps. The tag bobbles below his Adam's apple as he swallows. And the sight of him like that instantly feels so endearing to me that it almost hurts.

I stare at him, still not moving. Completely unsure of what to do, what to say. If he were just my regular friend Tyler, I would hug him goodbye. I wouldn't even think about it. But I can't bring myself to close the space, afraid of what it might lead to.

Then he smiles his slow-motion smile. A smile I've seen a million times, but now reinvented. He shakes his head. *"Fuck."*

And *whoa*. And everything in between.

"Yeah."

"I feel like I should apologize? But I don't know how to apologize for that." He pauses. "That wasn't normal, right?" It's like he's talking to himself. Then he looks me dead in the eye. "I have never felt anything like that in my entire life."

Instinctively, my fingers find my necklace. I let my eyes fall. Because I have felt something like that. But somehow it doesn't make this moment feel any less significant.

I look at him one last time, and the resulting pang in my stomach is something I'm not ready for. "If you have to apologize, then so do I." I nod toward the door. "But I have to go. She's my ride. We'll . . . talk about this later?"

"Okay. Later." His expression is goofy, and he says it like he's in a daze.

I press my lips together, and I don't wait for more. *More* is what got me into this mess. Instead, I leave the room to go find Becca. The whole way home, I'm not sure if I want to laugh or cry.

CHAPTER 28

"And it was good?" Becca looks delighted.

At least that makes one of us.

Sitting on her bedroom floor, I run my hands over her carpet. "Yeah. But I basically feel like the worst person in the world." The other night, after the party, I told her I wasn't ready to talk about it, so today, she's making up for lost time with the rapid-fire questions.

My phone buzzes.

"Hads? Is that him *again*?"

"It's not a big deal. Tyler and I have always texted."

"Right, but it's the *content* of these texts that interests me. Plus, you phone's been dying for like . . . hours. I'm surprised it can even get all these messages."

"We're just agreeing not to be weird. To give each other some space, time, whatever. To think about how the hell to handle this . . . situation."

"And?"

I'm ready to tell her that I haven't the faintest freaking

idea, that I'm the biggest mess of all the messes, when I hear my phone buzz again. I glance down to darken the screen, but it doesn't say Tyler's name.

It says Braden Roberts.

I slam my phone to the carpet, facedown. I press my hands against my chest and breathe deeply.

"Hadley?"

I pick it back up.

I'm so sorry, Hadley. And then a text bubble appears. He's typing more. He's typing *right now*.

He's awake.

When I look up, Becca is staring at me.

"You look like you've seen a ghost." She pauses, understanding. "Wait."

I nod quickly.

"What does it say?"

I hand Becca my phone. "He's typing!" she exclaims.

I leave my body, and I'm watching this from somewhere far, far away.

My phone buzzes again.

Becca's voice is protective. "Well, that's about the only acceptable thing for him *to* say."

I grab my phone from her. Three more texts come in quick succession.

It's killing me.

Almost literally.

Will you meet me somewhere? I can come to you.

The room is quiet as I hand Becca the phone again. "You're not going to, are you? What about Ty?" she asks incredulously.

But I don't even think about it. There's no answer but yes.

I text him back, telling him to meet me at my parents' house. Mom and Dad are at Mom's radiation treatment, and Judd has classes all day today. I have to go, *now*. But Becca's room is such a mess I can't find my sweatshirt and purse. "I have to. I've been losing my mind wondering how he is."

She has some counterpoint, but I don't hear it. "If I see him, then maybe I can move on. Figure out the Tyler stuff. Right now, it's all . . ." I make a wild gesture with my hands. "I need to untangle it." In the middle of this chaos, choosing to see him feels like the simplest decision in the world. I spot my bag. "Sorry to bail."

Becca is on her feet in front of the threshold of her bedroom. "Text me when you get there and when he leaves. Call me if you need me. And don't blow off Ty."

"Ty knows I need time to sort everything out."

"I know, but still."

I squeeze her arm. "It'll be fine." In this moment, I would say almost anything to get her out of my way. We both know that I may have just blown up our group of friends, but she doesn't say anything; just gives me a warning look and moves out of the doorframe, letting me pass. I bolt out of her room without so much as a parting glance.

CHAPTER 29

My purse lands with a thud on the passenger seat. It's less than a ten-minute drive to my house, but it feels endless. The whole way there, I fluctuate between driving like a maniac and remembering the accident and slowing down.

My heart feels like it might blow up.

When I pull into the driveway, I grab my phone and keep my promise to Becca to text her. Here. She immediately answers, but my phone dies before I can read it. I shove it back into my purse and take a couple controlled breaths.

Braden is going to be here any minute.

When I get out of the car and stand in the driveway, I feel like I'm using baby deer legs. I should go into the house, wait for him in the living room, do something. But my legs won't move.

I can't stop thinking of what the alternate version of this moment would look like, one where I speed off in my car and never look back. Where I text him and say, no, sorry. I can't. I remember his lies and my camera, and I simply say no. But in this reality, I stand paralyzed, afraid to look up from my shoes, remembering the other version of him. The one who let me pretend our first date was our fifth so I'd be less nervous, who couldn't wait until daylight to ask me to be his girlfriend, who comforted me after Mom was diagnosed. Sometimes I convince myself that the force of my will alone could bring back the boy I used to know.

Before I can make a decision, a car parks in front of my house.

The door clicks open and then closes with a thud. My eyes stay fixed on the ground, taking in the stains on my Keds. My hands tremble at my sides.

"Hadley." His voice is home.

I take a deep inhale and force my gaze up. He's stopped a few feet in front of me.

And he's the same but entirely different.

His hazel eyes are piercing, more nervous than I've ever seen them, accentuated by his green T-shirt. And the evidence of the accident is everywhere. Part of his head was shaved—the hair is shorter on one side than the other—and along the side, he has a healing scar from the stiches. His left arm is in a sling. He's littered with bruises. Frankly, he looks exactly how I have been feeling: shattered and put back together all wrong. Even though I still desperately miss it, I don't need my camera; I know the sight of him like that will stay with me forever.

We stare at each other for a few moments, silent except for my pounding heart. And his too. I can't hear it, but I know it as well as my own.

"When did you get out? Are you allowed to be here?"

"I'm so sorry, Hadley." His voice breaks at my name.

I don't move, but my heart throws itself at my rib cage. "You're okay?"

He nods. He's looking at me like I'm the answer to every question he's ever asked. "Are you?"

"Yeah." But my vision goes blurry with tears. "I don't know." I feel pulled in so many directions; I'm going to rip into pieces.

He takes a step closer, then abruptly stops himself. His brows are creased with pain. "Can I . . . ?" He offers his uninjured arm, reaching into the space between us.

"Braden—"

His arm falls. "I understand."

My heart fractures. Unable to find the words, I take a step closer to him.

"Oh thank god."

And when he wraps his arm around my body, all the pieces slide back into place. Feeling so suddenly whole makes my body ache. I grip on to him. "You're okay," I tell him, letting the weight of the world fall into his chest. "You're here."

He nods against my head as he rocks me. We move back and forth, and his hand twines in my hair, rubs my arm, rests on my hip. He touches me with so much love that it puts my heart back together and breaks it anew.

"Nobody would let me see you."

"I know," he whispers. "I'm sorry, Hadley. For all of it. *I'm so, so sorry.* The things I did—" He cuts himself off. "There's no excuse."

He's here. He's sober. He's him again. I talk through my tears. "I'm sorry too. I didn't realize . . . I should have—"

"No. What happened was my fault, okay? *Mine.*" He's

so close, I can feel his ragged breath, can see every shade of brown and green in his eyes. A gentle thumb traces my jaw. "I will never let anything like that happen again, okay? Ever. I love you, Hadley. *I love you so much.* I'm never risking you again."

My answer moves from my heart up my throat and out my mouth. "I love you too." And it's true, but it also tugs at something uneasy from deep inside me.

I watch him exhale, and then he's taking my face and bringing me back into him.

A memory of the party the other night makes me hesitate, but only for a second.

I kiss him to show how much I've missed him. To show how imagining a world without him made all the lights go out. I pour my every emotion into it, a kiss that hurts as much as it soothes.

I press a hand into his chest, and I'm shocked by the pained sound he makes.

I stop immediately. "Are you okay?"

He touches his chest with prudent fingers. "I'm fine. Just where the chest tube went in." He offers half a smile through his grimace. "It hurts like hell, but not because of you."

It's only a glimmer—something in the way he's standing, the light in his eyes—but it's the first trace of his personality that I've seen in weeks. And it makes me want to laugh out loud, maybe even dance a little. In response, I tease him, "Do you want me to call somebody? One of the nurses and I had a real bonding experience."

"Oh yeah?"

"Totally. I tried to break in at three in the morning."

Amusement flickers in his eyes. "My girl learned a thing or two, huh?" He reaches for my hand, and I let him take it. I marvel at the way our fingers still fit together so easily. The way his skin still makes mine feel electric. "And what nurse could deny you?"

I slide my hand back and forth against his. "I don't know her name. Thirtysomething maybe? Freckles, dark blond."

"Jeanette," he says.

"Of course you know her name."

"Jealous?"

"Of the women who kept you alive? No, I'm grateful."

He traces my fingers with his. "Speaking of nurses, how's Mia? I'm sorry. I should have asked right away." He looks at my mouth. "You distracted me."

I bite my smile. "She's good. Radiation is . . . It's not fun. She's really tired. She has to go every day. But the prognosis is good."

"She's tough as nails." He squeezes my hand. "Hadley?"

"Yeah?"

"I know everything is so messed up, and maybe this is stupid. But do you want to do something normal? With everything, I'm kind of dying for normal. Want to go for a walk? Go to a movie?" He laughs. "Is that boring?"

Relief courses through me. "A movie sounds sort of great, actually. I'm tired of thinking."

"Yeah, exactly! I knew you'd get it. I know we have a lot to figure out. But it can wait a couple hours, right?"

I nod, taking pleasure in his delighted face. "Yeah. It can wait." Because he's here. He's *him*. And just being in his presence sounds way better than sorting out our mess.

"Okay, you choose which one. I'm going to run inside and use the bathroom." He pauses. "Look up times? Meet you back out in a second; we can go to the soonest one?"

I agree, and he kisses me again, sweetly on the lips, before heading inside. My heart warms watching him walk into the house.

Retrieving my purse from my car, I dig for my phone. When I finally fish it out, I remember that it's dead. The closest charger is inside. I open the back door. Two steps into the kitchen, I see Braden's back to me.

He's digging through the cabinet.

The truth hits me before I have a second to think: *Mom's medication.*

When he hears me, he freezes.

And the second I see his reaction, I'm sure.

My whole body cracks and shatters.

I shouldn't be surprised.

I shouldn't feel this shock wave of betrayal.

I should have known better.

For a beat, we stand in total silence.

My eyes drill into his back.

He turns around slowly. "I had a headache—"

My throat is so tight I can hardly speak. "Don't."

"Had—"

"How *could* you—" It's a sob more than words.

"I didn't. Hadley—" He moves closer, reaches for me.

I take a step backward, reeling. "All the things you *just* said to me . . ." My voice is a whisper. "I'm so stupid."

"No. *No.* Hadley, don't say that. Of course you're not

stupid. I meant every word I said. I just came in here and I remembered she had . . . You know, just in case."

"In case of *what*? Look at you, you're not swimming anytime soon! And I told you she *needs* those. You *knew* that. Braden, think about what you're doing!" I shake my head, replaying the last twenty minutes in a darker light—seeing his real intentions. "This was a mistake. This was all a mistake."

He almost fooled me. Again.

Nothing has changed. He isn't two different people. He's just one person making terrible choices, again and again. And I can't, won't, be his collateral damage any longer.

"We are not a mistake." He turns and shuts the cabinet. "*That* was a mistake. And nothing even happened—I didn't take anything! We love each other. We'll talk through it, like we said. We can work through anything. . . ."

I take a step away from him, my mind racing. As he tries to justify his behavior, a realization dawns on me, like a punch to the gut: I *don't* love him anymore. It was easy to say because I've said it so many times before. Because I see flashes of who he was, and I miss that person so deeply that sometimes it feels like drowning. And while I certainly feel *something* for the boy in front of me, something big and undeniable, it's not love, not really. It's rotten.

Real love comes from safety, from trust; not this feeling rooted in desperation. It makes me want to scream and bang on his chest, demanding back who I used to know. But he's gone, and nothing is going to bring him back. What I feel now is the shadow of love, and all it has to offer is heartache.

"I can't do this."

"What? No—"

"Braden, I just caught you rifling through my mom's pills. My mom, who is *right at this minute* having radiation therapy." I let the brutal truth out. "You need to get help."

He pleads, "I didn't take anything. It was *one* misstep."

"*One?*" I shake away a million thoughts before I settle on what I want to say. I take a breath and look him dead in the eye. "I can't pretend to understand. It keeps me up at night, trying to understand."

He tries to interrupt, but I put a hand up in his direction.

I continue, "I *want* to understand. I keep making excuses for you. Or blaming everything on the drugs. *God*, Brade, I wish I could blame everything on the drugs." Emotion makes my voice waver. "But it's also *you*. *Your* hands on that steering wheel, *your* hands on those orange bottles, and *your* hands stealing my camera." My eyes drift to the medicine cabinet. "And this, now. You just chose those pills over me, again. It isn't *one*—"

Angry tears fall down his face. "*Chose?* Hadley, I didn't choose! I don't want to feel like this!"

"You keep choosing not to get help—"

His face is furious. "You know what? *You're right*, Hadley. It *is* me. *I'm* the one who almost died. *I'm* the one who lost *everything*."

"*Stop it!* Stop trying to make me feel bad for you! *I already feel terrible*." I take a shaking breath. "But you knew you had a problem, Braden, and you didn't do *a damn thing* to stop it before—" My voice cracks, thinking of all the things he could have prevented. I can't bring myself to list them. "You thought you could bury it, but you can't!" I stomp my foot in furious frustration as I gesture around us. "The secret is fucking out!"

"I didn't do anything! I didn't take it! You came in before—"

"Right. I stopped you." I pause, taking him in. There's still a small, urgent part of me that wants to pretend this never happened. To go along with his line of thinking. *He didn't actually steal the pills.* But that voice is easier to quiet now.

Because for the first time, I understand that Braden and I are irrevocably broken.

"Hadley, we can fix this. I'll get help. I'll go now. Today."

I shake my head. "I hope you do. But for us, it's too late, Braden. You made your choice before the accident, and you just made it again now."

"No, please, there has to be something. . . ." I watch a thousand thoughts cross his eyes. It feels like I'm watching our whole relationship pass by, up to this moment: the final realization. He knows it too. He knows that while I could look past him hurting me, I could never forgive him for taking advantage of the worst thing that has happened to my family. I could never forgive him for hurting Mom.

We both know it's over.

But still, one last time, he says, "Hadley, I didn't—"

"I can't. I wanted to. But this . . . I just. I can't."

I watch him swallow. Reluctantly, almost imperceptibly, he nods.

And when he leaves, the loss is sharp. I feel like I took a blade to my insides, carving him out before everything else started to rot. I'm bleeding, but I know I'm healthier too.

* * *

I sit at the kitchen table with the sound of the closing door echoing in my head. I'm not sure how long I'm there before I unclasp Braden's necklace and let it pool in my hand. A key to the room of a boy who won't be there, not as I remember him, no matter how much I want him to be.

And I know there's one last thing I have to do. Something I owe that boy. Something I should have done the moment I first suspected.

I pick up my phone, and it rings three times before a tense voice answers. "Hello?"

"Hi, Mrs. Roberts."

"Hadley?"

"Yeah." I pause, unsure how to tell her this. "Um, I just saw Braden."

"What—"

I cut her off and force myself to speak. I tell her about what happened. That there was no mistaking his actions. That I'm certain. "He tried to take more pills. And I don't know what he's telling you, but he hasn't stopped. Not since . . . your house." I push away the memories of that other morning. "And I just wanted to tell you that I'm so sorry for my part in this. I was trying to help, but I made it worse. And I can't fix it. I get that now. But I thought *you* might be able to help him. Maybe get him into a rehab facility or something? I don't know. I just needed to tell you."

The other end of the phone is quiet for a long time. And then she sighs, long and slow. I wish I could see the expression on her face. The silence stretches, until finally, she says, "Thank you for telling me, Hadley."

"I really want him to get better. I never wanted anything but that."

"Me too," she answers sadly before she hangs up.

And then, long after the line goes dead, I sit alone, doubting every choice I've made in the last year, running my finger along the sharp edges of his key, wondering how I'll ever live with all of it.

CHAPTER 30

"Hadley?" Remy stands at the doorframe.

I blink, letting my room come into focus. "Remy? What are you doing home?"

"I got a ride. I wanted to talk to you. Judd told me about Braden." Remy and I haven't spoken much since our fight, since she left for school, weeks ago. "Is it okay if I come in?"

I nod.

"Are you all right?" my sister asks, settling on the edge of my bed. "I called your name a couple times."

"Sorry. Distracted, I guess." The truth is, I'm second-guessing everything. *Should I be able to forgive Braden, because he's addicted, and it's out of his control? Am I being heartless? Is it even his fault? What if Braden's mom doesn't believe her son needs to go to rehab? What if, because I'm not there, something terrible happens? How would I ever live with myself?*

But at the same time, *how can I stay?*

I can't stand by and watch him ruin his life. I can't let him steal from Mom. How could I possibly condone that?

I can't bear leaving *or* staying. So I'm stuck, twisted in the covers of my bed.

Remy scoots closer. "Hads, I'm no stranger to heartbreak, so I get it, but you're worrying me. I've never seen you like this."

"I don't . . ." I exhale the next words. "I don't know what to do."

She looks around my room, the one I've hardly left in days, and back at me. And I know, to her, it probably looks bad. It's bordering on gross, but I can't bring myself to care.

"Do you want to talk?" she asks gently. "Maybe to get out of here?"

"Aren't you mad at me? Don't you think I'm weak or stupid or something?"

"No. And yeah. But everybody is stupid sometimes."

"Well, I'm mad at you." I grip on to my pillow. "And I can't leave."

She ignores the first part of what I said. "What do you mean you can't?"

Emotion settles in my throat, and I struggle to get the words out. I wrap my arms around my legs, buying time to find my voice. "He's in trouble. And he helped me through Mom's stuff, and now I'm just leaving him? But staying . . . I don't know how."

She sighs, tilting her head. "Hads."

My vision goes blurry. "It doesn't make any sense. *I know.*"

Remy climbs into bed next to me, ignoring the used tissues, and pulls me into her side. She presses her cheek into my dirty hair. "It makes sense to me."

The kindness undoes me.

313

I don't deserve it.

My breathing breaks, turning to gasps and sobs. "I think he needs me, Rem. He needs me and *I left*." She squeezes my hand, and my most fragile thoughts spill over. "I didn't want to leave. I love him, I love him so much, and I kept trying. But I could have tried harder. Better. Nothing I did was anything at all."

When I stop, my sister says, "I think you did everything you could."

"I gave him an ultimatum, Remy. It was for me. I was *selfish*."

"Hadley, you gave him a choice, and he made it. That's the opposite of selfish. You were prepared to give up somebody you love to help them."

I shake my head. "I did it because I was mad. And scared."

"No you didn't, not really. If he had been willing to stop, everything would be different."

I shrug.

"Did something change? Is he going to get some help?"

I remember Braden's empty promises, my heart aching for them to be true. "He said he'd get help. But only after he acted like everything was okay, and then I caught him . . . trying to get more. And he's been lying so much. I don't believe him anymore. But I feel guilty. Like I'm giving up on him when he needs me most."

Remy sighs. "It didn't feel like a real offer? Like too little too late?"

I nod, trying not to let my tears fall.

"If it helps, I wouldn't believe him either; not if he told me that way. It doesn't sound like he's trying."

My emotions are such a mess, and now anger flashes through me. "Remy, of course he's trying! It's just . . . It's like he thought that this scholarship was more important than anything else. Than his health. And then the accident, and withdrawal, and he thinks he lost everything. And who knows what the hell is going to happen to his swim career now. And it's not his fault the doctors prescribed some shitty, unsafe meds. *They're* the ones who should know better. And the pills made him, I don't know . . . He wasn't himself! And how is that fair?"

The way she looks at me, calm and sad, it's like she knows who I'm really angry with. "It isn't," she relents. "Hads, I'm not saying it's his fault. I think it's terrible. And . . . I get how it's confusing. But it did happen."

"What are you talking about?"

"It's just that, as bad as it sucks, *it happened*. He *has* an addiction. And you can spend as much time as you want being pissed about it, at him or whoever else, but it's still true. And the thing is, you tried to help. Even if your help wasn't perfect. You talked to him, you did research, you bought that medication, you called nine-one-one, you may have even saved his life, *and* you talked to his parents about getting him into rehab."

I'm annoyed Becca told her all that. "No, that's not— I did so many things wrong too. I made it worse. He said it wasn't a problem, and I believed him. Or maybe I pretended to believe him. I don't know, but I took the easy way out."

"Maybe. But it's hard to know; there's no right answer. And I do think you tried. Can you honestly tell me how Braden tried?"

"What? I just did."

"No you didn't." She looks at me, brows stern. "Because Mom . . . She had something awful happen to her too. Something she couldn't control, that wasn't fair. And you know what? She fought it. She did the hard, awful things she needed to, to get better. Surgery, chemo, losing her hair, months of nausea and pain, tattooing her body for daily radiation . . . she did *everything*. And she didn't just do it for her; she did it for *us*. The people she loves." Remy's lips are thin. "I did some research too, Hads. And if addiction is a disease, like cancer—like what Mom has—what did Braden do to fight his?"

I want to object. I want to say that Braden fought hard. He saw so many doctors. He *hated* feeling that way. But I keep coming up empty-handed. Did Braden actually fight the addiction, or did he only fight to keep swimming, to keep things the same?

He rejected having the surgery, because he was worried he wouldn't be as good after it. And maybe he wouldn't have been, but he also wouldn't have needed to keep taking those pills. But he wouldn't stop, because he was scared he wouldn't be able to compete unmedicated. Either of those decisions could have changed a lot.

Braden didn't like his options, so it's like he didn't make a choice at all. He just kept treading water, insisting he could handle it until his college plans were settled.

So I jumped in, too, trying to help. But I wasn't strong enough, either, and then we both couldn't keep our heads up.

I had to let him go or drown.

Remy squeezes my arm. "Hads, you can't fight somebody else's addiction for them. Just like I couldn't do Mom's chemo for her. *Braden* has to want to. He has to choose it himself, for himself. And your job is to take care of you."

I look at my sister. "You really think that?"

"Yeah, I do."

"But, Rem, I did mess up, though, a lot."

"Hadley, how could you *not* have messed up? You're a teenager. Your mom had cancer. You had no experience with addiction. What were you supposed to do?"

Be a life vest, save him. "I don't know," I tell Remy. "Know more. Be better."

"Well, okay, sure. But it doesn't really work like that, Hads."

"How does it work, then?"

"I don't know. I'm just saying that you're not perfect, and . . . I think you can handle that."

My chest tightens. "Even with this?"

"Even with this."

"Remy?"

"Yeah?"

"I'm sorry I was so awful, before."

She smiles. "I'm used to it."

"Hey!"

"I'm just kidding."

"You said you talked to Judd. Did you guys make up too?"

"Yeah. I'm kind of glad he stayed now. Who knew our almost-eighteen-year-old sister would need so much looking after?"

I roll my eyes. "I'm glad my misery was so helpful."

She looks around, taking in my piles of tissues and messy hair. "Hads, let's get you out of this room, okay? Soon?"

I nod. "Try again tomorrow?"

317

"I'll bring reinforcements."

"Not Becca."

"*Of course*, Becca."

"But she won't take no for an answer."

"Exactly." Her lips curl upward. "But, Hads, there is one thing you have to do, like, *right now.*"

"What?"

"Brush your teeth."

And when I laugh, I throw my pillow at her.

The clock ticks forward.

Bruised and exhausted, I finally get out of the pool.

❊   ❊   ❊

Two and a half hours later, an idea occurs to me, and I shoot out of bed. I haven't been able to stop thinking about what Remy said, and it suddenly dawns on me. I know exactly what I need to do.

My Great Lakes U portfolio assignment, the one for my application, is to create a collection around the theme that has most impacted my life. It can be anything in the world, and options were overwhelming. But suddenly it feels like the only way to tell a story about my life, something that feels important enough for *this* assignment, is to tell the truth.

I open my laptop and scroll through until I find it: the first picture I ever took of Braden. Thankfully, even though I threw away my actual portfolio, I had all my photographs backed up on my laptop. He's grinning in the leaves, the skin along his lean muscles glowing in the low light. I run my fingers along the screen, remembering that boy. Then I move on to the next. I chose only ten. Ten pictures to show how the most electric, vibrant person I've ever met turned into someone else. The life drains from his eyes; he's dazed and far away. It's a visualization of the addiction taking hold and Braden fading away behind it. It's something I couldn't see in the moment, but in my photographs, it's undeniably clear. In my head, I let an imagined photo finish the series: Braden lying broken in a hospital bed. I hope it never comes to something worse.

And then there are the pictures of Mom. It's still disease, but everything about her series is different. I start with a photograph of her at home, before she was diagnosed. She's holding a glass of wine as she tastes her spaghetti sauce at the stove, her eyes smiling and just barely meeting the camera before I snapped the shot. It's Mom as I picture her, even now. But in her images, as the cancer treatments begin, nothing takes hold of her. Nothing replaces the life in her eyes. Even when she shows me her arm where the IV of chemo left its mark, or as she takes a razor to her head, level eyes with a proud, naked scalp. Then there are the photographs of her sitting in a tank top, revealing part of her chest, before and after the small tattoos that were necessary for radiation. Again, ten images. This is a story of a woman who is throwing punches. She didn't become her disease; it never took over. She claimed what power she had and used it to fight.

In my entire portfolio, I'm not in a single image. Instead, I'm somehow stretched between the photographs. I'm the witness, connecting the two: the woman fighting for her life and the boy gambling with his.

And with these photographs lined up in front of me, it's a little easier to believe Remy. Walking away from Braden was hard—imperfect and maybe even brutal—but I have a responsibility to take care of myself too.

I'm going to survive all of this.

And as far as Braden goes, the only thing I can do is hope that he decides to fight for himself too.

CHAPTER 31

"I'm not talking you out of this. But are you *sure?*" Mom asks as she pulls her fingers through my dark blond strands.

"Absolutely." We're talking to each other's reflections in the salon mirror. My hair is in a low ponytail, and I'm sitting in a raised chair, ready to chop it all off. It's a surreal déjà vu moment, with me in the hot seat this time.

Mom objects, "But you have such pretty hair."

"You really do," Becca says.

"So did you," I tell Mom, glancing at her pixie cut, "and now you do again. It'll grow back."

Mom smiles. "Yeah, it'll grow."

We pause, feeling the weight of the moment, but then I shake it off. "Plus, I've wanted to cut it since you had to, but I let you talk me out of it. And then Braden cut his, and I thought that could count for me, but it doesn't. I have to do it myself."

"Right. Which we're totally behind. But just enough to donate, right? You're not doing a full Britney on me."

"Becca!"

"Okay, sorry!" Her hand moves into a gesture of surrender. "I support you. Even if I don't get it."

"I'm feeling very supported," I tease. "Will you take the picture now?"

She lifts her phone, but Mom stops her. "Actually, can you hold on, for just one second?"

She pulls a wrapped box out of her giant purse. "This was going to be a birthday gift, but, today just feels right." She smirks. "Here. Open it."

"Now? Here?"

"Yeah."

"Isn't this kind of a weird time to open a gift?"

"It's the perfect time."

"All right, well, thanks?" I carefully peel the paper away until I see a white box. Then I read one word: *Canon*.

Instantly, my heart is in my throat.

"Oh my god." I swallow and look up at Mom. Her eyes are bright. "Mom, this is too much. I can't."

"Yes, you can. You haven't been the same since yours broke."

My eyes fill with heavy tears. "Mom, my camera didn't break. . . ." The building emotion in my chest won't let me finish the sentence. *I can't believe she did this for me.*

She presses her lips together. "All the more reason for you to have a new one."

My smile tastes salty. "Thank you, Mom." It takes me a second to get the camera unboxed, but when I put the battery and memory card in, it powers up immediately. *It's beautiful.*

It's the newest model, and it takes video too. "I really can't believe you did this."

She looks almost as happy as I feel. "Well, believe it, baby."

I change the camera to automatic so Mom doesn't have to worry about the settings, and hand it to her.

Then I pull the hair tie out and shake out my hair. "Is my entire face covered?"

"Yeah, pretty much," Becca says.

"Pretty much or totally?"

She walks over and adjusts a few pieces. "Okay. Totally. Cousin It territory."

"All right, take a couple, Mom?"

She snaps a few pictures and then walks over to show me the screen.

I remember the night at the hospital when I caught a glimpse of the terrified girl in the mirror. This time, I'm *trying* to look like a Francesca Woodman, and it works. The girl in the picture is hiding. She looks afraid. But I'm not going to be that girl anymore.

"Yes, perfect. Thanks, Mom."

My hairdresser, Mandy, comes around the corner with the plastic bag to put my ponytail in, once it's no longer attached to my head. "Okay. I'm all set if you are. Take a seat."

What I think is: *Shit, shit, shit I really do love my hair.* But what I say is: "Let's do this." I put my hair back into a pony.

"I'm double-checking here: You said fourteen inches, right?"

My eyebrows join forces above the bridge of my nose. "Yes?" It sounds much more like a question than I intend. I try again, clearing my throat, and nodding. "Yes. I mean yes."

"That's a great amount for a donation. They'll be able to make a nice wig with it."

I squeeze Mom's hand.

Mandy eyeballs the length and adjusts my hair tie so that her cut will be right. Then she takes the scissors from her workstation and opens and closes them teasingly. I see my face flush in the mirror.

Mom squeezes my hand back, but Becca puts her hands over her face. "I can't watch."

I close my eyes. "Me either."

Mandy laughs. "Well, I have to." Then she moves the scissors closer to my pony. "I'm going to count to three, okay?"

"Mm-hmm."

"One."

"Two."

Ohmygodohmygodohmygod.

"Three."

I hear the crisp sound the scissors make as they cut my hair to my chin.

I make the highest-pitched noise I've ever made. With the final snip, I'm literally lighter.

My stomach is filled with helium. *"Holy crap, holy crap, holy crap."* My eyes are still closed. "Becca, did you open?"

"Not yet."

"Mom?"

"You look great, honey."

"You have to say that. Mandy?"

"Well, obviously *my* eyes are open. And I love it."

"Ugh, you have to say that too!" I complain. "Becca, you have to look before me. I know you'll tell the truth."

"Okay, opening." Her pause makes my pulse race. "Oh my gosh! Hads. It's good. It's *really* good! Open your eyes."

"I can't."

"I promise you on . . . Greg! It's amazing."

"On *Greg*? Are you kidding?"

"Just open your eyes!"

I peek one eye open and then the other. I don't even recognize myself. But . . . I like it. I think I like it? The girl looking back at me is bold. I like her. I think I like her hair too.

"Okay, I still have to even it out. But if you ask me, you look like a badass."

Becca answers for me. "That's exactly what she was going for."

I want to elbow her but am scared that I'll mess Mandy up. So instead, I just admit, "I kind of feel like a badass."

"Perfect. But don't move. I need to make sure you're even." She carefully trims along the edge, and in a few minutes, I have a wavy, very blunt bob.

"Do you want me to wash and blow it out?"

"No, there's no point. I'm going to yoga with my mom right after this." The oncologist finally allowed Mom to go back to her favorite studio, and to celebrate, I decided to go with her.

"*You're* working out?" Mandy has been cutting my hair for years.

"Is that so hard to believe?" I ask.

"Well . . ."

I object, "I totally did this hot yoga every day for a week, once, freshman year. As a new year's resolution."

Becca scoffs. "More like a new year's challenge. Mia said you wouldn't make it a week."

I look at Mom sharply.

"Well, you aren't known for early—" she starts.

"But I did it," I interrupt.

Becca makes an amused noise. "The point was that a week isn't a long time! You were supposed to go for a month."

"Whatever." I pretend to be annoyed, but the familiar back and forth is filling me with a warm glow.

"Well, all right, then. Case closed. She's worked out." Mandy is talking to Becca now. She moves back to her work-station and lifts my long, chopped pony into the air. I have a quick, passing urge to cry, but not really out of sadness, just out of change. Or maybe out of the memory of Mom's pony-tail and Dad's gentle fingers as he held it. Mandy carefully puts my hair into its designated donation bag.

"Hey, Mandy. This is weird, but can I actually see that for a second?"

"Your hair?" She laughs.

"Yeah, I want to take a picture with it."

"Sure." She waves the pony at me.

I hold it up next to my face, and Mom snaps a couple more pictures. Then I have her take one with my phone, and before I can think myself out of it, I text the image to Ty: better late—and not exactly how I pictured it—than never?

My phone buzzes quickly: I can see your face better. And then: it's perfect.

I try not to worry too much about what it all means.

And when I get up to hug Mandy, I shake my head and let the cool air tickle my neck. "Thank you. I wouldn't have trusted anybody else." Then I reach my hand out. "You can have this back now."

She wrinkles her nose and puts my hair back into the bag. "I'll get it sent over."

And it's as easy as that. It's not when or how I thought it would be, but I kept my promise to myself.

a new beginning

Senior Year

spring

CHAPTER 32

When I pull up to the yoga studio, my phone is lit up. It's a text from Braden's mom: Hi Hadley. I wanted to let you know that Braden gets out of treatment tomorrow. I didn't want you to be surprised if you heard from him.

My stomach flutters, but only a little. Thanks for the heads up. I hope he's well. It's a little stiff, but I mean it.

I know he's having a hard time, being out of school and watching his friends sign with universities that would have been thrilled to have him before the accident. And it makes my chest ache, thinking about how disappointed he must be. I hope that when he starts back at Lakebrook next fall, he's recovered enough to try again.

And I honestly don't know what I'd do if Braden called, but I did accept his letter of apology a few weeks ago. One of the twelve steps, to make amends. I told him I'd forgive him if he'd forgive me. I'm still working on both.

"Hadley!" Mom is outside with something flat in her hand.

"Hey, what are you—" I start to ask, but she interrupts me.

"Finally!" she exclaims, beaming.

"What are you doing out here?" I ask as I get out of my car.

She shoves the thick envelope toward me. "It's the big one!"

"What are you talking—" Then I look down at it and read: *Great Lakes University.* "Oh my god. It's the Big One."

"Big is good, right?" Mom is shifting from foot to foot, her grin spread across her face, reaching her ears.

"Yeah. Yes. Usually, I think." I don't want to get my hopes up only to have them crash down around me again.

"Well, hello? Open it up!"

"Here?" Nervous energy tickles my skin.

"Yeah, come on!"

Carefully, I shift my attention to the envelope.

Mom pulls at my T-shirt. "Did you have to choose something so wrinkly?"

"Mom, not now. I'm kinda freaking out here."

"Right. Sorry." But she doesn't stop messing with it, so I swat at her hand.

When I pull the paper out, I only read as far as *We are pleased* before I meet Mom's eyes.

"Are those happy tears or sad tears?"

"Oh my god!" I shriek.

"You got in?" she shrieks back.

"Holy shit, I got in!" I bounce up and down before Mom grabs my hands and we jump together.

"You got in!" And her words feel like the final piece of something sliding into place.

Mom looks back at the studio, and then at me, crinkling her eyes. "Forget yoga. We need to celebrate! Let's go get some margaritas and guac. Virgin for you. I'll drive. Call Becca to meet us."

Except Becca isn't the first person I want to tell. "Can I actually meet you guys there, maybe later tonight? I have something I want to do first."

❊　❊　❊

I can hear the doorbell ring inside the house from the front porch. My heart is hammering as the cool wind grazes the back of my neck. I run my hands along the ends of my hair, telling myself that I can do this.

I shift my weight from one foot to the other, impatient, until the door swings open.

"Hadley!" Tyler exclaims. I can't tell if it's a good or a bad exclamation.

"Hey." I smile nervously.

His head tilts. "What's up?"

"I got into Great Lakes." A little pride blooms in my chest.

"Holy shit! Congrats, Butler!" Ty moves to hug me, but there's an awkward beat between us.

Since everything went down, our friendship has remained firmly intact, but I needed some time before I could worry about anything else. He's been really understanding, and mostly, we've just been pretending it didn't happen. Until we get too close, and we're both painfully aware.

We're still not touching, but this time, I take in his proximity greedily. He's wearing an olive green hoodie, with shorts and black socks. I have the strangest urge to press my face against the cotton of the sweatshirt. *I've missed him.*

"That's so awesome. Looks like we won't be too far from each other, then."

"I think it's two hours to Chicago." *Two hours and eleven minutes.*

"Yeah, I think so too."

"But it's not why I came."

"Okay."

"I sort of thought we should talk."

"Now?"

"No time like the present," I joke.

"Okay."

"Well, first of all, I've been the worst friend ever."

"Nah." He teases.

"No, I have. And I'm really sorry for it."

He shrugs. "I told you, friends don't keep score."

"Well, I kept score. And I lost. And I'm ready to start over."

His brows furrow. "Start over?"

"I mean . . . Well, I think I sort of jumped the gun," I admit.

"What?"

"I just . . ." I'm so nervous, and I can't stop smiling. "I feel like if this amazing, totally unlikely thing can happen, and I *actually* got into Great Lakes, then other good things can happen too, right?"

"Okay . . ." His voice is tentative, following along.

I'm just going to say it. "The kiss . . . ," I add sheepishly. "Kisses? Whatever." I shake my head, embarrassed. "I mean, there's something here. Between us." I don't phrase it like a question, but I still find myself looking to him for an answer.

He nods without breaking my gaze.

I exhale in relief.

I've been thinking about this so much. Wondering if I could take any more risks after all the things that have gone wrong over the last year. But I've realized, slowly and deeply, that Tyler is a safe place for me. And I can only hope he feels the same.

"Do you remember when I told you what Remy said? Junior year. About how I'm afraid of losing people I care about, so I don't take enough chances?" I don't want to say Braden's name, not right now, but I think he'll get it.

He leans into the doorframe. "I remember."

"Well. She was right. But I don't want her to be right anymore." I force myself to look at him while I speak. "And when we were together, the thing I remember the most is being surprised. By my own feelings, I mean. Which . . . they were obviously there. But I really didn't know before then. And I think, maybe, it was because I was afraid to admit them. Because you're not just any guy, Ty. You're, like, one of my favorite people. Ever."

"Yeah?" His lips curve.

"Yeah." I nod.

Memories flood my mind. Ty listens and he shows up. He has faith in my strength in a way I'm only just learning to match. And since the first day we met, we've always had each other's backs. Tyler isn't going to sneak around or lie. He's not going to drive too fast, or go at the count of two when he told me he'd get to three. I'm *safe* here, with him. And I deserve to feel this kind of affection, the kind that doesn't hurt, that doesn't come at such a high cost. And so does he.

But it's not that simple.

I take a deep breath and say the hard part. "But the thing is, Ty, as much as I wish I were . . . I'm just not sure if I'm ready. Not yet."

His eyes are thoughtful as he shakes his head. "I didn't ask you to be."

"I know. I totally know. You've been super understanding, like, more than I could ever ask for. But I was just getting to my more important point."

"Okay." His voice holds a question.

"So maybe I'm not ready. But I don't want to close that door either."

"What?" He looks hopeful but confused.

"Well, like . . . I know we're going to different schools in the fall. And I know there are lots of reasons why this could be a mess. It kind of already is. But just . . . I'd like to keep the door open. Like maybe not walk through it yet. Or maybe never, if you don't want to. I'm not going to assume you'll wait around for me. But I'd like it to be open, if you want it to be."

"The door?"

"Yeah. The door." The absurdity of it all is nearly making me lose my train of thought.

"We're not really talking about a door, are we?"

"Am I totally sucking at this?"

I think he's enjoying my nervousness. "No. You're not. I get it, I think. And I'd like to keep the door open too. See what . . . um, happens to it."

Relief courses through me. "Okay. Whew. Great. 'Cause I have sort of an open-door question."

He lifts his chin. "Yeah?"

"Um. Yeah." I swallow. My heartbeat accelerates. "I was sort of wondering if you had any plans for prom."

He bites his grin into his mouth. "Well, Lauren Brooks asked me last week."

"The clarinet player?" I say it like *clarinet* is the dirtiest word I know. "In *March*? You've already been asked to prom in freaking March."

"Yeah, she plays the clarinet." His eyes are teasing. "And yeah. To the other part too."

"Did she ask you in some cutesy way?"

"She put a sign on my chair in band."

"What did it say?"

He battles with his smile. "'I know we can make music together, but can we dance?'"

Ugh. I'm too nervous to laugh. "And?"

He doesn't answer for a minute; just looks at me. An eternity later, he says, "I thanked her, but told her I was hoping to go with somebody else."

"Somebody else?" I ask breathlessly.

He shrugs. "You kind of sounded like you were leading up to something."

"Yeah. But I didn't know I needed a sign."

"You don't need a sign, Hadley."

I gather all my remaining nerves and take a leap of faith. "Well, do you want to?" I can feel my heartbeat in my throat.

"I'm sorry. I'm not sure what you're asking. Do I want to . . . ?" His face moves into phony confusion.

A ball of nerves explodes in my stomach. "Ugh, Ty! Do you want to go to freaking prom with me?"

"Well, since you asked so nicely." He pauses. "Yeah, Hads. I would like that."

"You are the worst, you know that?"

"I thought *you* were the terrible friend."

I swat his shoulder. "You didn't have to make that so hard."

"'Cause you've made this whole thing a real breeze for me."

"All right. Fair." I exhale a million pounds of worry, of expectations, of all the things it took to get to this moment. "But okay. Cool. We're going to do the prom thing."

He laughs quietly. "Yeah. We are."

"Okay. Well. Now that that's over, I have one last thing."

"More?" he says incredulously.

"Do you want to go for a drive?" I nod to the Jeep. "I kind of miss hanging out with you. And I made a playlist." I've been working on it for a while, compiling every song that explained how I felt about him, in words I was too afraid to use myself. I might not be ready to make any actual decisions, but being honest felt like a good place to start.

"*You* made a playlist?"

I nod.

His amber eyes are sparking. "Where'd you find these songs? What's in store for me?"

"Are you coming or not?"

"Oh, I'm coming."

"All right, let's go."

And as we walk, shoulder to shoulder, I look up at the evening sky. Half of it is glowing with low yellow and pink sunlight, and the other is darkened by heavy rain clouds. I unlock the car, get in, and plug the aux cord into my phone.

I turn to Ty. "No peeking. Just listening."

"Got it." He moves my camera out of the way and leans back in the passenger seat.

The music fills the space between us, and I roll the windows down to the let wind comb through my short hair. And as I drive, with no destination in mind, I feel like the sky: full of both darkness and light. It will probably be clumsy, and definitely flawed, but I can handle it—whatever life throws at me—rain or shine.

And when I look over at Tyler, he lifts my camera and snaps a shot of me, frozen forever in this perfect moment of hopeful uncertainty.

ACKNOWLEDGMENTS

This book has been years in the making, so bear with me as I try to express my major gratitude.

First, I'm so thankful for my agents, Garrett Alwert and Mandy Hubbard. I'm the luckiest writer to have this incredible team supporting me. From signing, to revision, to submission, to landing me at my dream publisher, I'm endlessly grateful for your hard work and support.

Audrey Ingerson, my editor, you saw the heart of this story and helped me bring it to the page. Your notes were astute and thoughtful, and they kept me up all night trying to figure out how I could get to your level. I am so thankful that my first book was in your capable hands. I'm also grateful to Wendy Loggia and Alison Romig, who stepped in after Audrey's departure and helped this book make it out into the world. Thank you.

I'd like to thank Random House Children's Books, and specifically Delacorte Press. Thank you to Beverly Horowitz, for leading this team, which has taken such good care of me. Thank you to Casey Moses, the cover designer; Pedro Tapa, the illustrator of my gorgeous cover; and Alison Impey, the YA art director. For interior design, thank you to Trish Parcell and Stephanie Moss. Thank you to the copyeditors, Colleen

Fellingham and Alison Kolani. The managing editor, Tamar Schwartz, and the production manager, Jonathan Morris, thank you! I have admired Delacorte Press books for years and years, and I'm still pinching myself that I'm being published at your imprint.

I'd also like to thank my early readers/editors, Corey Ann Haydu, Jill Dembowski, Debby Duvall, and Kerry Kletter. This book would never have found representation or a home without you. Kerry, you were the first person in the industry to tell me I could do this, and I'll never forget your encouragement.

To my friend Paul Young, thank you for patiently answering all my questions about high school swimming, even if it was after midnight at a bar in Brooklyn.

I want to thank the Tyndall-Schultz family, my in-laws, for their support, cards, and bottles of bubbles throughout this long process.

To my best girls/Ace Gang/friends with the Hearts of Gold: Angela, Lia, Susan, Casey, Laura, Danielle, Jeanette, Trish, Caroline, and Andrea. Having all of you in my life is an embarrassment of riches. Thank you for being women who root for and support one another. I can't imagine my life without you.

To my family, thank you for living the real version of this story with me.

Alex, in one of my biggest moments of self-doubt, you admitted that this story made you shed a tear—which I took as the biggest compliment in the world. In my gratitude, I will now tell everybody about your crybaby tendencies. Love you.

Allie, I'm not even sure how to thank you. You've read more versions of this story than anybody. You're the first person I go to with every new idea, because I know you'll always tell me the truth. Thank you, thank you, thank you forever. Hadley and I both have wonderful sisters, but mine is better.

Dad, this book wouldn't have happened if you hadn't shown me what I'm made of. Nobody pushes me harder or believes in me more than you do. Thank you for your willingness to be my teacher, even when I'm a resentful, stubborn student. I'm so lucky to have you.

Mom, just typing those three letters is making me cry. Thank you for always picking up your phone, even when I've already called you three times that day. Thank you for listening to every worry and sharing every joy. Thank you for being the light in even the darkest situations. Thank you for inspiring this story.

To my husband, Matt: you always believed I could do this, even at the very beginning, when we were looking up at what felt like an impossible mountain to climb. Thank you for supporting me while I did it, even when it took longer than we imagined. The only thing that has ever made me happier than getting this book published was marrying you. I'd do it again and again and again. I love you.

The last thing that I want to say is that this story is a piece of my heart. I spent years drawing it out, trying to get the words just right. It started as pages from my high school journal, and now, somehow, it's a real book. And I want to say that I'm grateful for that sixteen-year-old girl who was brave enough to write down all the ways she hurt, and that she was able to take some of the hardest moments of her life and turn them into my proudest accomplishment. It's been an emotional, wild ride. But we made it.

ABOUT THE AUTHOR

NICOLE B. TYNDALL grew up in a small town in Michigan and lives in Brooklyn, New York, with her husband, Matt. She graduated from Grand Valley State University with a bachelor's degree in art history and a minor in philosophy and French. *Coming Up for Air* is her debut novel.

Visit Nicole online at nicolebtyndall.com and follow her on Twitter and Instagram at @nicolebtyndall.

 t